The Heart's Filthy Lesson

A NOVEL

Written by

Sheldon L'henaff

Caroline, (a.k.a Fleur)
Thank you always for a
fabulous year ...
HERE WE GO AGAIN! !!
Much love,
Sheldon
L'henaff

Order this book online at www.trafford.com
or email orders@trafford.com

Most Trafford titles are also available at major online book retailers.

Printed in the United States of America.

ISBN: 978-1-4269-6551-7 (sc)
ISBN: 978-1-4269-6550-0 (hc)
ISBN: 978-1-4269-6552-4 (e)

Library of Congress Control Number: 2011905979

Trafford rev. 07/12/2011

 www.trafford.com

North America & international
toll-free: 1 888 232 4444 (USA & Canada)
phone: 250 383 6864 • fax: 812 355 4082

The Heart's Filthy Lesson is entirely a work of fiction. Names, characters, businesses, places, and incidents either are the product of the author's imagination or are used fictitiously. Any resemblance to actual persons, living or dead, or events is entirely incidental.

For El Riz. . .

Chapter one

He stood against the escalator railing as it slowly glided up towards the second floor. The huge sign that proudly displayed Home Department Store greeted Dutch as he began the walk to the escalator to third. As he looked around, he noticed the mall was desolate with the exception of the odd panhandler that scurried underneath him on the bottom floor in the food court. Dutch focused his gaze upwards as the escalator finally presented him to the non-descript entrance of Go Credit. When he arrived at the entrance a young blonde-haired girl looked up from the computer screen at the desk while he scanned his card to release the door.

She smiled sweetly and said, "Good morning Dutch."

He leaned in to her and kissed her on the cheek as he replied with a smile, "Good morning Miss Dawn. How goes the battle this morning?"

She replied, "Usual morning at Go Credit."

He then asked, "And the date this weekend?"

Her smile weakened as she then deadpanned, "Yeah…I think he and I are done."

Dutch shyly smiled as Dawn then mentioned, "I'm supposed to tell you breakfast is served."

He smirked and said, "That's a sign." She shrugged as he swiped his card against the access pad and said, "I'll stop by at lunch."

A few feet in from the second set of doors, the hallway widened out to a huge call center that, proudly, was the nerve centre for Go Credit. To Dutch's right was customer service, his initial home for the first few years working there. People moved back and forth between cubicles as he quickly gazed at the perpetual motion and energy that began to flow at seven a.m. while the office filled up. To an extent he missed the starting point of his career path in customer service. Further right was a small flight of steps that led to an open balcony type landing which housed the collections department and staff lounge.

Dutch continued forward as he passed the manager's office as well as the glass enclosed main conference room to his left which signaled the end of customer service and a small group of cubicles, similar to the ones in customer service that were designated for the Elite loyalty team. For Dutch's last two years this area had been his home. As he set his messenger bag down he quickly turned on his computer, glancing briefly at his reflection in the monitor screen. His bleach blond hair seemed to reflect off the screen as he leaned back in his chair, gazing at his surroundings. Upon logging in he opened up his e-mail and began to sift through all of his messages. He opened each one until he saw the most recent one at the top which proudly announced in bold letters:

BREAKFAST IS SERVED

Dutch faintly smiled as he picked up the steaming coffee that was left on his desk and walked towards the far back of the call centre. The left wall was nothing but tinted windows that stretched from floor to ceiling and was an open invitation to gaze at downtown Edmonton's skyline. When he passed the small block of three offices to his right, he turned and pushed open the door into the men's washroom. Once through the second set of doors he strolled past the urinals and a couple of stalls and then turned to his left as a voice announced, "It was about to get cold." His smile widened and he walked over to the four stalls which were tucked away from the main part of the washroom. He gazed into the mirror and adjusted his suit and tie.

He asked, "The main part or the coffee?" He saw the stall door unlock and Dutch gently pushed inwards. He saw Eli bent over while Eli took a deep breath and stood up, wiping his nose and turning towards Dutch.

Eli grinned as he handed the clear straw to Dutch and announced, "It's all yours."

Dutch walked in as Eli began to adjust his suit in the view of the mirror. He stood about the same height as Eli, his face more filled out and his hair a jet black. Unlike Dutch, whose hair was spiky, Eli's hair only stood in a little tuft at the front. Dutch asked him, "I know that it's early to ask but what's on the agenda this weekend?" He pulled out a credit card while Eli adjusted his tie.

Eli said, "Apparently there's a huge entourage from Calgary coming up this weekend."

Dutch chipped away at the lines of white powder as he mused, "Pink Bar it is then." He then pulled out the straw as he continued, "Those fuckers are so caught up in themselves down there that they really need to take lessons from those who party properly and come to Edmonton to do it." Dutch then asked, "Did you get a meeting request this morning?"

Eli replied, "No I didn't. Why do you ask?"

With one deep inhalation the first line disappeared and Dutch explained, "I dunno Eli. It just seems kind of fucked. There's about ten of us who will be in attendance at the meeting."
Eli replied, "Not sure." As Dutch came out of the stall he smiled, Eli grinning back. He then asked, "Did you clean it up?"

Dutch grinned wider as he confirmed "Dishes are cleaned and put away in the cupboard boss." Eli's smile then vanished while Dutch's facial expression changed to confusion. Eli then took his thumb and wiped from under Dutch's nose. Dutch laughed while Eli took the powder covered thumb and rubbed it into his gums.

They walked out of the washroom as Dutch then asked, "So what else did you have in mind?"

As they walked towards customer service Eli explained, "Was thinking the usual haunts this weekend. Some of the girls were thinking Vivid on Saturday night and we're not that far away from Friday."

As they stopped at Eli's desk Dutch suggested, "You know that Bliss is having a DJ event?"

Eli rolled his eyes and said, "Bliss is a fucking mom and pop fag coffee shop and really who needs that?" Dutch grinned as a younger redhead walked by them both.

Eli called out, "Hey copper top" as he looked over.

Dutch then said, "Eli, he's done fuck all to you. He's not worth it."

Eli asked, "Who Stewart?" Dutch shook his head as Eli said, "Oh come on Dutch. He's as flaming as the hair on his head."

As Dutch looked over at the entrance into collections he noticed a blonde spiky-haired boy talking to Dutch's supervisor as Eli looked over at them and scoffed, "If you really like that…"

Dutch said, "What?"

Eli rolled his eyes then said, "I'm gonna clock in Dutchie. E-mail me later."

Dutch headed back to his desk and sat down while a hand lightly crossed his back. He turned around in his chair as the brown haired woman in front of him asked, "Are you ready for the meeting?"

Dutch looked puzzled as he asked, "Marie, what is this meeting about?" She neatly smiled as she leaned back in her chair, her straightened hair flowing over her shoulders as she began to click her mouse onto her browser.

Marie was Dutch's supervisor that had specifically hand-picked him for Elite. She had begun to form the team by moving some of Go Credit's top performers. Dutch's summoning was two years to the day that this meeting was about to take place.

Dutch mused, "So I noticed you were sizing up the cute blonde jock."

Marie made eyes at him, smiled and said, "Soooo not my type…"

He sat up and teased, "Bullshit Marie."

She grinned and said, "You'll see at the meeting."

As Dutch turned around to his computer, a pop up announced the meeting as Dutch sighed. Marie asked, "What's the matter?"

Dutch weakly smiled and said, "They're shutting us down."

He stood up and slapped her with a pad of paper as she said, "Get to the meeting mister…"

He walked over to the glass conference room as Eli came up and pointed in the direction of the main entrance as he slyly said, "Let's include that in the weekend agenda."

Dutch glanced over and saw Christine and her fiancée Nicholas as Dutch said, "You so do not want to fuck with that Eli."

Eli said with a grin, "It would a lot of fun."

Dutch argued, "No Eli. You fucking know better."

Eli said nothing and just casually smiled as he then said, "Get in your meeting."

Dutch walked into the room as Marie closed the blinds to the conference room. As he sat down at the table he noticed the blonde haired boy standing at the screen along with Natasha. Natasha was the call centre manager for Edmonton, and the prime mover and shaker with Go Credit. For the past ten years Go Credit had moved from being an upstart credit card company based out of Alberta, to a Canadian financial powerhouse. It had inked a national deal with supermarket chain Marketplace to be its stand alone credit card. With the addition of offices in Vancouver and Montreal, Go Credit became poised for North American expansion. Natasha had seen it through up to that point, and was ready to move it forward.

Christine appeared from the entrance and promptly sat down at the table across from Dutch. She smiled at him and asked, "And how are you this morning?"

Dutch shrugged and half-smiled. "Just a regular morning, and you?"

Christine flashed her smile and said, "Nicholas took me out for breakfast this morning."

Dutch teased, "So you and Nicholas are on an on day today?" She only smiled as Daniel entered the conference room.

Daniel was another customer service agent who stood about 5'11 sporting a shaved head and small patches of facial hair. He also sat opposite Dutch and beside Christine as she nudged him and teased, "Running a bit late as always."

Daniel's face reddened as he reasoned, "I had to pick up a prescription for my mother this morning."

Dutch said, "Now now Daniel, using your mother an excuse for your tardiness? Tsk tsk…"

Marie and Stewart were the last ones in as they sat down beside Dutch while Natasha dimmed the lights. She said, "I'd like to introduce you to Antoine. Antoine is a senior support representative from the Montreal office and is also one of the people involved in the Regenesis project which we're all here to introduce you to this morning"

Antoine smiled shyly as he quickly glanced over the room, letting his gaze linger a little longer towards Dutch. He then began, "As you already know Go Credit has recently become a major player in Canada. We scored a major agreement with Marketplace as their official credit card for the entire chain. Right now we're in an excellent position to move into the American market." As Antoine continued with his speech he handed out a booklet to each person at the table, Dutch couldn't help but notice that Antoine continuously eyed him while Antoine delivered his presentation. Dutch would momentarily gaze down at his booklet, only to find when he looked up that Antoine would quickly move his eyes back to the presentation on the screen.

Two hours elapsed and the lights came on while everyone shuffled out. Dutch waited until everyone had left and then stood up to leave when Antoine glanced over and asked, "So what do you think of the Regenesis project?"

Dutch looked around and then asked, "Who me?"

Antoine replied in a thick French accent and a grin, "Well you are the only one left in the room…"

Dutch glance around embarrassed and replied, "Oh…" He then said, "It's a lot of what loyalty does now."

Antoine nodded in agreement, "You're right. But this is so much on a larger scale. We really want everyone to be involved." He then said, "I'm sorry I didn't quite catch your name…"

Dutch extended his hand and said, "I'm Dutch."

Antoine clasped it and replied, "Antoine."

Dutch then asked, "How long are you in town for?"

Antoine shrugged and replied, "I'm here for a few weeks. I'm designated to help out with collections team and give them a chance to get started."

Dutch breathed in and said, "Wow, this is quite the big deal."

Antoine nodded and he explained "They're making a huge North American push right now. With a few million under our belt and the backing of three Canadian financial institutions that want the card and out of the grip of American credit card companies that wont give them a break."

Dutch said, "Sounds about right to me."

Antoine then said, "Natasha and Marie both highly recommended you for Regenesis."

Dutch blushed as Antoine said gazing to the screen, "I hope to work more with you on this project."

Dutch shyly smiled and replied, "Nice meeting you Antoine."

They shook hands again as Dutch left the conference room. He walked back over to his desk where he opened his e-mail. The fist one that sprung up from Eli read – SO WHEN IS THE CLOSE DATE? Dutch chuckled and typed back SPECIAL PROJECT ASSHOLE. He shut down his e-mail as he stood up and walked over to Eli's desk.

Eli had just finished a call when he looked over and asked, "So who is he?"

Dutch explained, "His name is Antoine. He's from the Montreal call centre."

"Greeeatt…" Eli drew out as Antoine walked by the small flight of steps into the collections part of the call center. Eli glanced, then circled around and said, "He looks fucking French to me." Dutch began to say something as Eli then said, "You know what that means, right?" Dutch shook his head as Eli grinned and said, "He's a hoodie."

Stewart turned around and then asked, "Say what?"

Eli then said to him, "You weren't a part of this conversation ginger."

Stewart focused back on the screen and mumbled, "Fucking asshole"

Eli then elaborated, "He's uncircumcised, means his dick is in hiding."

Stewart then piped up, "But French guys are very well equipped in the sac, especially from Montreal."

Eli turned around and said, "Shut up. I won't tell you again…"

Stewart stood up and walked away as Dutch looked at Eli and asked, "Do you have to be such an asshole to him?"

Eli shrugged and replied. "It passes the time." Dutch shook his head as Eli began to pack up his bag and close it as he stood up.

As Daniel walked by he waved at Eli and said, "Hey dude."

Dutch and Eli looked at him as he continued to walk up towards the steps and through credit to the lunch area.

Eli sighed, "Now there's a closet waiting to be ripped open."

"Fuck you Eli" Dutch said as he argued, "Did you see how he was chasing Shantal this summer?"

Eli chuckled as he replied, "Now there's someone who wouldn't give him the time of day."

Dutch added, "He chases after the impossible. Everyone he runs after is taken. And I can tell you Shantal is definitely not willing to give up her current boyfriend for that douche."

Eli then logged out of his phone as he turned off his computer and said, "I hate to dispense with pleasantries but I have a political science class I have to be at."

Dutch teased, "You mean a political science intern to fuck."

Eli smiled and explained, "I'll have you know that that's not the reason why I have A's in that class." And with that Eli took one last look at the call center floor and made his exit out.

With Eli gone he took a look over to where Stewart sat as Stewart finally returned back to his desk and sat down. Dutch could sense the anger seething from him as he went to say something to him when he heard Marie call out "Dutch?" Dutch quickly turned around as Natasha was standing beside her.

Natasha looked concerned and asked, "Is everything okay on the floor Dutch?"

Dutch replied, "Yeah, everything is fine."

Natasha then said, "Marie needs to discuss your schedule with you back in your area, because there's going to be some changes." She then turned quickly to Marie and said, "I'll leave it to you two."

As they walked back over to the Elite department Marie asked, "What's up with Stewart?"

Dutch replied, "Ahh Eli was just teasing him. Nothing major."

Marie asked, "Teasing, or being vicious?"

Dutch said, "You know how Eli is."

She argued, "That's what I'm afraid of."

Dutch then said with a smile, "You know it's all in good fun Marie."

Her look of disapproval hadn't disappeared as she explained, "What would you think if we brought Stewart over to Elite?"

Dutch immediately replied, "I think Stewart would be an excellent asset for the team. He's got the drive."

She then smiled and said, "I'm glad you agree. Because I think he's my next Elite star."

Dutch then sat down at his desk and asked, "What about Eli?"

Marie replied, "He gave up the team leader application because he had two other people up against him. He didn't think he should have to earn it and for that reason he was passed over. Now…"

She sat down then explained to Dutch, "I need you to work a different shift during the duration of the Regenesis project."

Dutch's eyebrow lifted as he asked, "And what kind of shift are you thinking?"

She explained, "I need you to work one to nine-thirty on the weekdays for the next few weeks. You're going to be helping Antoine run the show at night."

Dutch nodded and said, "Count me in Marie."

She grinned and said, "I'm so thankful Dutch. I knew I picked the right person for this project." She patted him on the shoulder and explained, "I'll let Natasha know you are one of the people identified for this project. Thank you so much Dutch." As she walked back over to Natasha's office he continued to file through his e-mails and snickered when he saw the company-wide announcement of the Regenesis project.

By the time his shift was over he had shut down his computer and Marie had returned back to the pod. He stood up and said, "I'm out for the night Marie, when do you want me on late shift?"

She pulled back her hair and replied, "We'll start you tomorrow. Gives you an excuse to sleep in."

Dutch grinned and said, "I guess we'll be seeing each other later then."

She then pointed out as he began out towards the entrance, "This does not give you an excuse to go out and party young man." Dutch winked at her and he then made his way out the double doors and into the mall towards Jasper Avenue.

LOVE'S SWEET EXILE: DISC 54 - 34 minutes

When Dutch unlocked the apartment door he quietly stepped in and looked around. It seemed that the apartment was much brighter to him as he walked into the living room where the television was on to find Erin laying on the couch, remote in hand.

She then said, "Well look who's home for the first time in...how long has it been?"

Dutch smiled at her and playfully argued, "I'm always home, just you never see me get in." He then walked over to her and kissed her on the forehead while he asked, "How's my little radio lady?"

She sighed and deadpanned, "Fucking frustrated." She added, "I feel like my whole existence in radio is going to be nothing more than some DJ's administrative assistant."

Dutch asked, "Have you slipped a demo to the manager yet?"
She frowned and replied, "No yet."
Dutch the offered, "Did you want to work on something this week?"
She shrugged as Dutch then said, "You know what you need?" I think you need a night out this weekend." He then asked, "Did you want to do Pink Bar with me and Eli?"

She responded, "And watch a bunch of hallow empty twinks claw each other to shreds?" Dutch only shrugged as Erin said, "Let me think on that one okay?'

Dutch nodded and he explained, "I'm off to my room. Got some work to do."

She shot him a look of disbelief as she complained, "You've been in your room a lot lately." Dutch shrugged and explained, "Nature of the beast I guess."

He closed the door behind him and placed his bag on his bed while removing his shirt. Sitting on his bed he gazed at his computer. It was a basic set up, a poster of the Manic Street Preachers towered above his desk with the words *This Is My Truth Tell Me Yours* emblazoned across the bottom. He reached over to the left to access his CD player while he opened the desk drawer and retrieved a minidisc. While he carefully removed the wrapper, he moved from the bed to the chair, fishing out the minidisc recorder and began to insert the new disc inside. The player was a gift from his parents when he was sixteen. Sixteen when the entire world changed. Sixteen when he'd come out. Sixteen when he'd met Eli.

Once plugged in he reached further back into the drawer and pulled out a small black pouch. When he loosened the string he opened it and pulled out a frosted glass pipe. He opened the little Ziploc bag and tipped it upside down, emptying its contents into the bulbous end. He looked up at the picture of him and Eli at sixteen, then at the few pictures taped to the side of the computer tower. Dutch pulled out his lighter from the drawer and began to flick the switch as he let the flame lick the bottom of the pipe. Once he could see the smoke start to form and escape from the pipe's opening he began to inhale deeply, the smoke flowing from the tube into his mouth. When he finally stopped he exhaled above the bed and with that began to speak into the microphone that stood on the desk.

"I've been working on this journal now for close to seven years. Seven years worth of minidiscs full of the exploits of Dutch and Eli, two best friends living in Edmonton Alberta." He paused for a moment then continued, "Seven years…of ups, downs, ins and outs. But the one thing that has always been consistent over time is the fact that I've known for seven years." He sucked back on the pipe again and quickly exhaled as he breathed with an enforced hush, "That I've been in love since the first day we met." He lovingly ran his fingers over the pictures as he explained, "It's the only thing that has been consistent over all of these years. Never mind that his idea of relationships is nothing but one night stands."

He then said, "But not just any one night stands. First of all, you have to be his type. Secondly, you have to have something he wants. Third…"He paused for a moment then sighed, "You have to be ready to be discarded as soon as the next best thing comes along, and with Eli the next best thing comes along a half hour after."

"Something's changed. He's become especially morally devoid over the past eighteen months. It's like he's thriving on blurring the lines. Fuck knows he's made his way through a third of the male population that have come and gone in Go Credit."

"This brings me to Antoine and the Regenesis project." He lit the pipe again as he inhaled and shortly exhaled after. "He's sworn up and down he's not into Antoine. And as far as anyone knows he's straight…but if Eli had his way he'd try and coax him into having sex." He then sighed out. "He has no fucking shame. No morals, and definitely no consideration for anyone else. This begs the next question…why am I still here?"

"It's because I'm really the only one left. I'm the only one who's stood by him. For as long as it takes him to work through his shit and then maybe realize that I unconditionally love him. That he'll maybe see I'm always going to be there for him." He looked back at the pictures and grimaced. "It's been seven years. I've kept this secret for so long, somewhere deeply locked away. The right moment hasn't come along, but it will…and I'll be there."

He stopped the recording and on one of the adhesive stickers wrote the date, and placed it on the case. He carefully put everything away and turned the light out, escaping into the living room. He passed by Erin as she said, "Hey Aimee called for you today. She wants to have lunch with you."

Dutch sighed and replied, "I guess that means the fucking family's in town." He headed to the fridge, pulled out two beer bottles and walked back into the living room, passing one to Erin.

She asked, "Are your parents done disowning you yet?"

Dutch shrugged and explained, "Not while daddy's in office and until he fucking retires he'll still be getting fucked up the ass by Big Oil and still hiding his queer son in Edmonton." He then asked, "So when did you want to do the demo?"

She smiled as he continued to finish his beer and asked, "How about next week?"

He chugged the rest of the beer and smiled, "Done." He then placed the bottle in the kitchen and leaned against the doorway. He explained, "I'm out for a little while. Gonna meet Eli at the club."

She smiled sweetly as she took another sip of her beer and said, "Enjoy your evening."

chapter two

Thursday night saw the customer service floor quiet as Marie packed up her bags and said to Dutch, "Enjoy your evening Dutch."

Dutch explained, "I will Marie. It'll be a little lonely here now that I'm on the new shift."

She then said, "Well it's making you a bit more money. Besides..." She smiled as she squeezed his shoulder playfully, "Keeps you out of mischief."

"Ha ha" he replied sarcastically as she walked away.

Since the beginning of the Regenesis project began, Dutch had agreed to work the later shift and on the project on his own. In a way he was relieved, as it had given him an excuse to skip breakfast. Eli quickly rescheduled "breakfast" to "morning coffee break" and shortened it so Dutch could be back out on the floor. However, since the shift switch something had been nagging at him that he couldn't place his finger on it.

Two hours passed and Antoine appeared at his desk. "Hey Dutch" he said with a smile as Dutch looked up and smiled.

Dutch replied "I didn't think you'd be in tonight."

Antoine sighed, "I've been doing a lot of overtime as of late. Just haven't had the chance to slow down." Antoine then asked, "Are you the only late night rep from Elite?"

Dutch nodded as he asked, "Who's with you in customer service?"

Antoine replied, "I have Ariel, Daniel, Christine as well as a couple others." He then sat down across from Dutch and said, "She seems nice enough. Her boyfriend is like sex on a stick."

Dutch chuckled and replied, "You and every woman and gay male in the call centre." Dutch then added, "And it's fiancée. They just announced their engagement three months ago."

"Shame" Antoine said.

"Then this must make you…" Dutch pointed out.

Antoine nodded with a smile as Dutch mentioned, "You don't give it off…"

Antoine stood up and said, "Kinda wished I did." He then asked, "Are we still on for tomorrow night?"

"Yeah absolutely" Dutch said as the alarm on his cell phone went off. As he gazed at it briefly he asked Antoine, "I'm going for coffee. Did you want to come with?" Antoine nodded in agreement as they headed out towards the front cell centre entrance. They stopped as Antoine walked up to Daniel and Ariel. After a few moments Dutch saw Daniel give the thumbs up.

As Antoine rejoined Dutch he said in a relieved tone. "They don't need anything. Let's go."

Dutch then said, "Follow me. I know this really amazing organic coffee place just by the mall entrance."

Antoine followed him as he asked, "Is the mall always this quiet for a Thursday evening?"

Dutch replied, "Everyone pretty much hits West Edmonton Mall. I believe it's still one of the biggest malls in the world."

Antoine asked, "If you're not busy sometime, would you show me?" Dutch nodded and tried not to blush as they crossed the pedway across the street underneath and towards the down escalator.

After turning south at the bottom of the escalator they crossed the intersection and Dutch pointed to the marble building that was sandwiched between the National Bank and Telus. They walked in and Dutch led him up the stairs as the barista finished serving the customer at the till.

He waved at them as Antoine scanned the room. The café itself was a basic white walled space, pictures neatly spaced all around. People bustled in and out of the main café space while jazz music floated above the many conversations that had blended together.

The barista asked Dutch, "The usual?"

Dutch replied, "Two please." Antoine looked at him in confusion as Dutch reassured, "Trust me this will be amazing." After Dutch was handed two cups he asked, "Can you get lids?" Antoine reached over and handed Dutch a lid. He smiled at the barista as he explained, "He's from Quebec."

The barista ahhhed and said, "Have a good night guys."

They headed out the door while Antoine took a sip of his coffee and immediately made noises of approval. Dutch beamed, "See?"

Antoine explained, "This is amazing Dutch. I can't even get coffee like this in the village."

When they reentered the mall Dutch offered, "At some point I could take you over to this little café called Bliss on the edge of Jasper Avenue. It has even more amazing coffee then what you're drinking now and maybe one morning you and I can do breakfast there."

Antoine grinned, "I would really like that Dutch."

Dutch let them both back into the office as Antoine explained, "I'm going to clean up my e-mails and get lost. Have a good night Dutch."

Dutch raised his coffee cup to him in a toast and he began to walk towards his desk when he heard, "I can't fucking discuss this with you right now and especially on the company phone! These calls are recorded you asswipe!!" He discreetly walked to the back row where Christine was sitting while she navigated on the computer, anger distorting her face. "Nicholas you're being childish, and this call is being recorded. If I get written up…"

She then slammed down the receiver and sighed in frustration as Dutch went over and satin the desk next to her. "Are you okay?" he asked as she slammed her fist down on the desk in frustration.

"It's always the fucking same with him." She continued, "He always picks the stupidest shit to fight with me over. And on my time too…" Her facial expression simmered down from anger to disappointment as she said, "I don't know if this was a good idea."

Dutch reasoned, "Its okay Christine. Couples do this all of the time. It's just growing pains. You and Nicholas will make it.'

Christine sighed as she stared blankly at the screen. He knew that she was trying to hold back her tears as she explained, "You know the fighting was never this bad. Some days I feel this is all he wants to do."

Dutch went up and hugged her tightly as she sniffled a little bit. He whispered in her ear, "It's going to be okay I promise." He then joked, "Just don't let Eli near him."

She started laughing as she replied, "No fucking kidding." Her smile reappeared as she said, "You know it's funny after the Christmas party last year he came back to our place." She continued, "He tried to convince Nicholas that he might be bisexual and asked us if we ever tried a threesome. I mean for fuck sake, he never gives up."

Dutch reasoned, "He does that once in awhile."

Christine sighed and said, "I don't understand Eli. He just seems so empty."

Dutch said, "Nobody understands him Christine. Even I don't understand him sometimes." He glanced out at the call center floor and watched as Daniel talked to Ariel. Uneasiness washed over him as he walked back over to his desk and sat down in his chair.

His watch beeped and he looked at his computer clock as he cleaned up his papers and shoved everything into the bin underneath the desk shutting the screen off and picking up his bag. He walked out of the office and out back towards the east mall entrance and to the intersection overlooking the library. He walked past Churchill Square and through the gate which decorated the entrance of Chinatown. He then stopped for a moment and dialed numbers on his cell phone, waiting for a response. A voice on the other end responded, "Hello?"

Dutch said, "I'm on my way. Where you at?"

The voice said, "The Mohawk on Jasper. I'll meet you there."

A few blocks passed and Dutch arrived at the gas station. He dialed the numbers again and the voice only said, "Be right there." Dutch waited around the other side of the convenience store as a taller, deathly thin figure in soiled jeans, greasy t-shirt and jacket seemed to almost float over to him. His ballcap shadowed his sunken face, as he looked up at Dutch.

Dutch smiled and said, "E." He nodded as he replied in kind, "Dutchie" and motioned him to follow. E was the cleverly abbreviated version of his full French name Etienne, hinting at one of the many party pharmaceuticals he sold for a living.

They walked up to E's building whose outside appearance was that of disrepair. He opened the door and ushered Dutch in as he then walked up the two flights of stairs to the top floor. E let him into the apartment and said, "It's been awhile since you dropped by. You'll have to excuse the mess." Dutch looked around as he saw plates piled up in the sink, clothes in a pile in a basket. As Dutch walked into the living room E said, "Sit down I'll be right back."

He watched as E disappeared into the bedroom. He looked around as music came out from the speakers of a portable stereo. E returned as Dutch pulled out his wallet. E sat down at the end of the coffee table. He then handed Dutch a bag and said, I hope you like these green macs. One a day keeps the doctor away."

Dutch snickered as E set down two more bags, one blue in color, and the other clear. E then explained, "The blue bag is ketamine. The clear one is cocaine." Dutch handed him the money as E then pulled out a pink bag as Dutch plucked the other two from the coffee table and stored them in his bag.

He then asked, "What's in that one?" He pointed at the pink baggie as E reached under the table and pulled out a glass pipe.
He opened the little bag and started to put some of the substance into the pipe while he lit it, watching the substance bubble and then inhaled slowly. The smoke disappeared into E's mouth as he then turned away and exhaled a huge cloud of smoke from his lips. E then handed the pipe over to Dutch as Dutch lit it and explained with smile, "This new shit's got kick. It's really amazing stuff." Dutch exhaled the largest cloud of smoke

that he had ever exhaled. In a matter of seconds he could feel the surge start to flood through him.

Dutch's eyes widened as he said, "No kidding." He pulled out his wallet and asked, "How much?"

E waved it away and replied, "This bag is on me." He sealed it and tossed it in Dutch's direction. "Just remember where you got it from."

Dutch then smoked the pipe some more and mused, "I may have someone that may be interested in this. I'll keep you informed." E nodded as Dutch looked out the patio door window to see that the metal bars that held up the balcony were horribly bent. He asked, "What happened there?"

E said nothing as he snatched the pipe from Dutch's hand and inhaled again, this time black smoke fuming from what was left in the pipe. E exhaled as he asked, "So I take it you don't pick up for just yourself."

Dutch shyly smiled as he replied, "I pick up for a couple of people. Nothing big."

E explained, "If you pick up even more you and I can work out an arrangement."

Dutch then stood up and said, "I will take that under advisory."

E then showed Dutch the door as Dutch said, "I'll call you next week. Let you know how this pink stuff works out."

Dutch began down the stairs as he opened the apartment complex door. The temperature seemed to sharply drop as he zipped up his jacket. He continued down Jasper Avenue, carefully watching as he moved further into downtown. Dutch arrived at Commerce Place and as he sat down on one of the benches in front, he noticed a disshelved man propping himself up with a cane stop and start his way to the bus stop. His glasses magnified the beady pools of black as Dutch tried to decipher what the old man was explaining. He knew that years of drugs, sex and self-abuse had eroded away at him. Dutch had seen him times before at The Cactus and at The Pink Bar's upper level lounge.

The old man slurred out, "Those boys at the Pink Bar are not very nice people. They're all rude and they don't give a shit about us older guys."

Dutch asked, "You think Peter?"

Peter then said, "You know we built this community and it's like they don't care about it. They just throw it away and take it all for granted." Peter then grew silent as he made a disgruntled look. Dutch noticed that Peter's teeth were all misaligned as the look of disapproval disappeared as quickly as it had appeared.

Peter then began again, "So many people are two faced. No one cares about each other anymore." While Dutch knew that Peter was old and dementia was beginning to set in, he also understood in many ways that Peter was right. The chemicals may have destroyed his motor skills, but some of that mind was very intact.

Dutch watched while he garbled some more and eventually propped himself up with his cane, beginning the walk further west. He fidgeted in his bag and after making sure that no one was watching, he opened the clear bag while taking one of his keys and scooped a small pile onto the edge and snorted it. As he leaned back he texted Eli, GOT THE GOODS.

He could feel the cocaine start to supplement what the crystal had done an hour before as he decided to make the walk home from Commerce Place.

His walk coupled with the effects of the crystal and the coke helped him to arrive back to his building in record time as he looked up towards his window. While it wasn't one of the massive new towers that had started to squeeze all of the walk ups out of the downtown core. It was the classic façade outside that had attracted Dutch to this twelve story building. Within moments he took the elevator up to his floor and let himself in to his suite, heading immediately to the fridge. When he opened it the light shone on a lasagna pan and the note above that read WORKING LATE. He immediately wedged a slice on to a plate and placed it into the microwave, scurrying to his room to set down his bag. Upon his return to the kitchen, he felt his phone vibrate, the message SEE YOU TOMORROW ran across the screen.

After checking his e-mail and messenger, he spotted Eli on his chat list and opened a window, typing ARE YOU AWAKE? He waited a few minutes as the next few words were being typed out. The screen read, CALL ME. He dialed the numbers on his handset in his room.

Eli answered, "Yes Dutchie?"

Dutch explained, "I saw Pete today on Jasper Avenue."

Eli asked. "And how was that?"

Dutch replied, "He looked like a shell."

"Well that's what disco, drugs, and flashbacks will do to you."

"Are we going to end up like that?" Dutch asked

"I hope the fuck not. I hope I'm dead before that happens." Eli replied sarcastically

"Shit he must have done a lot of drugs." Dutch replied almost worried.

Eli chuckled over the phone and said, "They didn't have ecstasy, ketamine, and pot back then. It all evens out."

Dutch sighed and replied, "I really hope so."

Eli reiterated, "We'll eventually get bored and drop out of this scene. They'll have to make the drugs stronger, the music faster, better, and the sex more dangerous."

Dutch laughed as he began to juggle the pink bag between his fingertips.

"Get some sleep" Eli said. "We've got a long weekend ahead of us."

Chapter Three

Dutch heard the phone ring as he stepped out of the shower. He glanced at the call display and upon noticing it was the front door pressed nine while he scurried back into his bedroom. He opened up his closet and began to pore through the clothing, trying to find his favorite French Connection shirt. Moments later he heard a knock at the door while he threw on a pair of jeans. When he peered through the peephole he opened the door to find Eli standing outside.

Eli shot him a half smile as Dutch suggested, "The door is wide open. You could have just come in."

Eli replied, "Oh" and stepped inside.

Dutch plucked the vodka coolers out of Eli's hand while he asked, "Did you manage to get a nap in before you came over?"

Eli casually wiped his nose and explained, "About as much as I could. Today seemed a little bit more high-strung than usual out on the floor."

Dutch explained, "With all the changes going on in the office I'm not surprised. Everyone's wondering when the next shoe is about to drop in customer service."

Eli smiled and said, "Actually that's not the case at all…" As Eli sat down at the dining room table he asked, "Did you pick up the groceries for the next three weeks?"

Dutch handed Eli a bottle and explained, "Thirty tabs of ecstasy, an eight ball of both coke and ketamine."

"Good job" Eli beamed as Dutch pulled his shirt over his head, and down over his chest and sat down.

He noticed how much Eli had been wiping his nose and asked, "Are you okay Eli?" Eli sipped his drink and leaned back as Dutch added, "Chinese should be here any minute."

He then scowled as Eli replied, "You said that fifteen minutes ago when I was at the fucking liquor store."

Dutch shrugged as he then went to the fridge and asked, "So what were you talking about?"

Eli said, "Stewart has a crush on someone. You can just see it all over his face." Eli took another sip as he commented, "It's kind of cute in a sad, pathetic way."

"Why do you have to be such a bitch to him?" Dutch asked irritated.
Eli replied, "More entertainment for me I guess."

Dutch protested, "You know you've been pretty vicious with him since he started a few months ago."

"Someone's got to be. Unfortunately queer life is harsh" Eli replied matter-of- factly.

"That doesn't mean you have to be such a cocksucker to him." Dutch replied getting angrier.

"But I am a bona fide cocksucker aren't I?" Eli said with a touch of humour.

Dutch said "Why would you want to fuck up his and Daniel's relationship?"

"Why would I need to do that? Stewart will do that all by himself." Eli said in a familiar dismissive tone.

Dutch sighed and shook his head while he said, "I really don't think you should fuck with their friendship Eli. Let them sort it out."

Eli smiled and replied, "Stewart's an easy target and…"

Dutch spat out, "Daniel's something you can't have. And as much as you try to deny it and keep it buried, I know you want him."

Eli said, "We don't even know if he's gay. Although I don't know any fag who would be caught calling people 'Dude' and 'Man'."

Dutch said, "Well, he still does have his v-card at twenty-one. But that's because he's a fuck up when it comes to girls."

Eli chuckled and added, "Did you know that he did actually ask out Shantal?"
Dutch asked, "How did you know?"
Eli grinned and said, "She told me. But she's not having any of that. She thinks he's a pot-smoking shit-show."
Dutch cocked his head and he said, "Oh-kay…"

Eli then out-of-the-blue said, "I really wouldn't mind getting into Nicholas' pants."
Dutch interjected, "Engaged Eli…"
Eli smiled again and said, "Where there's a will there's a way."
"Fuck off Eli" Dutch said hotly
Eli then innocently asked, "Where's dinner?"

Dutch looked at his cell phone and groaned, "Fuck, it's been an hour." Dutch dialed the number and asked, "Hello I'm still waiting for my order. It's been an hour and twenty minutes." After a few moments Dutch frowned as he then said, "Please cancel my order, we don't want it anymore." He hung up the phone and explained, "The cocaine is in the bathroom Eli. Cut us a few lines before we go out."

As Eli darted for the bathroom Dutch's home phone rang. He picked up the handset and said, "Hello?" Moments later he explained, "I'm sorry but it doesn't take an hour and a half for you to kill a couple of Chinese children and make food out of them. We don't want the order anymore." Dutch hung up the phone and he walked back towards the kitchen while the phone rang again. He walked back over as he picked up the handset again.

Upon seeing it was the delivery man's cell he groaned as Eli came out of the bathroom. He asked, "What's wrong?" Dutch said nothing as Eli then said, "Give me your credit card Dutchie. I'll fix this."

He did as he was told and Eli stormed out of the apartment and boarded the elevator, pressing the lobby button. When the doors opened he walked over to the landing where the driver stood, bag of food in hand

and grease bleeding through the bag. The driver's broken English resonated as he said, "Order for you mister."

Eli sighed as he watched the pudgy man hand the bag to him. Eli pushed it back and said, "It's been an hour and forty-five minutes. We're not paying for that."

The driver's frustration began to crack through his sentences. "You need to pay. We made food for you."

Eli could see his eyes bulge through his glasses as Eli said, "I'm sorry but I know it does not take that long to deliver Chinese food. We don't want it."

The driver then protested, "I can't take this back! I give you discount for food!" Eli argued back, "We're not taking this Chinese food! It's cold, not tasty and you probably made this shit from cats and dogs!"

The driver then yelled, "I make you pay! You buy dinner you order!"

Eli then plucked the bag of food from the driver's hands. At first the driver smiled and Eli began to walk towards the elevator.

The driver then shouted, "I need payment for order!" Eli then turned around and launched the bag at him. Upon contact an explosion of sweet and sour sauce, breaded shrimp, rice, and steamed vegetables covered the driver, the door, and the windows. Eli walked into the elevator and pressed Dutch's floor as he chuckled to himself and stood against the wall.

When he reentered the apartment, Dutch came out of the bathroom while Eli grinned and handed him back Dutch's credit card. "What the fuck did you just do?" Dutch asked.

As Eli snorted both his lines, wiped his nose, and said, "Let's take the stairs down to the back entrance tonight."

Dutch followed Eli's lead down the stairs as they finally made it to the alley that eventually opened to Jasper Avenue. The smell of freshly baked bread wafted from Earl's to his right, tickling his nose which at that point Dutch's stomach protested. They walked over to the intersection as Dutch pointed to the billboard that hung on what looked like an empty McDonalds.

Eli growled, "They're fucking putting high-rises up everywhere downtown any building that had any type of architectural substance they've torn down."

Dutch shrugged and replied, "You can't stop progress."

Eli looked at him and asked, "Progress at what price?"

Dutch only smiled as the walk light signaled them to cross.

They finally made it to the huge neon sign that read PINK on its side. While Dutch had never really paid attention to the sign before, there was something this particular evening that made him gaze upwards in awe. Eli dragged him to the VIP entrance where the bouncer stamped their hands and said, "Enjoy your evening guys." They walked down the flight of stairs and past the pink mirror ball as the final flight of steps led down to the coat check where the corridor opened up to the Pink Bar.

The club's interior itself was the furthest thing from pink as forest green with black stretched across the walls. Overhead the din of top forty diva remix bled through the speakers as people shuffled through the crowds back and forth.

Eli said, "Get us some drinks and I'll meet you in the back men's room." Dutch nodded as he got into line and began to search the crowds for familiar faces.

It was the same pattern every weekend. Dutch would wait in line for drinks while Eli disappeared to the back washroom where Eli would prepare the two vials of illicit powders for consumption. He sighed as he inched closer to the counter. The bartender looked up at him and smiled as Dutch made his order when someone tapped him on the shoulder. As he looked over the person waved and smiled.

Dutch asked, "How are you Paul?"

Paul replied, "I'm not too bad Dutch. How is your evening going?" Paul stood a little shorter than Dutch and had a darker complexion that mirrored off his hazel eyes. His choice of jeans and a basic black t-shirt aided in drawing attention to Paul's facial features, especially his immaculate smile. He then asked, "Are you not out with Eli tonight?"

Dutch announced proudly, "He just stepped into the bathroom. He'll be out shortly."

Paul appeared disappointed as he suggested, "Well come swing by our booth at some point tonight." He motioned up to the booths by the washrooms near coat check.

Dutch paid for his drinks and replied, "Will do" as he took the bottles and started to head towards the washroom by the back bar.

He noticed that Eli stood leaned back against one of the half walls that separated the back area from the main area. Eli had a scowl on his face as Dutch walked over and handed him his drink.

Eli asked, "What did the greasy Mexican want?"

Dutch chuckled and said, "You were always one with words weren't you?"

Eli then leaned over and said, "Behind me" while Dutch reached behind Eli, he pressed a small vial into Dutch's hand.

Dutch explained, "He asked me to go swing by in a bit."

Eli grinned while he pointed out to Dutch, "When it comes to the A-gays Dutchie, you becomes us. You know the rules."

Dutch said as he discreetly lifted the vial to his nose and inhaled deeply. "You know they fucking hate us."

Eli then added, "The A-gays hate everyone Dutchie."

Dutch leaned back and watched the crowd of men on the dancefloor while the lights overhead bounced off the mirrors that partially surrounded the dancefloor. He teased, "Then you should fit right in."

Eli complained, "Not since I fucked Keith's ex…" Dutch's jaw dropped as Eli hissed, "Oh fuck off Dutch, like you didn't know. It was all over the call centre floor."

Dutch said, "You fucked Samuel when those two weren't dating."

Eli took a sip of his drink and elaborated, "Actually, we fucked before they split and then during."

Dutch asked shocked, "So you were Samuel's rebound while he and Keith were broken up."

"As far as Keith knows." Eli smiled.

Dutch peered over to the dancefloor as Eli said, "Keith and him got back together, and when Samuel told him it gave Keith even more reason to hate me."

Dutch said, "In the time I've known you, you've never had an official relationship. Admittedly that's scary."

Eli responded mildly offended, "Why would I ever want to tie myself down to such bullshit? Besides I've been out as long as you have been…"

"…and we've been best friends for just about the same…" Dutch responded distantly.

"Speaking of relationships Dutchie, what are you waiting for?" Eli asked

He remained silent as for a few moments the thumping of the music seemed to drown out any indications of thought in Dutch's head. He then blurted out, "Aimee called yesterday. She didn't leave a message as to why."

Eli grimaced and muttered, "Mother is probably wondering how you are."

Dutch grunted and said, "Yeah like that's the case at all."

Eli reasoned, "I'm sure your parents have a very legitimate reason as to why they gave you relocation money to stuff you in Edmonton."

Dutch said, "It's because my dad is one of those crazy fuckin' redneck conservatives under Klein who thinks you should be burned at the cross if you're gay. Fucking pathetic."

Eli then popped a tab of ecstasy in his mouth and said, "It's no excuse to not send a postcard, or call your mom."

Dutch argued, "The problem is he controls her. We talk on the phone and I can feel that she channels him." While Dutch guzzled the remainder of his drink said after, "I think between myself and Aimee we're the only sane ones in the family."

Eli sighed and asked, "How is she doing anyhow?"

Dutch said, "Good as ever I guess. University is keeping her busy and she's dating that French guy from Quebec City."

Eli rolled his eyes and deadpanned, "Fuck, the French are taking over Dutchie."

"Why do you say that?" Dutch asked kind-of shocked.

Eli replied incredulously, "Cause they're everywhere. I mean, look at Go Credit…"

"That's only Antoine, Eli…" Dutch replied getting irritated.

Eli then grinned and said, "Looks like someone has a crush…"

Dutch glared and then laughed. He then reached into Eli's pocket and fished out the vile of cocaine, unscrewing the lid and inhaling deeply.

Eli prodded, "You have getting into my pants down to science."

Dutch then teased, "Fuck you Eli, I'm going to get drinks."

Dutch walked over to the lineup where he quickly wiped his nose and inhaled deeply. Once his drinks were purchased he walked around the bar where he spotted Eli in conversation with someone. And while Dutch could not decipher the words, he knew clearly what was going on and what was about to happen shortly after. The person was Asian, not Eli's type at all. Shorter and skinnier than Eli, his sunglasses masking his eyes, while his black hair had carefully been spiked upwards. Within moments Dutch could read Eli's facial expression that he was clearly not interested. Finally the stranger stormed off as Eli shuddered while Dutch arrived and shoved the drink in his hand.

Dutch said, "That looked painful."

Eli elaborated, "It never ceases to amaze me that when you tell them you're not into foreign food, they don't get the hint."

"Ouch" Dutch said as he started to work on his drink. He then added, "Don't you think that was a little harsh?"

Eli shrugged and asked, "I didn't come to pander to anyone else."

As Dutch took another sip of his drink, he could feel the waves of ecstasy start to progress from its minor ripples which seemed to happen only moments before. The cocaine began to coarse through his system as Eli's sentences seemed to melt together. They weaved in and out of the dancefloor lights and finally Dutch snapped out of his higher state of consciousness when Eli sharply jabbed him.

"Earth to fucking Dutch." Eli intoned sarcastically.

Eli then grinned as Dutch sighed, "Sorry. These pills are really kicking my ass." He then looked over and noticed that Eli's attention had shifted to the dancefloor.

Eli asked, "Are these the pills you got from E?" Dutch nodded and Eli smiled and pointed out, "See? Even our drug dealer is French." Dutch groaned and shook his head with a smile as Eli said, "C'mon, lets go out to the dancefloor."

Dutch followed along as Eli planted them in the middle of the shirtless, sweaty crowd. While Dutch found his dancing partner in the music, he noticed that Eli's focus was not completely on his surroundings. He followed Eli's gaze as it moved along with someone whom he'd spotted only minutes before. He stood about the same height as Eli, and Dutch could visibly see the muscle pattern defined under his shirt. While his ball cap partially hid his face, he could see the brilliant smile and not that he shot at Eli as Eli said, "Don't wait up for me. I'm going to go play."

Dutch stopped dancing, left in the opposite direction, and peered over to see if Keith and Paul were still seated. He sighed and sat down at the back bar, briefly watching Eli and the capped stranger make conversation.

As Dutch ordered another drink he heard, "Does he always just leave you in a lurch like that?" He glanced over and saw Stewart and half-smiled.

He asked, "Hey Stewart how are you?"

Stewart only shrugged as he sighed, "I'm feeling a little off right now. Otherwise…"

Dutch then asked, "How do you like customer service?"

Stewart smiled and said, "I really like it. Everyone seems like a fun bunch." He then said, "My only problem is that."

Dutch echoed, "That?"

Stewart paused and replied, "I shouldn't be telling you. You're really tight with Eli."

Dutch reassured him, "Just because Eli's my best friend doesn't mean that I report back everything to him." Stewart then said, "I just hate how he rides my ass all the time on the floor. It makes me fucking mental." He added "And all the shit he gives me because I apparently like Daniel." Dutch remained silent as Stewart pointed out, "He's told half the fucking call centre."

Dutch then said, "Eli only does that because he's very insecure about himself." He then added, "Plus he's a gossip queen who can't keep his mouth shut." He took a sip of his drink and said, "You and Daniel seem pretty tight."

Stewart explained, "When all that shit with Darcy happened a few months ago, Daniel really pulled through for me as a friend." Stewart then said, "He was supposed to come out with me and some of my friends but he bailed last minute."

Dutch then asked, "Is everything okay?"

Stewart explained, "His mom passed out at bingo last night. He had to take her down to the hospital."

"Fuck" Dutch mumbled as he said, "I knew his mother was quite sick, but I didn't know it was this harsh." Dutch then continued, "It's just him and his mother Stewart. Daniel doesn't really have anyone else."

Stewart nodded as Dutch then said, "Hey Stewart I'm not making an inference here, but please be careful with him. He's not as reliable as you think."

It was at that point that Dutch could read it across his face. He tried his best to mask his concern which was easy enough given his chemical rush.

Stewart then asked, "So what about you and Eli?"

Dutch's eyes suddenly widened as he then asked, "What about me and Eli?"

"Well you seen like a perfect fit. I mean, you would think that you two would be living happily ever after."

Dutch was silent for a few moments, stared down at his drink then back up at Stewart as he replied, "If you hadn't already guessed, Eli's perfect fit is exceptionally impossible compared to anyone else's. In other words Eli's perfect fit doesn't exist."

Stewart chuckled and said, "For his best friend you sure are upfront."

Dutch then grinned and replied, "I've just learned to live with the idiosyncrasies."

Stewart's phone then vibrated as he gazed at the caller ID. He apologetically said, "I have to take this call. I'll talk to you later."

Dutch raised his drink and said, "Enjoy your night."

Stewart sped off towards the DJ booth while Dutch scratched his head and gazed around as he discovered Stewart's question had significantly depleted his high. He discreetly popped another tab in his mouth and finished his drink as he felt his own phone start to jiggle in his pocket. He opened it up and spotted the text message that read UPSTAIRS IN LOUNGE.

He got up and made his way up the steps, each step feeling a little heavier as he could feel his second pill start to dissolve and travel to the furthest points in his body. When he arrived outside he went up the next flight of stairs to the lounge where Eli sat laid back in a booth, a pint of beer in his hands.

Dutch sat down and said, "That was quick."
Eli replied, "We're going to the bathhouse next door."
Dutch then protested, "I really wanted to go to Factory tonight and check out the DJs."
Eli snapped, "Dutchie those places are dirty and everyone who goes is all fucked up on something."

Dutch glared at him as Eli asked, "What?"
"Just listen to yourself and what you just said for a moment."
"What do you mean?"
"And you're telling me a bathhouse is not fucking dirty."

Eli said, "Dutch you know my position on all that sketchy music you listen to."
Dutch could start to feel a vein pop out of his forehead as he said, "Fine. Go to the fucking bathhouse without me Eli. I'll go to Factory by myself."

Eli half-whined, "Oh come on Dutchie. Come to the bathhouse with me tonight." He then tried to entice him with, "You'll get laid…" Dutch grunted as Eli poured him a glass of beer from the pitcher close by and cautiously pushed it forward in front of Dutch. Eli then reasoned, "If I don't meet Guy at said bathhouse, we'll get dressed and go to Factory. I promise." He then pointed out, "Plus I've taken an unhealthy mix of drugs and alcohol and you'd be quite upset if for some reason I react badly and suddenly die in the sling room due to my over consumption…now wouldn't you?"

Dutch was not happy as he finished his beer in record time and they both headed down the steps and towards the building next door. Eli led him down the pathway between the two buildings and into a nondescript entrance that led them into the bathhouse. The whole way Dutch beat himself up for not protesting loud and aggressive enough at the lounge. When they arrived at the window next to the entrance Eli said, "Two please" and the attendant asked, "And how are you boys this evening?" Dutch remained silent as Eli replied, "Fucking fantastic." The attendant let them in and handed them towels.

Eli handed him a key and explained, "You're locker thirty-three." Dutch asked, "And you are?" Eli grinned and replied, "Room eighteen."

Dutch scowled and said, "It fucking figures as much." He started to walk away and said, "I'll be waiting in the lobby dressed."

Eli headed over to the maze of rooms and found room eighteen, quickly undressing once the door was locked behind him. Finally clad in only his towel he locked the door and began back down the hallway. A few people slowly passed Eli in the hallway trying to make eye contact which Eli quickly avoided.

When he arrived in the shower area he saw the man with the ball cap from the Pink Bar hang up his hat on one of the hooks with his towel hanging underneath, and opened the glass door into the shower cubicle. Eli waited a few seconds then quickly followed suit, opening the door and stepping in. The person smirked and asked, "Don't you ever think to knock before you enter?" Eli only let out a small chuckle and closed the glass door behind him.

When he secured the door shut he stepped under the rush of water while the person leaned in eyes closed to prevent chlorine sting and kissed Eli passionately. Eli could feel his penis stiffening as the stranger moved from Eli's mouth, down his neck and chest, then finally to Eli's erection. Eli positioned himself in the path the water while the stranger began to engulf him fully, one hand holding Eli steady while the other hand wander up and inside Eli. Eli moaned in pleasure as his hips began to slowly rock in approval.

Within minutes Eli could feel it welling up inside him as he finally achieved climax and pushed himself further into his companion's mouth. He held Eli during his orgasm and slowed his sucking rhythm as Eli pulsed and came. He then regained his balance on his feet and stood up putting his head back under the shower.

They kissed again as the guy with the ballcap asked, "You got a room?"

Eli smiled and said, "Follow me." They stepped out of the shower and Eli grabbed his towel while he watched his shower companion reach over and started to dry off from the top. He then gazed a little lower to see his erection still half ballooned. It poked out as he wrapped the towel around his waist and pulled the ball cap on his head. Eli motioned and they both disappeared into the maze of rooms.

Meanwhile Dutch had resigned himself to soaking in the whirlpool as he pulled his clothing, stuffed them into the locker, and headed to the shower area. He saw the ballcap and grunted as he turned on the water in his stall and began to let it wash over him. The ecstasy had begun to work even deeper as with each shift in the water's temperature he could feel the sensation start to elevate. A few minutes later he turned the water off and wrapped the towel back around his waist. He took one look at the whirlpool and decided before he would sit in he would wander around the hallways and venture through the main area. In a darkened corner of the complex he spotted someone who looked a little younger than he was eyeing him up and down. Dutch returned the gaze and followed him over to the glory hole booth where the person quickly inspected to ensure vacancy.

Once sure that the booth was empty, Dutch entered the one beside it. He closed the door behind him as Dutch could feel the fingers from the other side clumsily prodding at Dutch's crotch area, finally finding the erection and guiding it towards the hole. Dutch properly positioned himself and slid in, promptly feeling the mouth on the other end tug at his erection. While the room was already pitch-black Dutch closed his eyes and began to focus on the other persons sucking motions. Dutch however didn't think of the person who was on the other end, but visualized who he wished was on the other end. He placed a hand behind him, imagining that it was His as he could feel himself nearing climax. The pace was consistent as Dutch felt the tongue circle around the shaft and his head as he crested, Dutch letting out a high pitched moan as he violently shook and came.

Within the moments it had finished, he leaned back against the wall catching his breath, then picking up the towel from the floor. He wrapped it around his waist and opened the door, the area empty as the din of electronic music bounced from the overhead speakers. This promptly reminded Dutch of where he really wanted to be instead of here as he walked back through some of the hallways which were deserted. He circled past room eighteen slowly three times, the last time strumming his fingers on the door as he walked away and back towards the lockers.

He pulled on his shirt as he saw the message light on his cell blink. He opened the phone and sighed as the lone message read DON'T WAIT UP read across the screen. The momentary feeling of bliss caused by the ecstasy was quickly replaced by disappointment as he hurriedly pulled his jeans on. He tightened his belt and walked to the front to drop off his towel. He sighed as the attendant smiled and asked, "How was your night?" Dutch sighed and shot him a pained expression. He deadpanned "Business as usual…"

Once he left the bathhouse, he strolled across Jasper Avenue and into the main entrance of his building. What once was a steady stream of vehicles was now desolate and empty. Upon arrival he was greeted by the same mess of Chinese food that Eli had caused hours before. Dutch did not realize that this was their order that has been strewn over the panes of glass and carpet. When he finally let himself into the apartment, he walked into the kitchen and pulled out a vodka cooler and a bottle of water. As he walked into his bedroom he spotted Erin asleep in the couch. He carefully pulled the blanket that was on the couch over her. She stirred briefly as he then crept to his room and closed the door behind him.

LOVE'S SWEET EXILE
DiSC 54 - 63 MiNUTES
50 SECONDS

"And here I am once again. Friday night at the Pink Bar was full of the usual vampires and pretentious fucks that inhabit the majority of Edmonton's queer population. Although I'm told that admittedly Calgary's community is not that much better. You even classify as fresh and the fangs are automatically out."

"Although I wouldn't even be so sure of that myself because of the fact that I alone was excommunicated from the family, all thanks to a patriarchal system that existed so that Alberta's forefathers could still inbreed. It was good to see Stewart out though. I feel bad for him because Eli makes his life miserable in Customer Service, and he can't do anything about it. I really hope for his sake either Daniel comes out, or at least gives a fuck about their friendship. Maybe that will put some responsibility into Daniel. But then again if Daniel is already ditching out on Stewart it's going to make life that much more difficult."

"Eli should know better. He really needs to learn to leave things be and not try to fuck over Stewart just for the sake of destroying someone else's life. Just because Daniel can't make up his mind sexuality-wise, it doest not give Eli the right to walk all over their friendship. Then again you can see it in Eli's eyes even though he swears up and down he does not want Daniel. He can say it all he wants but there's a look in Eli's eyes that just oozes that he's not completely given up on the idea."

"It's the way he looks when he wants something badly. For the most part I swear to God some days he knows. It's like he sees right through me and takes a key and unlocks it. It's almost like he knows that my heart breaks when he goes off, gets what he wants, and makes a point to throw it in my face as if I was fucking blind…"

"Maybe its time I told him. I'm getting tired of waiting…thinking he'll come around…thinking he just might return to me…"

Chapter Four

Eli fumbled for his keys and opened the door to his apartment situated only blocks away from where Dutch lived. He immediately looked around and headed for the bathroom as he checked the clock on he wall which read noon. He peeled off his clothing and walked out into the living room as he set up his laptop at the kitchen table. He opened the vile of ketamine and laid it on a mirror beside the laptop, using a credit card to start cutting the lines as he logged in. With his wireless mouse he navigated onto the internet and aimlessly began to surf as he waited for his messenger program pop up. As he searched for Dutch, he discovered that his icon was set on away. He typed, AM HOME…VIVID TONIGHT?

There was no response as Eli leaned over and began to snort up one of the perfectly formed lines when a sound announced the arrival of someone online. Upon looking up he wiped the drizzle from his nose and at the bottom of the right hand corner a window popped up. The name on the top of the window read Sammy as Eli quickly maneuvered the mouse and clicked on the screen as the message ARE YOU THERE popped up?

Eli smiled and typed in OF COURSE I AM as the ketamine began to instill a feeling of vertigo.

He waited and watch as DID YOU JUST GET HOME? popped up on the screen.

Eli sat back for a moment watching the computer screen. He then typed, JUST WOKE UP. He knew that he lied, a flat out direct lie. The moment of guilt he felt vanished quickly as the next message that popped up caught his attention.

Samuel typed PLANS FOR THE DAY?
Eli typed back that he was planning to spend the day with Dutch.
Samuel wrote back HAVE TO SPEND THE DAY WITH KEITH.

Eli sighed as he tapped the straw on the table. He snorted another line and typed in the words I MISS YOU on the screen. What was actually minutes felt like hours as Eli waited for the words to be typed back.

Finally I MISS YOU TOO showed up on the screen. With one hand he closed the laptop and stumbled into the bedroom as he laid back on his bed and stared at the ceiling. In a matter of minutes he'd fallen asleep on his bed, woken up a few hours later by his cell phone alarm clock.

He rubbed his eyes as he looked at his cell phone and groaned. He walked into the bathroom and turned on the shower as he stretched and quickly dashed to his laptop and opened it up. As he looked at the screen he saw his original message to Dutch and the message underneath that read WILL DO. He quickly returned and stepped into the shower and he let the water cover him. The smell of soap filled the room as Eli carefully washed himself down, making sure he cleaned everywhere. When he stepped out of the shower he walked back into his bedroom, and pulled out an undershirt and found another dress shirt. As he buttoned it up he shot a glare at the mirror reflection, quickly dashing back to the closet to find a pair of pants.

He took the elevator down to the parkade and quickly hopped into his car and quickly donned a pair of sunglasses, then began the drive towards the most southern tip of Edmonton suburbia. As he drove down 109th Street he opened his phone and started dialing the numbers. Within two rings he announced, "I'm on my way down mom. Did you need me to pick up anything?" A few moments passed as he turned south onto Calgary Trail. He then said, "Fair enough. I'll pick some up on the way."

Eli always thought that the drive down Calgary Trail was empty and desolate. Motels coupled with car dealerships lined either side of the route, the odd fast food restaurant or liquor store punctuating the stretch before another exhausting row of dealerships and motels would pass him by. He finally took the off ramp that was just by South Edmonton Common and stopped at the Real Canadian Liquorstore just before he traveled another off ramp that signaled the entrance to a cookie-cutter suburb that his parents called home. Eli raged that every house looked exactly the same, distinguished only by the BMW's, Mercedes-Benz and Volkswagens that graced either the driveways or lined up on the streets. It was partially why Eli wanted to burn down every house in this neighborhood, concluding they would just all burn down into toxic heaps of nothing. It was also the reason Eli would miss his parent's house every time he drove by.

When he was sure he had arrived, he pulled up into the driveway and turned off the ignition. He stepped out and slowly paced up the steps and knocked on the door. Moments later a middle-aged woman opened the door, paused for a moment then smiled, "My dear boy."

"Hey mom" he blushed as he gave her a tight hug. He followed her in and closed the door behind him while she beckoned,
"Come in. Dinner's just about ready!"

He glided over to the kitchen, set down the paper bag on the counter as he glanced over, and spotted his two sisters as well as the older one's girlfriend. His youngest sister Chelsea brought in a plate of food while his mother said, "Come sit down before it gets cold." She then asked, "Where's Dutch?"

He weakly smiled and mumbled, "Not too sure" while everyone sat down. He then looked over at Chelsea and teased, "I didn't see you at work as of late miss."

She shrugged and explained, "I haven't been taking a lot of shifts lately because I've been swamped on campus." She then sweetly asked, "Has anyone said anything?"
He said to her as he began to sip his drink, "I would never gossip about people outside of work." He then asked, "Where's the darky?"

She frowned and said, "Fuck you Eli if you can't use proper terminology." She then added, "And you gossip all of the time."

His eyes widened as he then demanded, "With who?"

She began, "Let me see you gossip about Sherry, Alex…" She then put a finger to her chin and rolled her eyes. "Your favorite person of late has been Stewart."

Eli then shot back, "Not quite. He's a piece of gossip that writes itself."

He sighed out as she argued, "You know its people like you that prevent him from meeting someone nice."

He asked, "Like who? Daniel?" Chelsea shrugged as Eli said, "Daniel is the hopeless, straight cheese head that will be forever tied to mommy, who will keep him on a leash by methods of fainting. She'll turn a blind eye to his pot smoking which of course keeps him heavily sedated and stupid." He flatly blurted out, "No thank you, I'm not into that fucking shit show."

Chelsea said, "Even though you like to create your own?" He said nothing as she continued, "And you wonder why everyone thinks you're the abnormal one in the family."

He opened his mouth to say something when his older sister Jade said, "It's true Eli. Even when I was a team leader on the floor people thought we all turned out normal and somehow the Antichrist just seemed to show up somewhere in between…"

With that comment she promptly slapped some food onto his plate while his parents sat down and Jade snapped, "Now eat you little drama queen."

His mouth became unhinged as he protested, "The abuse I get here." He said, "Your only gay son being beat up by a lesbian and someone who dates darkies."

Chelsea stabbed him with his fork enough for him to wince in pain as she said, "Keep up that shit, and you won't live to see your next night out."

His mother chimed in, "Y'know, next time you come around bring Dutch along." She added, "I'm sure that kid needs a family too."

Eli huffed out, "I'm sure he's fine mom."

His father chimed in, "Your mother's right Eli. Dutch doesn't have a lot of people here in Edmonton."

Eli argued, "Aimee just moved up to Edmonton in the spring for university."

"Still it's not right" his mother said, "Disowning your kid because he's different."

Eli knew when his mother was passionate and dead serious about how she felt when it came to subjects of family and sexuality.

He coldly repeated, "I'm sure he's fine…"

The rest of the meal left Eli detached from the conversation the family was engaged in. It was becoming common ritual as he said nothing and finished his meal. This last year alienation had really seeped into the family meals as his disdain had become more and more vocal. When he finished his meal, he stood up and took his plate over to the sink. He then opened the bottle of rye in the fridge, and after digging in the freezer for ice, poured himself a glass and escaped out the door and onto the patio.

His gaze moved from the backyard out to Edmonton's empty outskirts as he held the glass up to his nose, sniffed it in approval and swallowed the first gulp shaking his head to go down his throat. He gazed at his phone as he debated whether or not he wanted Dutch to pick up more chemicals. As he leaned back on the wooden bench, his father came out and spotted him. He sauntered over to Eli as Eli tried to notice how years of unforgiving labor had taken its toll on him. Like Dutch's parents Eli's father was a card carrying Alberta politician. After the more recent housecleaning of Alberta Liberals out of the legislature, Eli's father shifted his focus to teaching political science on University of Alberta's main campus. Legislature was where Dutch and Eli's respective parents met and eventually would be how they would meet as well.

He sat down beside Eli, after plucking the drink from Eli's hand took a swig, and mused, "You know we love you Eli. We also know that Dutch is still without family here in Edmonton." He stared at the glass and then said, "Fuck Eli, don't you still have to drive?"

Eli smugly replied, "I'll be fine dad." His father then lit up a cigarette, took a puff then handed it over to Eli. He said, "Then give us something to work with kid. You know your mother hates it when…"

"When you don't get the whole picture."

He said, "I get e-mails from his mother still."
 Eli sucked back on the cigarette and said, "If she really cared…"
His father countered, "She does. But she's worried that Dutch is not telling her the truth."

Eli flatly said, "He has a lot of trust issues right now, but honestly he's okay." Eli handed the cigarette back and his father finished it. Eli continued, "Dutchie's got strong survival skills. I mean, he's made it this far."
His father smiled in agreement and added, "He's not the only one Eli."
Eli smiled and said, "I learned it from you both." He squeezed his father's shoulder as he explained, "I gotta go dad. Dutch and I are going out tonight." He then looked back at him on the bench. "Finish the drink off for me?"
His father held his up in salutation and said, "Cheers."

Instead of through the house Eli opted to sneak through the side gate and out to his car. With keys in the ignition and car backed out of the driveway, the rye was beginning to seep out of the meal as a lightheadedness started to move slowly from his legs and up into his arms. It was at this point he decided to stop the car on a corner and fish for the small vile of cocaine. When he finally found it he cautiously inspected it, ensuring that the vile was not the one with the ketamine. Once sure he poured a little onto the back of his hand and quickly snorted it up one of his nostrils. He then checked in the rear view mirror for residue and leaned back closing his eyes.

He wished that Chelsea had not brought up work at the dinner table. Eli was fully aware that family was not only apparent at home but also at work, but he questioned it's validity at the diner table. It was only one more reason to avoid the house, and overall the family.

It was the rush of adrenaline and anger that dissipated the intoxicated feeling. When he opened his eyes to feel his phone vibrate in his pocket, he pulled it out and saw the screen. Dutch had called. He quickly dialed the number. When Dutch's voicemail picked up he said, "Dutchie its Eli. Bring more." And with that he turned the ignition back on.

Chapter Five

When Eli first walked up into the main entrance of Vivid he quickly shot the text R U HERE? The instantaneous response was missing as he glance at the lineup behind him and then back into the entrance. The thirty-something bouncer nodded and said, "Good evening Eli." She placed a plastic wristband around his arms while he dryly thanked her and walked in.

Eli scoured the main floor as he huffed and debated where to venture first. He then followed the flight of stairs down, under the playground crossing sign, and into the dark. He looked to his right and saw the overflowing dancefloor, while he stretched to try to spot Dutch. While a green laser ricocheted overhead to the bass, he inched his way in a little closer while trying to peer through the crowd. The thump of the music continued to vibrate around him as finally Dutch appeared up at the shooter bar just across from the dancefloor.

He walked up to Dutch as Dutch immediately spotted him and waved. Dutch asked, "How was family dinner?"

Eli rolled his eyes and groaned, "I really should have done a little more K before dinner."

Dutch chuckled then asked, "Are you sure that would have been a good idea?"

Eli pondered for a moment then said, "You're right. That might have not worked out too well."

As Eli was handed a drink he asked, "What did you do this afternoon?"
He replied "Pretty much nothing. Just couldn't have been bothered."
Eli then said, "I should have done the same."
Dutch then pointed out, "Your family would have been up your ass in no time." Eli grinned and asked, "You wanna trade?"

Eli then felt a hand slide into his pants while Dutch leaned in and whispered in his ear above the music, "The red vile will speed you up nicely and help you fire all synapses. The blue one will stick you further down the rabbit hole."
Eli asked, "And tonight's plans?"
Dutch smiled and replied, "Freshly pressed white doves."
Eli grinned and added, "The symbol of peace and tranquility." Eli sipped his drink and suggested, "Let's go up to the lounge. This music makes my fucking head hurt."
Dutch protested, "What's the point of dropping a perfectly good pill if you don't have an equally good soundtrack?" Eli shot him a glare as Dutch then said, "Fine. Your loss." Eli beckoned him up the steps, and out of the basement towards Vivid's main foyer. The deep blue glow warmed them as Eli led the way up the steps while Dutch scanned the lounge. Everyone seemed bathed in blue as the thump from the lower level was now a distant echo, replaced by the mesh of strings and sporadic beeps and bleeps. They both looked over to the left as Dutch pointed out two stools over by the bar. When they sat down Eli casually held the red vile up to his nose and inhaled deeply. Dutch looked over and with his thumb rubbed under Eli's nostrils. Eli chuckled while Dutch wiped it on his jeans. Within moments Dutch could feel his tab of ecstasy start to flood his senses. He looked over and saw Keith and Samuel standing not too far away, ready to order drinks. Eli then breathed, "It's time to go make nice I guess." Dutch trailed behind him as Eli went up and greeted Keith. "Hey Keith" he said as Keith looked up and asked, "Where's your little assistant this evening?"
Eli was fumbling for the words when Dutch stood out from behind Eli and said, "Hey guys."
Keith glanced at Samuel and said, "Look Sammy, if it isn't sketchy and sketchier." When Eli went to say something Keith spat out, "You really should know better Eli. You don't just home-wreck as you please and walk away thinking karma's not going to bite you in the ass."
Keith walked away from them as Samuel apologized, "You know how it is."

Eli calmly replied, "It's not an issue." Samuel laid a twenty dollar bill on the counter and explained something to the bartender while he then turned around and said, "The next round's on me you guys." He then walked up to Eli and said, "I'll text you later." Eli watched as Samuel rejoined Keith and they walked down the stairs.

Dutch handed him a drink then observed, "Yup. Keith fucking hates us Eli, which nullifies any remote chance of..."

"I fucking know that Dutchie!" he spat out, then added, "I'm heading to the washroom. Don't fucking wait up."

Eli headed down the stairs and made his way over to the men's washroom on the main floor. He could have stayed and used the men's room in the lounge, but something inside him wanted to see Samuel again. He slowly pushed his way through the crowd that moved slowly towards the back. At the best of times on Saturdays he tried to avoid the main floor. However the impromptu sighting of Samuel made him yearn to clear his head chemically.

His walk to the bathroom was stopped short when he felt a hand tug at his shoulder. He stopped and looked over as he heard, "Hey Eli how have you been?"

When he looked he saw someone about his height and build as Eli weakly smiled and said, "Good-bye."

When he went to turn around the hand tugged again and the person asked, "Don't you remember me?" Eli cocked his head to the side as the person continued, "Ricky. We hooked up last week at Pink."

Eli then said, "Oh riiigggghhht..." Eli then explained, "We then started off in the bathroom at Pink and headed to the bathhouse after."

Ricky said, "You're there."

Eli then barked, "Yeah, goodbye" and proceeded to walk away.

Ricky raised his voice a little in agitation. "Do you pride yourself on being a prick?"

Eli turned around and began to inch closer to Ricky. He sneered, "When the sex is mediocre and not worth remembering, you tend to forget pretty fast." Eli then said, "Now I'm going to head over to the washroom to actually piss, which I've been trying to do since I was so rudely interrupted."

Ricky gave him the once over and replied, "Fuck you Eli."

Eli then snapped, "Not worth a second round."

When he walked into the bathroom he quickly headed to the stall at the very end. He closed the door behind him, and pulled the vile back out deeply breathing in. He then downed his drink and wiped his nose while he headed over to the sink to wash his hands. Upon arrival back into the main foyer he saw Dutch in conversation with a blonde-haired male that appeared to be not much older than them. He sauntered over as Dutch looked over and then said, "Sean, this is my best friend Eli. We've known each other now for at least seven years."

Sean extended his hand and slithered, "Hi, I'm Sean."

Eli's prompt reply was, "Fuck, are you ever dirty."

Suddenly the half crooked smile was gone as Sean asked, "Excuse me?"

Eli then continued, "Now really why would I want to fuck, or let my best friend fuck someone that for the most part looks like he was born with down syndrome?"

Sean just stood there glaring as Eli grinned, "Still mentally processing that one eh?"

Sean then spat out, "Fuck you." and stormed off.

Eli hollered after him, "Someone make sure that boy don't get a pair of scissors!!"

Dutch smiled and said, "Thanks" as Eli asked with a smile, "You weren't seriously thinking on going home with that were you?"

Dutch shook his head no as Eli replied, "Good. Because unlike you, it looks like the bleach really affected him."

Dutch laughed as Eli suggested, "Let's go back downstairs and have a drink."

They walked downstairs as Dutch asked, "How are those pills treating you?"

Eli replied, "These are actually really good Dutchie. Did they come from E?"

Dutch explained, "He got them from Amsterdam. Apart from pures, they're the next best thing."

Eli nodded as he said, "I'm going to the washroom. I'm going to drop another one before the feeling starts to dwindle."

Dutch said, "I'll get drinks."

He walked over to the back bar when Keith quickly approached him. Keith said to Dutch, "I have nothing against you Dutch. But do you honestly want to spend the next few years being a little bitch to someone who doesn't really give a fuck about you?"

Dutch bit his lip as he said, "Eli and I are best friends Keith. We've stuck together this long."

Keith chided, "With all of the drugs that he's ingested over the years on your dime, I would stick with you too. In fact I'm pretty surprised that you've survived."

Dutch then said to him, "Funny cause the same could have been said about you."

Keith argued, "You can't be his wingman forever Dutch."

Dutch turned to Keith and responded defensively, "And you can't beat him up forever for fucking Samuel when you two were broken up."

Eli quickly rejoined Dutch as Keith stood there and glared at them both. Eli asked, "Is everything okay?"

Dutch grimaced as he explained. "Keith was just leaving."

Keith then snapped, "It's deeper than you think" and walked away. Eli looked at Dutch as Dutch forced a drink into his hand. "It was nothing. Just start drinking."

Eli remained silent as he mumbled, "Okay" while they watched a full dancefloor.

When Dutch could feel the second tab start to move through his body he said to Eli, "I want to dance."

Eli frowned and asked, "Do I have to?" Dutch grabbed Eli's free hand and pulled him onto the dancefloor. As the lights seemed to almost guide them onto a free space on the dancefloor Eli leaned into Dutch and said, "You're lucky I'm high and you're my friend Dutchie." Eli then added, "Especially to this rave shit."

Dutch playfully argued, "If you came out with me to the afterhours once in awhile we would not be having this discussion."

Eli reasoned, "Fair enough."

Minutes later Eli felt his phone vibrate. When he pulled it out he read I'M FREE splashed across the screen. He knew exactly at this point who it was as he leaned into Dutchie's ear. "Dutchie I've got a two a.m."

Dutch asked, "Where? At the bathhouse?"

Eli said, "If that's a request to tag along, the answer is no."

Dutch shrugged and replied, "Fine. Suit yourself."

Eli disappeared to the foyer shortly after and he texted I'LL SEE YOU THERE. He then raced up to the stairs and out to his car, sniffing a little more from the red vile before he drove off towards Jasper Avenue, Dutch furthest from his mind.

Chapter Six

Dutch got out of the cab and stared at the huge yellow sign that was adorned with flashing lights, some wildly blinking, some completely burnt out. Dutch felt a familiar chill as he walked into the adult entertainment store. He walked past the tired-looking and overweight prostitute, then pushed open the door as he looked at the empty store. It was deserted save for one older man casually glancing at the videos. He looked up as Dutch shuddered and turned to the counter. "Evening" he said to the clerk as he smiled and handed Dutch tokens.

He sighed as he felt the surge of his high begin to pick up speed despite the dirge of eighties music that played overhead. After a brief glance of the empty back area, he quietly made his way towards the corridor down the stairs and into the main area. Four men sat in the TV lounge area while someone passed him, clunking up the steps. As he looked around he began to fumble in the darkness, following the half – lively set of Christmas lights around a corner and then another into what looked like rows of doors on either side. He cautiously made his way in as people crisscrossed the main aisle into other booths. As Dutch could clearly hear the sounds of porn in a surround-like state, he walked through the main area and peered around while outlines quickly faded behind booths or in the dark corners.

He could clearly hear over the din of squeals layered with the music above, Eli's voice resonating through his mind, reminding him of how this place was dirty and was infested by trolls, prostitutes, and crack-addicts. The irony was that Eli had actually shown him this place within the first years of being relocated from Calgary. Before they'd graduated to bathhouses they would make the peeps the second afterhours stop. Eli had stopped making the trek to the peepshows after awhile and Dutch would make the trek alone, despite Eli's veiled objection. However the last year he had learned to keep that from Eli, surmising it would be better if he just not knew at all. For what it was worth he knew it would be better to just not say anything at all.

After one quick tour around the main area, he decided to sit down back in the main lounge area and watch the big screen television. Someone had left it on one of the religious networks as a cruel joke, and as he gazed at the poorly resembled news program he wondered how much plastic surgery the female co-host had adorned over the years. The last pill he ingested seemed to amplify the sound as he quickly glanced to his left and found an older man asleep on the chair opposite side him. He then looked to his right where the lone 8-bit arcade games stood and momentarily flashed bright lights or spat out the random beep and bleep of badly constructed melodies. His eyes then focused back onto the screen as a few minutes later he could hear the door open upstairs and footsteps overhead. After a few minutes the steps moved over to the right and then disappeared towards the back of the main floor as the mock newscast focused on the snowy white male anchor. Beside him was a newspaper clipping of a world event that he dissected inside and out and painfully tried to match it to scripture. Dutch half smiled as he remembered where the verse was from. He knew it was somewhere in Revelations, somewhere very close to the end of the New Testament.

Dutch became very bored at that point and quickly walked up the steps and to the counter. He asked, "Can I get the remote control for the downstairs television?" The clerk nodded and handed him the remote as he sped downstairs and sifted through the channels quickly. When he finally found MuchMusic he returned the remote control and then sat down while the other person sat, still motionless in his chair. People shuffled in and out behind him, momentarily stopping to glance at him, then either arriving or disappearing up the stairs and out.

This continued for an hour as finally he opted to get up and start walking around again. He had just barely heard the door open and a lighter pair of footsteps move a long with the creaks and snaps of the floor. He returned to the maze and finally leaned against the back wall while he watched people move in and out of one booth to the next. He briefly closed his eyes and inhaled deeply. The smell of stale air and smoke filled his lungs and caused him to suddenly exhale in a cough. When he opened his eyes, the pair of footsteps that he had hear upstairs had belonged to someone sporting a leather high school jacket that turned the corner while looking around. When he disappeared into one of the side corridors Dutch sighed out as a few seconds later he reappeared and opened the nearest booth by Dutch. He quickly stopped and glanced in Dutch's direction as Dutch returned his gaze and began to inch forward.

He locked the door behind him as the jock had already lowered his jeans halfway down, his hand already manipulating his erect penis. Dutch quickly got on his knees as he leaned forward onto the jock's erection. A few minutes passed and Dutch gazed up while sucking to see the jacket come off and onto the bench as Dutch unzipped his own pants. He then pulled his mouth away as he started to remove his pants. Dutch lay back down on the other bench, and spit on his fingers then applied them around and inside himself while the jock began to position himself over Dutch. Dutch looked into his eyes as the jock then began to push inside him. Dutch grunted as he relaxed a little, letting him gain complete entry while the television screen broadcasted straight porn behind them.

With each deep thrust Dutch grunted as the usual small jabs of pain were dinned by the healthy mixture of ketamine, ecstasy, and alcohol. The rhythm seemed forced as Dutch tried to get more comfortable while his partner tried to move deeper. In the awkward position, Dutch almost felt like he was being pulled part. Finally the jock pushed all the way in while Dutch tightened up to feel the spasms inside him. He then pulled out of Dutch and put his jeans back on, disappearing shortly after, leaving Dutch alone in the light of the monitor screen.

He sat there for a few minutes as he caught his breath then quickly looked at the screen. As he began to fish for his underwear from the heap of clothes on the floor an older man walked up to the booth entrance and began to fondle himself in front of Dutch as his coke bottle bottom glasses reflected the television screen. Dutch looked up and after finally finding his underwear in the pile looked up and said to the stranger, "Not a fucking chance old man," reaching for the door and locking it shut in his face.

chapter seven

Sunday night had appeared all too soon as Eli finished his first drink and tried to let the badly sung karaoke drown out all of his thoughts. He sighed and watched the bartender float effortlessly between the register, the customers by the computer and then back over to Eli.

As the bartender glided back he asked, "Another beer hon?"

Eli nodded as finally through the entrance to the left he saw Dutch stroll in. He walked over and sat down while Eli then stood up and hugged him tightly. "You look freshly fucked" he grinned as Dutch began to redden.

"Nah just slept really well when I got in this morning."

Eli then asked, "Did you finish the vile?"

He shook his head no. "Thought I would save it for coffee break tomorrow."

Eli replied, "Good plan"

Dutch asked the bartender, "The usual." He produced small bottle of Jagermeister and a can of Red Bull, flawlessly combining the two as Dutch apologized. "Sorry I didn't text you last night. I was over at Lockers." He then took a sip of his drink and asked, "Where did you end up?"

Eli breathed in and simply explained, "I was at the other bathhouse last night. Fuck, was it ever boring."

Dutch quickly scanned Eli's face for any traces of guilt and immediately knew that Eli was lying. Dutch only smiled in agreement and nodded as the volume of the sounds around him began to increase. When he finished his drink, he loudly set the glass down as he commented, "Well at least one of us had a productive evening."

The bartender casually strolled up and asked, "More?"

Dutch put a twenty dollar bill down and nodded in agreement as Eli deadpanned, "Edmonton is such a dead city Dutch. It's no wonder that people are so quick to fuck off elsewhere."

Dutch explained, "Funny. I'm sure that people everywhere else say the exact same thing." Dutch then pointed out, "It's a common fact that we're never happy where we are." He sipped his drink. "It's why gay guys come from the small town to the big city." Eli then added, "Then to the even bigger city. Until you're right back to where you started."

"And that's why…" Eli began to sip his drink. "That there's no point in leaving where you are." Dutch only shrugged as Eli then asked, "It wasn't that retarded fucking blonde was it?"

Dutch grinned and replied, "No Eli." He then protested, "He's a hair stylist."

Eli then snapped, "I'm sure he cuts his own hair." He polished off his drink and said, "I wouldn't let that fucker near me with a pair of scissors or a child-proof razor."

At that moment they both looked over and saw a spiky-haired Asian boy walk in, sporting sunglasses and a tight long-sleeved shirt that matched his painfully skin tight pants. He strolled up to the bar and as the bartender began to pour four shots, he smiled over and nodded at Eli and Dutch. Eli groaned, "Oh fucking great…"

Dutch reasoned, "He's only trying to be nice."

Shortly after the bartender set down two full shot glasses in front of them. "Sambucca" the bartender said as Dutch watched the bartender and Asian guy down their respective shots. Shortly after, he inched his way over to them, Dutch quickly ingesting his shot.

He then said, "I'm Tom."

Dutch said, "Hey Tom thanks for the shots but we're just hanging out tonight." He then watched as Tom tried to rub Eli's chest, to which Eli grimaced with displeasure.

Tom then said, "I want to go home with you."

Eli then turned to him with shot in hand and explained, "Sorry. I'm on a no MSG diet."

He then lifted his shot glass and said, "Cheers" while Tom just stood there frozen.

Dutch grinned as again Tom tried to say something and reach for Eli's crotch when Eli shouted in his most horrible knock-off Chinese accent, "No MSG! No MSG!"

This signaled the cue for Tom's abrupt departure as his face reddened and he disappeared out the door. The remote area around them erupted in laughter while the person on stage fumbled two of his notes to the song.

Dutch had to wipe his eyes from the sting of tears from laughing so hard. Eli mused, "Aggressive little fucker."

Dutch said, "Oh come on Eli."

Eli only grinned as he picked his drink back up and started to finish it off. After his swig Eli said, "You know I hate everyone equally Dutchie."

"Except those that have money and look airbrushed."

"You also can't come in thinking the world is your noodle house." Eli replied matter-of-factly.

"Fair enough" Dutch sighed as Eli only shrugged. They both watched the television screens above as Dutch then asked, "Are we going to be like this five years down the road?"

Eli replied as he set down his glass, "I don't even want to think about that. I can't sign off on a future that feels like fucking nowhere other than Go Credit, Pink, Vivid, The Cactus, and the two bathhouses."

Dutch reasoned, "Hence why a change of scenery would do you good."

Eli then argued, "Everywhere is the same Dutch. We just don't realize it until six months into actually being there. Trust me Dutchie. Somewhere else is the same as everywhere else."

Eli finished his drink and said, "But right now a change of scenery would do use both some good. Downstairs?" Dutch silently nodded in agreement as they made their way down the stairs back out to Jasper Avenue and the Pink Bar's main entrance.

Love's Sweet Exile - Disc 55: fifteen minutes, twenty-five seconds

"Eli brought up a very valid point about how someplace better really isn't. I remember meeting someone who came from St. Brieux, Saskatchewan. He told me that he'd been terrorized growing up there for being gay. At seventeen he ran away to Saskatoon, finished high school and started university. However it seemed like every gay guy there absolutely loathed him. He wasn't ugly. He seemed like a really nice guy, maybe a little too friendly. He came across to them as wanting sex, or wanting a relationship. Six month to a year in he was beginning to feel very isolated and lost. So what was his next step? Fuck off to Calgary."

"He swore up and down to his family and friends that Calgary was the promised land. Instead it was quite the opposite. At least in Saskatoon he had a bit of a fighting chance. If they didn't hate him before, they definitely did in Calgary. They. Absolutely. Fucking. Hated. Him. After two years he finally found himself a nice boyfriend in Calgary. Nice as in jumped ship and started fucking a condom hating crack addict who liked to shoot it between his toes. I happened to meet him just after he'd finished falling apart in a rehab facility in Lethbridge. He told me he was moving to Vancouver. I wonder if he did make it to Vancouver? Or is he back in St. Brieux?"

"Something else Eli just seemed to casually ignore and that I'm beginning to find is that after our lost weekends, I'm beginning to wonder what is going to happen down the road. I'm in my early twenties and I don't feel like I've completed a fucking thing. Part of me wants to just keep things the way they are and hope something better comes along. Part of me wants to just leave it behind and be somewhere different. But I really don't want to leave Eli behind. He feels like life is so fucked for whatever reason and it shows when he goes off and fucks up someone else's."

"Is he really that unhappy?" I don't even know anymore. I'm supposed to be his best friend, and even some days I don't have a fucking clue. Even though I do love him, I can't read his mind. Especially recently. It's almost as if he purposely sours things. No explanation, no reason, no apologies."

"Myself, I didn't run away from where I was. Okay, not exactly. I was forced up here. Part of me wishes I would have run away instead. I might have avoided all of this, maybe with Eli somewhere where things would be very different between us. But that also begs the question, would we be back here anyways?"

Chapter Eight

When Eli walked into the call centre he noticed it seemed busier than usual as he set his bag down at his desk and checked his watch.

He looked over and spotted Stewart as Stewart looked over after releasing his call.

"Morning Eli" he said as Eli shrugged.

Eli then asked, "How are you Stewart?"

Stewart explained, "I'm fine Eli."

As Eli went to say something, Ariel had appeared from the lounge as she adjusted her glasses. Her expression was of frustration as she at down beside Stewart. Stewart looked over and said, "Just in time too…" She had darker brown hair which fell over her glasses, her presentation simple as she sighed. Stewart asked, "What's wrong?"

She frowned and replied, "Last night Jeremiah and I went to the Ranch with our friends. I ended up being bored because they drank so much. Finally, I told Jeremiah I wanted to go home. He started ignoring me and I started getting upset. He kept ignoring me so I finally told him to give me the keys to the car."

Stewart said nothing as she continued, "He finally fucking followed me to the car. And as if he didn't know what was wrong…" Eli tried to focus on his e-mails as she said, "So finally I said to him that sometimes I wish we would just break up and he agreed with me." Stewart's eyes widened a little as she sighed and in near tears explained, "It's so fucking frustrating. He's being such a jerk and it seems like it's been forever since we started discussing marriage."

Eli then pointed out, "He's just pissed off because you've lasted longer working here than he did." He then turned to Ariel. "This is a pretty simple job to do and really why would you want to fuck an idiot like that for the rest of your life?"

Ariel tried to choke back tears as Eli stood up and explained, "If Dutch happens to ask I'm gone for coffee break."

As Eli left she said, "Christ, he's so insensitive."

Stewart said, "He's Eli and he's gay."

She was silent and then after a couple of minutes asked "What do you think Stewart?"

Stewart shrugged as he explained, "I'm not really one to dispense advice right now. I have relationship issues of my own." She said nothing and continued to text while Stewart grabbed the next call.

Eli pressed the door and headed to the back stalls where he found Dutch already separating the lines on the toilet paper dispenser.

He said, "I thought you weren't coming."

Eli sighed and explained, "Ariel has to stop dating stupid people. Everyday it's a new fucking episode of drama with her."

Dutch asked sarcastically, "Really?"

Eli then said, "Michael was smart in firing Jeremiah's dumb ass." Dutch tried to focus on the cocaine and not spill it as he restrained his laughter. Eli continued, "Their soap opera style relationship was beginning to distract the rest of the floor."

Dutch moved out of the way and let Eli in as he said, "Now don't tell me you didn't enjoy watching that gong show."

Eli said, "It's a typical Friday night on the Pink Bar's dance floor. But here's the twist…" Eli bent down and snorted his line and said, "Ariel and Daniel have been e-mailing back and forth over the past couple of months. Daniel is well aware that Ariel is taken but that's not stopping him."

Dutch sighed as he said, "I really don't understand him Eli. I mean, he fucking chases after girls that are not available to him, or choose not to be available to him." Eli wiped up the rest of the leftover cocaine with his finger and rubbed it into his upper gums.

Eli then said, "I remember when he was running after Lisa in credit." He opened the stall door and said, "It was kind of pathetic actually. She agreed to go on a date with him and she would continue to put him off. Actually when it comes to women he's a bit socially retarded."

They walked to the washroom entrance as Dutch then said, "And that's the reason why you would never fuck him."

Eli grimaced and explained, "Too flaky for me, way too flaky…" Dutch followed Eli down the main aisle as Lance, the company's human resources director and Natasha passed them. Natasha said "Hi guys" as Dutch greeted them back. Lance only glared at Eli as they disappeared into Lance's office.

Dutch then asked, "What did you do to piss off Lance?"

Eli quietly replied, "A-gay. He hates me because of Keith." Eli then added, "And I let his ex-boyfriend fuck me."

Dutch only shook his head while he sat down at his desk and said, "Later."

Dutch spotted Marie as she sat a coffee down beside him. She asked, "How was your weekend?"

He smiled and replied, "Nothing new, was quite typical."

Marie then said, "Translation, Eli hooked up while Dutch did not."

"Hey now" he protested as he took a sip of his coffee.

She then asked, "Don't you ever get tired of being Eli's wingman?"

He shrugged and said, "It keeps me safely entertained." He then opened his e-mail as he said, "Plus I don't quite know what I'm looking for if at all."

Marie then asked, "What about Antoine?" She said, "You mean you haven't talked to him yet?"

He asked, "Should I?" Marie said nothing and just smiled as more and more members of the Elite program began to fill up.

She neatly explained, "Just remember nothing is what it seems."

As Dutch began his shift he started to sort through his e-mails and his calling schedule. One of the foremost responsibilities Dutch was assigned was the follow up with customers who hadn't been using their credit card and ensuring their needs were being met. As the Elite area was beginning to teem with work, and sounds of productivity, Dutch systematically went through his list and began to tackle his duties.

Upon first break he turned to Marie and said, "I'm going for coffee. Did you want anything?"

She smiled and explained, "Large mocha if you wish." He nodded as he began to head out towards the entrance.

On the way he saw Daniel and he said, "Hey dude"

Dutch asked "I'm going into the mall for coffee. Did you want anything?"

Daniel replied, "Coffee would be nice dude, just black." Dutch then spotted Antoine at reception talking to Dawn and cautiously made his way over while Antoine spotted him right away.

Antoine said, "Hey Dutch how are you?"

He replied, "Off on a coffee run, how about you?"

Antoine asked, "Do you mind if I come join you?"

Dutch smiled and said, "No not at all."

They headed down the escalator as Antoine said, "I've been here just under a week, and I've been so bored. I've been pretty much sticking to the mall just because I'm not sure where anything is."

Dutch then asked, "Where is the Montreal office located?" Antoine explained, "The office right now is on Langelier Boulevard in St. Leonard."

Dutch fell silent as Antoine asked, "Have you ever been to Montreal?" Dutch shook his head no and Antoine elaborated, "St. Leonard is an old Montreal suburb that's to the north. It's mainly industrial business up there. We're in a two story building out there." He then said as Dutch slowed down and lined up on the pedway that stretched across to the east part of the mall. "With the Regenesis project they're moving us hopefully downtown into the financial district."

Dutch asked, "What is the call centre like?"

Antoine chuckled, "It's quite small actually. Not like here where it's a huge centre." The line inched closer to the coffee counter as Antoine explained, "Of course Montreal is mainly home to the French speaking client base when it comes to 'Go Credit'. But Regenesis is putting a lot of important and exciting changes in motion."

They reached the counter and Dutch made his order as Antoine then added, "An espresso and a caramel latte." When the total rang up Antoine pulled out his wallet and handed her cash.

Dutch protested, "You don't have to…"

Antoine smiled, "I can expense it."

Dutch said, "Thank you"

Antoine replied, "No worries." As the barista handed Antoine a tray along with one to Dutch he asked, "Shall we?" and gestured back to the office.

"So what do you enjoy doing?" Dutch innocently asked.

Antoine replied by asking, "What are your clubs like for electronic music?"

Dutch thought for a moment then replied, "There's a few really amazing clubs left. Vivid is one of the longest running clubs in Edmonton and has three levels." Dutch then asked hesitantly, "Do you like afterhours?"

Antoine grinned and said, "I'm a Stereo boy through and through."

Dutch breathed a sigh of relief and said, "Finally someone who's not anti-afterhours." Antoine cocked his head to the side and glanced over at Dutch as he explained, "The majority of my friends hate the afterhours, so I never really go."

Antoine asked, "Do you want to go?"

"When?" trying not to sound too excited.

"I don't know. How about this weekend?"

"That sounds good. Friday night you could come out with us to the Pink Bar as a warm up."

"Who's us?"

"Eli, myself, and maybe my roommate Erin."

Antoine thought for a moment and he then asked cautiously, "How long have you known Eli for?"

Dutch replied, "We've been best friends since seventeen. Why do you ask?" Antoine smiled as they began up the escalator. Dutch sighed, "Fuck"

Antoine explained, "Eli has a bit of a reputation on him." Dutch's eyes widened as they walked into the lobby. Antoine handed Dawn her coffee as he said, "I'll tell you what. I'll e-mail you my number and we can talk more on our night out?"

Dutch nodded and replied, "I look forward to your e-mail."

Dutch watched as Antoine walked through customer service and up to the collections department. He strolled right by Daniel and Stewart who both were talking on the floor. Dutch noticed that Stewart seemed a little agitated as they talked. He neared closer to them and after wrestling the coffee from the tray handed Daniel his coffee. Dutch teased, "Black, just like how you try to act sometimes, and quite poorly I might add, when really you're from Claireview…" Stewart laughed as Dutch then handed him a coffee. "I don't know what you drink, but enjoy." Stewart thanked him as Dutch left a coffee on Eli's desk and headed back to his pod.

Dutch sat down and handed Marie her coffee as she teased, "That took a little bit longer than usual."

Dutch explained, "Yeah I got a little sidetracked on the way to grab coffee."

She then asked, "By who?"

 "Daniel stopped me mid-run to see if I would…"

"No, who?" she demanded.

Dutch said nothing as Marie began to smile. Dutch then said, "He asked me about Eli." The smile vanished and she scowled as he continued, "Yeah I thought the same."

Marie said, "That's quite a waste if you ask me." Dutch shot her a glare as she said, "Please don't ask me to apologize, because you know I won't…" The smile returned as he then continued to work through his list.

As he was busy typing notes into an account, an e-mail popped up on his desktop. He noticed it was from Eli and clicked it open. It read YOU WILL NEVER GUESS WHO ELSE LIKES DANIEL. Dutch smiled and shook his head as he checked his watch. He sighed then explained, "I'm off for break Marie. I'll be back."

As he walked out of the pod he headed back into customer service where Eli was just finishing up with a customer over the phone. As he hit the release button he leaned back and deeply exhaled. "What a fucking morning" he said.

 Dutch said, "I'm going to the lunch room. Do you want to come with?" Eli stood up and followed him up to the staff lounge which was a glass enclosed room that sat closest to customer service. As they walked in they noticed Stewart sitting and reading a newspaper.

Eli sat at one of the computers and began to surf the internet as Dutch asked, "Ever get the feeling that we're in an aquarium?"

"I kinda like this" Eli explained. "I feel in a way that it has the illusion of openness when in all actuality it's closed in."

"Let me guess kind of like you eh?"

Dutch grinned as Eli shot at him, "Fuck you Dutchie."

Stewart then walked by them both and Eli quickly glanced out to the floor as Dutch said, "You don't think…" he smiled as Dutch then asked, "How do you know that she also…"

Eli shrugged and explained, "You need to see Stewart when he's around Ariel. Ariel talks about Daniel all of the time and you can just see how Stewart gets. It's so funny 'cause poor Stewart looks like he's going to cry."

Dutch then said, "I don't think it's just that." He shifted his eyes around and continued, "It's because you keep riding his ass all the time and makin him feel like shit."

Eli then said, "It's what happens when you're an obese fucking redhead with a uni-brow."

Dutch shot a glare at him and spat out, "Fuck off Eli. Stewart's not even fat. Now you're just being fucking rude."

Eli asked, "Can I say that he looks like Bert then with his uni-brow?"

Dutch said, "If he's Bert, You're fucking Ernie."

Dutch then flung open the door and stormed out and down the steps into customer service. As he walked back into his pod, he sat back down when his phone began to vibrate. He saw the call display and answered, "Hello?" He then walked back towards the washroom area as he leaned against the windows that gazed out over the rest of downtown. He watched as people bustled in and out of buildings and to their cars. He explained to the voice on the other end, "I'll be in on Thursday night to pick up." He quickly scanned the area around him and said, "Some vitamins, some fast-forward and breakfast cereal." He then said, "You know my favorite…"

Chapter Nine

As Dutch and Eli arrived outside the Pink Bar's entrance, Dutch quickly scanned the lineup and the crowds outside to see if Antoine had arrived yet.

"What the fuck are you looking so sketchy for?" Eli asked accusingly.

Dutch answered preoccupied, "Maybe he doesn't know where to go"

Eli sniped, "It's fucking Edmonton Dutchie. There are three gay bars downtown. How can you fucking miss it?" Dutch shot a glance at Eli as Eli then said, "Oh right, he's French."

They walked in and down the steps as Dutch could feel the ecstasy that he had taken only twenty minutes before start to boil up inside him as the music started to dictate its crescendo as Pink was already busy as people wandered around the main area. Dutch continued to look around as Eli said, "I'm going to the bathroom to reload. Get us some drinks." Dutch watched him leave as he began to line up behind some of the other clientele when he received a tap on his shoulder.

He looked over and saw Antoine, dressed in jeans and a black t-shirt with his blonde hair spiked up. Dutch smiled and said, "Hey."

Antoine leaned in and kissed Dutch on each cheek. "How are you?"

Dutch replied, "I'm good. Ready to take on the weekend..." Dutch then asked, "Did you find the Pink Bar all right?"

He explained, "I got lost but made it here eventually." He then looked at Dutch's pupils and asked, "Are you high?"

Dutch began to sweat and worry as Antoine whispered in his ear, "I won't tell anyone I promise. What are you drinking?"

Dutch replied, "Vodka and Red Bull."

Antoine then asked, "Are you with anyone?"

Eli sauntered up to them. "Dutch do you have our drinks yet?" At that point he looked over and glanced at Antoine. Antoine extended his hand as Eli shook it.

"Eli" he said as Antoine responded back.

Dutch then explained, "Antoine is the collections rep that is working on the Regenesis project from out of Montreal."

Eli beamed, "Pleased to meet you."

Antoine then asked him, "What are you drinking?"

Eli looked over and said, "Pretty much the same thing that Dutch is having."

He then put his arm around Dutch and said, "Me and Dutch go way back. We both started out at Go Credit together."

Antoine then explained, "I was told you two have been best friends for a very long time."

Eli nodded and as he then turned to Dutch. "Can you reload for me?"

Dutch began to protest as Eli reasserted, "Dutchie. Please. Reload. The. Vile."

Dutch rolled his eyes as he headed over to the washroom. Antoine motioned Eli to follow him as they stood at a side counter. As Antoine set the drinks down Eli went to reach for him when Antoine backed away.

"What are you doing?" Antoine asked

"I was hoping I could interest you in a little bit of fun after the Pink Bar." Eli said lasciviously.

Antoine said, "I heard you thought I was too French." He then continued, "And I thought you thought I was a steroid junkie." Eli said nothing and grinned.

After a long pause Eli said "Oh that's just a front I put up at work."

Antoine then said, "It didn't look like a front to me." He then began to stir his drink and he said, "Whatever you're thinking...don't."

Dutch reappeared at that moment as he discreetly forced the small vile into Eli's hand. Eli said, "I'm gonna go reload..." and with that he quickly dashed off.

Dutch asked Antoine, "Is everything okay?"

Antoine shook his head and muttered, "Fucker creeped me out..." He then looked at Dutch and said, "Sorry."

Dutch shrugged as he tried to explain, "He's...just Eli."

Antoine asked, "Has he always been like that?"

Dutch sipped his drink as he thought for a moment then replied, "Yeah, as far as I can remember."

They both nervously chuckled as Antoine asked, "So what did you take?"

Dutch asked, "You really wanna know?"

Antoine nodded as he replied, "A tab of ecstasy with a little bit of coke."

Antoine thought for a moment then asked, "Do you have any more?"

Dutch nodded as Antoine inched a little closer to him. He leaned into Dutch's ear and asked, "Which pocket?"

Dutch's high suddenly elevated as while Antoine's voice seemed to spark something inside him. He could feel himself start to flush as Antoine's hands lightly skirted Dutch's arms. Dutch stammered in a whisper, "It's… it's in the l-left pocket." He felt Antoine's hand dig ever so lightly into Dutch's jeans as he fumbled and found the bag that contained the pills. He fished around some more as Dutch neared a little closer and Antoine plucked one out of his pocket and quickly popped the pill into his mouth. As Antoine pulled away Dutch breathed, "I didn't think you…"

Antoine then teased, "You didn't think I was gay either."

Dutch frowned as he asked, "Who told?" Antoine laughed as he grabbed Dutch by the hand and said, "Let's dance."

Dutch couldn't pinpoint it but he felt at the moment that he and Antoine hit the dance floor that it was as if it was the two of them. Dutch pulled him up to the platform partially encased by steel fencing. All the while Dutch's rush began to playfully seesaw. He glanced around as he watched his packed surroundings. Eli as nowhere in sight as Dutch carefully watched the floor, and then shifted his attention back to Antoine.

This lasted for a good forty minutes as Antoine then said, "Let's go get another drink" as they both headed down the stairs and to the back bar. Dutch ordered this time as he handed the money to the bartender in exchange for a drink that he quickly handed over to Antoine.

He asked Dutch, "Do I owe you anything?"

Dutch only shook his head no, and smiled as Antoine held up his drink and said, "Cheers." They clinked glasses as Antoine asked, "What time does the afterhours open?"

Dutch replied, "We should probably get going soon. The club opens up in about a half an hour." Dutch finished his drink and said, "Let head over by cab to Factory. We can line up there and be ready to get in." Antoine nodded as they finished their drinks and Dutch reached for his hand, guiding them out to the club's entrance. He didn't understand why he had done it, except that there it was.

They hopped into the first available cab and as they went down Jasper Avenue Antoine asked, "Are you okay to be leaving Eli there on his own?"

Dutch replied, "He's a wet blanket when it comes to afterhours. That's why I wanted to high-tail it before he found us." Antoine laughed as the cab pulled up in front of the huge stone church. A smaller building sat beside it which housed a pizza place, and an unmarked entrance where a small line of people had already formed.

Antoine paid the cab driver and they both lined up and began to wait. Antoine mused, "I'm really surprised that Eli doesn't like afterhours."

Dutch explained, "It's hard for him to tolerate that kind of music. He thinks it lacks originality and soul." Dutch then said, "It's a surprise I can drag him out at all. He fucking hates thumpa-thumpa."

The bass started to vibrate the building, a signal for the bouncer to arrive at the front of the line. The entrance opened and a muscular bouncer with shaved head appeared at the front of the line. He looked up at the line announced, "Make sure you got your IDs ready!" He then looked up and upon spotting Dutch and Antoine trumpeted, "Dutchie!" Dutch spotted him right away and promptly hugged him.

Dutch turned back to Antoine, waved him over and explained, "Dom, this is Antoine. He's from Montreal."

Dutch then said to Antoine, "Antoine this is Domenic. Dom worked part time at Go Credit."

Antoine shook his hand as Domenic explained, "I was only there for about half a year."

Antoine asked, "What made you leave?"

Domenic explained, "Just needed a change of pace. Call centre is not quite my scenery." Domenic then asked, "You guys coming in?" Dutch nodded as Domenic then said, "Dutch I never see you out anymore. What gives…" Then Domenic glanced over at the line and asked, "Where's Eli?"

Dutch gave Domenic an over-exaggerated I don't know expression. Domenic then smiled and ushered them in. "Admission's on me you two. Enjoy your night." Dutch walked in and Domenic stopped Antoine with his hand. As Antoine looked over Domenic leaned in and said, "Be good to him, because the other one can't." Antoine immediately understood and nodded as he followed Dutch into the club. The club itself was very different than Dutch had remembered. To his immediate left lay the bar, while right behind him was the DJ booth elevated six feet off the dancefloor. The walls had been painted black where the glitter sprinkled blue had been along with mirrors. Where the bar had been towards the very back, had now been relocated or even more seating.

Dutch gazed in astonishment as he said to Antoine, "I feel like I'm in a completely new club."

Antoine asked, "When was the last time you were here?"

Dutch smugly replied, "Three or four years."

Antoine's eyes widened as he then asked, "Why so long?"

Dutch shrugged and replied, "No one to go with." He then explained, "I've been hanging out with Eli for so long on the weekends you kind of forget where other places exist."

Antoine then said, "Find us a place to sit and we'll chat some more."

He found a seat that straddled between the lounge and the dance floor and promptly leaned back. His eyes shifted between the steady trickle of people that started to congregate in the main area. Dutch closed his eyes for just a moment as the ecstasy began to intertwine with the music, his high beginning to move with the melody. In the back of his mind he couldn't help but think of Eli's whereabouts. Part of the euphoria began to evolve into paranoia and discomfort as he started to regret ditching Eli at Pink. He knew that if he'd stayed with him he and Antoine would not get the time alone. Dutch would have been at Lockers right now watching helplessly as Eli bedded his next conquest. He would have left angry and bitter, and ultimately alone.

The swelling of self-loathing suddenly washed away as Dutch felt a hand gently touch his knee. He opened his eyes again to find Antoine seated beside him, Antoine handed him a fresh bottle of water as he asked, "What are you thinking?"

Dutch began to stammer out, "I'm beginning to think about how fucked up I am right now…" which prompted laughter from the both of them. While it was truth, it was a cover-up of what really was on Dutch's mind.

He then turned to Antoine and asked, "What about you? What are you thinking?"

Antoine was silent for a moment then explained, "I'm thinking about home. About Montreal." Antoine sucked in his breath and elaborated, "There's a club on St. Catherine Street just on the outskirts of the village called Stereo." He then looked out towards the dance floor and continued, "You would love it out there Dutch. It's one of the world's best clubs. The sound is so clear and crisp that you can feel it move through your body and still be able to think." Antoine was silent for a few minutes, eyes closed and after opening them again said, "Not just Stereo. There's tons of afterhours and clubs worth checking out. You'd be like a kid in a candy store."

Dutch could feel Antoine's hand move to his right shoulder as it began to massage and knead the tightened muscles. Antoine could feel Dutch start to relax and said, "Your muscles are so tight Dutch. You really need them to relax a bit."

Dutch moaned, "That feels so amazing…"

Antoine then let his hand work its way across Dutch's back as he could feel the tension release and his body start to get even higher. Antoine asked, "How does that feel?" Dutch only nodded in approval as Antoine then said, "So tell me about work. Tell me about the office."

Dutch asked, "What do you want to know about the office?"

Antoine shrugged and said, "Tell me about some of the people."

He started to describe his co workers thinking of the most logical place to start, "Well our most notorious people are in customer service. It's pretty much the starting point at Go Credit." He thought for a moment and then said, "There's Ariel, who's a friend of the daughter of one of the customer service supervisors." Dutch grimaced and continued, "She's a fucking neurotic idiot. Supposedly she's happily engaged to her boyfriend Jeremiah who was just fired for being an overall dumbass." Antoine chuckled as Dutch said, "Then Ariel's also into Daniel, who's either so straight and dumb that the tries way too hard on purpose. Or he's so fucking gay that his closet might as well be the doorway to Narnia." Dutch sipped his water and looked around. "Then there's Stewart who is supposed to be Daniel's best friend…"

Antoine interjected, "The redhead."

Dutch nodded in agreement and replied, "He's in love with Daniel. But Daniel's a fuckup by nature. He cancels plans at the last minute, and also runs after girls who have no interest in him whatsoever." He then looked at Antoine. "Its kind pathetic, but Eli rides Stewart's ass about it every opportunity he gets."

Antoine then said, "So how does Eli fit into this picture?"

Dutch said, "Eli and I started off in customer service together. This was before Go Credit was about aggressive expansion." Dutch looked down at the floor and back at Antoine. "I've seen him ruin a few relationships in the call centre He has the largest sexual appetite I've ever seen."

Antoine's eyes widened as he asked, "Really?"

Dutch explained, "He doesn't ever fucking stop." He then sighed and pointed out, "He's the biggest hypocrite. He doesn't practice what he preaches. Especially with Stewart."

Antoine asked, "What do you mean?"

While Antoine continued to work on Dutch's shoulders, Dutch said, "Eli picks on Stewart for being gay. He totally points out his effeminateness, which Stewart hardly has at all. He also gives him shit for being a redhead."

Antoine said, "That's fucking shameful."

Dutch added, "That's not even the half of it, trust me."

Antoine asked, "Then why you remain friends with him?"

Dutch breathed out, "Because I'm the only one who will." He then added, "We're just two lost souls that happened to have found each other."

Dutch then looked up at Antoine who leaned in and pressed his lips against Dutch's. The first second was a quick synapse of awkwardness as Dutch felt a momentary flash of Eli, then the thought of getting involved with someone in a position of management which all became dispelled the moment he leaned in and his mouth connected with Antoine's. He knew it wasn't the ecstasy, but somewhere between them a connection had been made. Dutch felt that all was right in the world around him. For that moment he let the energy draw him in. He could feel it when Antoine's tongue pressed into his mouth, meeting his.

When Dutch pulled away Antoine asked, "Why don't you have a boyfriend?" He could only swallow as he shook his head and leaned back in. They began kissing again as this time Dutch pulled Antoine closer to him. Antoine asked, "Am I okay to kiss you here?"

Dutch whispered, "Its okay…" as he leaned in and kissed him again.

Dutch then felt his phone vibrate as he continued to focus solely on Antoine. When Antoine pulled away Dutch asked, "Did you want to go back to mine?"

Antoine looked at his watch and said, "It's only four-thirty." Dutch looked confused as Antoine pulled him up and guided him out to a full dance floor. Dutch smiled as they began to lose themselves in the mixture of crowd and music. Any remnants of Dutch's hesitation had by this point disappeared as they continued to dance. That moment Dutch focused solely on the waves of pleasure the ecstasy had dictated in movement.

After what seemed like hours, Dutch began to slow down and made his way back to the seat, Antoine trailing right behind him. He wiped the sweat off his forehead with his arm while Antoine asked, "How are you feeling?"

Dutch smiled and replied as he nuzzled his head under Antoine's arm, "Pretty good…pretty fucked." They both chuckled while Dutch closed his eyes again, listening to Antoine's heartbeat. It was the one moment that the music intertwined with the natural rhythm. Antoine let his hands brush along and massage Dutch's upper body while Dutch began to rub Antoine's leg.

Minutes and mixes passed as Dutch sat up and finally checked his phone. Antoine continued to rub his shoulder muscles as Dutch finally leaned back letting Antoine drape his arm over him. He then blurted out, "I want you to come home with me."

Antoine kissed the side of his head and asked, "When?"

"Right now."

Dutch didn't remember what happened next, but it all moved with such a blur that within what seemed like moments they were in Dutch's main entry. Antoine pressed him up against the wall and into him as their kissing became more passionate and intense. Dutch then slightly nudged him away as Antoine asked, "Are you okay?"

Dutch then replied, "One moment."

He walked over to Erin's room and quietly opened her door. He noticed it was empty as he breathed out a sigh of relief and headed back to the living room where Antoine was now seated. Dutch motioned Antoine to follow as Antoine then stood up, his erection clearly bulging from his pants.

When inside Dutch's room he closed the door behind them and moved to the bed where Dutch had sat him down and began to let his hands undress Antoine while his mouth and tongue moved from Antoine's mouth down his neck and chest. Dutch's hand unbuckled his belt and began to pull Antoine's jeans down while Dutch pulled away long enough to let Antoine reach over and pull Dutch's shirt over his head. After he threw it onto the floor Dutch started to kiss, lick, and suck his way down Antoine's chest when Antoine pushed him away and said, "Stand up."

Dutch stood up as Antoine pulled him close and began to explore him in the same fashion that Dutch had done. Dutch moaned as his hand rested on the back of Antoine's neck, starting to guide him further down as Antoine unbuckled his belt and opened his cargo pants. Antoine started to let his hand start to fumble inside while Antoine's other hand gradually started to pull Dutch's pants down. He suddenly stopped as Dutch watched Antoine stand up and move Dutch onto the bed. As he laid down Antoine began kissing him while his mouth moved back down to his cargos. Antoine pulled them completely off a he then followed suit with Dutch's boxer briefs.

He snickered when Dutch looked up he asked, "What's so funny?"

Antoine smiled and replied, "Calvin Klein." Dutch snickered and they came off, Antoine commenting, "God you're huge." Dutch glanced down as he watched Antoine press his lips down on the circumcised head, letting his mouth then move down to the base and back up again.

He writhed under Antoine's touch as after a few minutes Antoine let his fingers run gently over the smooth contours of the sack of skin beneath Dutch's erection. One finger wandered a little further down while Dutch opened up a little more under Antoine's touch. His tongue moved along with his finger as Dutch spread his legs open a little more, Antoine finally starting to let his tongue push inside while Dutch let out a loud moan. Antoine's hands held him steady while he continued to lick, prod, and push.

Finally Dutch breathed, "If you keep that up I'm going to come all over the place."

Antoine then stopped as he smiled and leaned into Dutch, passionately kissing him as Antoine started to pull his own underwear down. Dutch watched as Antoine half-erect, uncircumcised penis flopped out as his eyes widened momentarily. Dutch then reached for it and began to fondle watching it thicken while Antoine grunted in approval. Dutch then said, "Come here" as Antoine straddled his chest pushing his erection downwards while Dutch positioned himself, letting Antoine easily slide it between his lips and down his throat. He slowly thrust in while Dutch's left hand steadied Antoine's thighs while the other one began to push and poke inside Antoine, first one finger then two as Antoine tightened up.

Antoine used one hand and steadied himself with the wall while the other held onto Dutch's head. Dutch continued to let his tongue lick and twist over the shaft while every time he licked the head Antoine would moan and twitch. After a few minutes Dutch could feel Antoine stiffen even more as he finally pulled out of Dutch's mouth and began to move down between his legs. Antoine pushed his legs apart as he began to insert a finger back inside Dutch, then a second while Dutch moaned loudly.

Antoine asked, "Do you want me to use a condom?"

Dutch asked, "Are you clean?"

Antoine nodded as Dutch inhaled while Antoine's penis gained entry inside of him. He pushed in all the way as Dutch yelped a little.

Antoine asked, "Are you okay?" Dutch nodded as Antoine lowered himself down further on top of Dutch almost completely out.

He then leaned in and kissed Dutch deeply as he thrust back in. Dutch's hands pulled Antoine closer as he continued to push inside him. Dutch pulled Antoine closer while he focused solely on Antoine, him gazing down at Dutch lovingly. Dutch would arch his back, trying his hardest to take in as much of Antoine as he could. Antoine's hands caressed Dutch's thighs while Dutch pleaded, "Stay with me Antoine."

Antoine breathed, "I'm right here Dutch. I won't let you go." Which each thrust Dutch had never felt more complete. For all of the times that Dutch had experienced intimacy with the same sex, he'd never felt as intimate with someone as he had with him.

Dutch sensed that Antoine was getting close as he began to thrust quicker inside him. Dutch could feel his thrusts become deeper and more erratic as Antoine's breathing became heavier. He breathed, "Dutch I'm going to come…"

Dutch pleaded, "Inside me..." while Antoine grunted and pushed in as deep as he could. Dutch could feel the warmth flood inside him as Antoine thrust back in all of the way, the pulses weakening as he collapsed on Dutch.

They kissed passionately as Dutch could feel Antoine slowly pull out. Dutch sighed as Antoine kissed him again, reassuring him, "I'm still with you Dutch." Dutch nuzzled into Antoine and whispered in Dutch's ear, "I'm still here."

Chapter Ten

Sunday, 3 a.m.

Eli still lay wide awake staring at the ceiling. He'd agonized and pinpointed that it was exactly twenty-five hours since Dutch and Antoine had vanished from the steps of the Pink Bar and out into the vastness of downtown Edmonton. Eli was abandoned in a sea of twinks as his resentful glare followed their every movement of the pair up the stairs until they disappeared. While he hated the fact that Dutch had ditched their regular Friday night sacrament for what he considered to be the French steroid monkey from Montreal, he also realized that he was able to engage in a distraction that Dutch may have not approved.

He'd made the connection the following afternoon after a long night at the bathhouse. Saturday night and Samuel had arrived at Eli's doorstep, peacefully asleep hours later. Despite this, Eli's mind still raced in frustration. Eli wanted to believe it was the comedown effects of the cocaine that augmented his thoughts. He'd lied to himself and reasoned that it was because of Samuel's naked presence in bed. All of those shallow explanations could not disguise the fact that he was sorely angry with Dutch for his defection on Friday night.

He rolled over as Samuel stirred awake, peering over at Eli. He mumbled, "What time is it?"

Eli peered over Samuel and at the alarm clock. "It's about three forty-five." He replied as Samuel rolled onto his back and heavily sighed. Eli gave a faint smile and reassured him, "Keith doesn't get home from Factory until at least six." He brushed his hand onto the side of Samuel's face as Samuel frowned and then abruptly sat up. Eli asked, "What?"

Samuel rubbed his face with his hands and sat on the side of the bed. He said, "I told Keith I was with the family tonight out in Beaumont." He then looked back at Eli and said, "You know Keith would kill both of us if he knew right?"

Eli then sat up and leaned back against the wall. He stared at his hands and then said, "He doesn't have to know. It's just between the two of us." Samuel stopped rubbing his face then leaned back, relaxing his head against Eli's stomach.

He explained, "I know it's just..." He paused for a moment then thought, "I don't understand why he fucking hates you so much." Samuel then stared up at the wall and said, "All he cares about is his fucking appearance and whether or not his six pack is intact or his cock is still nine inches."

Eli shyly smiled and mused, "I guess you picked him for the latter."

They both chuckled as Samuel explained, "It's just he thinks he's invincible and he feels like he can treat anyone any way he chooses. And the drugs..." Eli was silent as Samuel continued, "He does so much coke Eli, that it's a surprise his whole nasal cavity hasn't caved in yet." Eli yawned as Samuel then asked, "How come you're not out with Dutch?" Samuel then gazed up at Eli. "Don't the two of you usually go out and go mental on a Saturday night?"

Eli only shrugged and deadpanned, "He dropped me this evening for some juice monkey from Montreal. The guy is from the eastern office."

Samuel was stunned and replied, "I'm really surprised. You guys are tight, but it doesn't seem like him to just fuck off like that."

Eli stared out of his room into the apartment and sighed out, "Believe me. These days, nothing surprises me about him."

They were both quiet for awhile when Eli asked, "So when do you start the internship downtown at the firm?"

Samuel said, "I'm thinking in the next week. I'm excited. Even though admittedly working closer with Keith will be an interesting experience."

Eli suggested, "You'll be just down from the Go Credit office. You and I can definitely do lunch."

After a few moments Samuel then asked from out of nowhere, "Why don't you two ever date?"

Eli chuckled nervously while Samuel nudged him. "Oh come on you two look like a perfect match." He then smiled and asked, "What are you waiting for?"

Eli said nothing and he glanced down at Samuel. Samuel shifted his gaze and sat back up as he leaned over and began to fish the floor for his underwear. Samuel then pointed out, "I just don't understand how someone so amazing isn't snapped up yet." He pulled his boxer briefs up as he smiled back at Eli.

Eli asked with a grin as he handed him his shirt, "Are you talking about me or Dutch?"

It was always the same routine since the first time Eli had sex with Samuel. A string of quick and urgent text messages which resulted in Samuel carefully appearing at Eli's front entryway, as drunk as Eli was high. It was the most erratic however fulfilling sex that Eli experienced. It all happened under Keith's nose, and Samuel was beginning to show threads of strain. Eli then stood up and stretched as he said to Samuel, "You know you're gonna have to sort it out with him sooner or later." It was Samuel's turn for silence as Eli said, "You know what you need to make you happy."

Samuel then smiled and asked him, "Would that include not sneaking around anymore?"

Eli smiled and leaned in kissing Samuel. When Samuel pulled away Eli said, "I'll walk you out."

Samuel said, "Text me later" as Eli closed the door behind him then leaned back against it completely naked. After a few minutes he then decided to hop online and see who was cruising for quick company.

Hours later and a few blocks away Dutch could feel the warm nuzzle next to him as he began to stir. He looked over and saw Antoine sleeping peacefully beside him as he turned over and draped one arm over his chest. As Dutch began to fall asleep again, he could feel Antoine's penis hardening against him. Antoine half-mumbled, "Are you awake?" as Dutch inched closer and started to kiss him. Antoine responded in kind and smiled.

"Good morning" Dutch said as he opened his eyes. Antoine started to kiss him as Dutch continued, "Well afternoon actually."

Antoine asked, "What time is it?" as he looked at the alarm clock. It read one thirty-five as he groaned and slowly sat up in bed. He then asked, "How high did we get on Friday night?"

Dutch quietly thought for a moment then said, "I believe you and I did two pills each, in addition to a couple bumps of K." Antoine chuckled as Dutch continued, "We left Factory about six thirty."

Antoine asked, "Does Eli normally stay out with you that late?"

Dutch sighed, "Normally, it's the other way around. I'm the one who's out with him. His fucking wingman while we're out at the bar, then the bathhouse." Antoine said, "Duly noted for when I have to kidnap you next." They both laughed as Antoine mused, "So you two are really best friends eh?" Dutch nodded as Antoine pointed out, I wasn't feeling the love on Friday night at Pink Bar. It didn't look like he was your best friend at the bar." Antoine watched as Dutch was silent. He then said, "I'm sorry if I'm treading on thin ice here. He should just learn to treat you better."

Antoine said to Dutch as he began to massage him, "Eli tried to pick me up at Pink Bar the night you and I were out."

Dutch said, "That doesn't surprise me at all." He then asked, "Why didn't you?"

Antoine's hands worked their way down as he explained, "Because I had my eye on someone much hotter and more interesting." He then said, "Ever since I laid eyes on you Dutch, I knew that I had to get to know you. You were the book that I had opened, and I need to know that much more…"

Dutch looked behind him and asked, "Really?" Antoine nodded and Dutch leaned over and passionately kissed him.

Antoine then said with a smile, "So tell me something interesting about you." Dutch blushed as Antoine prodded, "Oh come on Dutch. I know you have a lot to tell me."

Dutch stood up and walked over to the CD player turning it on. Antoine gazed up at the life sized posted that hung above Dutch's computer. Antoine said, "You're really into the Manic Street Preachers aren't you?" Dutch smiled as he tossed the jewel case towards him. Antoine's fingers ran over the smooth cover of the three members on the beach with the words *This Is My Truth Tell Me Yours* emblazoned on the cover. A drum beat, then coupled with an acoustic guitar crept from the speakers as Dutch crawled back onto the bed beside Antoine.

Dutch said, "They're one of my favorite bands. I really wish that I could have been around for their earlier years."

Antoine asked, "When did you start listening to them?"

"I started listening to them when I was about fifteen. One of their albums, *Everything Must Go* unlocked something deep inside me. I couldn't explain it at all."

Antoine asked, "Why's that?" as now the bed covers had been peeled down to his waist. Dutch elaborated, "It was 1994 and their album *The Holy Bible* became one of the most important releases of the year. Well, right behind Oasis's *Definitely Maybe*." Dutch leaned back and said, "February 1st, 1995 and enigmatic lyricist and guitarist Richey James Edward disappears from a London hotel, the site was well known for suicides." He then looked at Antoine and said, "No one has seen him since." Antoine hmmed as Dutch said, "One year later they released *Everything Must Go*, then two years after that this album." He then looked back out towards the computer. "This is my favorite Preachers album ever."

They listened for a few minutes then Antoine leaned in, starting to kiss Dutch passionately while he crept out from under the bed sheets and pinned Dutch on the bed. Antoine then mused, "Makes you wonder what happened that would have driven him to just disappear."

Dutch said, "Maybe it was the pull of stardom he couldn't handle. Or maybe he really thought being alive and isolated was the biggest downer of all."

Antoine thought for a moment and said, "Maybe he was pining for anonymity. Maybe he wanted a normal life again."

They said nothing as Antoine leaned in and brushed his lips up against Dutch's, carefully mounting himself on top of him as Dutch's tongue met his, Dutch beginning to moan. He could feel Antoine's erection, completely hard as they began to move along with the discs melody. While Dutch had yearned for this, he sensed an empty longing that had began to haunt him. It cautioned him to finally look at his cell as it blared out its ringtone. Antoine stopped kissing him as he looked over and reached for it. Upon seeing the number he handed the cell phone over to Dutch. Dutch said nothing for a few seconds and finally blurted, "I don't have to answer it." They both looked at the phone as Dutch quickly opened it and with a flip turned it off.

Antoine smiled and said, "Clever." They laughed as Antoine leaned back in to kiss him again. Hours later, they showered together and as Antoine dressed, ready to go back to the hotel Dutch offered, "You could come to Pink Bar with me tonight for a drink."

Antoine asked, "Wind-down drinks?"

Dutch nodded as he reasoned, "Eli and I carry this tradition every Sunday night for years.

Antoine thought for a moment then replied, "I'll take a raincheck. Thank you though."

He leaned in and kissed Dutch as Dutch pulled him close. He then breathed, "Thank you for this weekend."

Dutch then asked, "I'll see you tomorrow?" Antoine nodded and kissed him again as Antoine smiled, "See you tomorrow."

LOVE'S SWEET EXILE – DISC 55: SIXTY MINUTES, TWO SECONDS

"Any author will tell you that any good story has its twists and turns and that when it comes to what we hope the ending is going to be, that there has to be a few detours in the way, or a significant change in plot. But this past weekend was a twist in plot that I did not see coming."

"He chose me."

"Out of everyone that he could have gone home with that Friday night, he made the decision to pick me. I can't make sense of it. It's something that has completely blindsided me and left me lost for words. Antoine appeared out of nowhere and out of all things at work. I'm surprised that he's even gay, let alone interested in me."

"Admittedly, I kind of saw the indication in Eli's eyes that signaled how badly he wanted Antoine. When I looked in his direction at the Pink Bar, that glance had appeared. It was his determined to fuck glance that appears anytime Eli sees something he wants, and wants badly. But for whatever reason he passed on Eli, and not only went home with me, but also to Factory as well. It was an amazing weekend. I never felt so close to someone as I did that night.

"I need to run with this. Even if Eli and I don't end up together, and happily ever after. Antoine's unlocked something in me that I thought Eli might have only ever had the key to. But I guess now that's not completely true. And while I'm excited about this new development, I'm nervous too. Because I know that Eli will carry that rejection with him and wont fucking get over it until something better comes along. "

Chapter Eleven

Sunday evening, 9 p.m, and Eli was not happy.

He sat at the center bar in Pink, steaming over Dutch's inability to answer the phone. What irritated him even more was Dutch's sudden disappearance from Pink Bar that Friday night, almost sure of what had happened next. The more Eli thought about it the quicker his beer disappeared. Despite the fact that even though it had bought Eli time to spend with Samuel on Saturday night, it had also prevented him from the Friday night conquest in where he would eventually find himself at the bathhouse beginning the comedown process. A small breeze had quickly danced through his room as Eli woke up to discover Saturday morning's companion was in the form of an enormous dehydration headache.

It had taken a Red Bull and three lines of Coke to even himself out at the bathhouse. At that point Eli could have cared less about his penis temporarily retreating into his body. No one would have seen under the bleach-ridden towel anyways. A walk home and an encounter from Samuel had kept him distracted up until Sunday morning when he had made the decision the begin all over again, visiting the bathhouse and after doing just enough coke to even out the alcohol and let him focus firmly on the coat-check. Luckily for him, there was enough of a cross-section of characters who pretty much picked up his drinking tab.

Four beers, a jack and coke, and a shot of tequila later peppered with more cocaine and still no Dutch. Dutch was always properly on time, always had let Eli know where he was and when he would meet him at the bar. Except this weekend. The one weekend that in a way, had meant some sort of importance. Eli couldn't pin it down, but either way Dutch's absence signaled something very wrong. As he continued to focus on the entrance, Dutch's bleach-blond top finally appeared, simply sporting a French Connection shirt and cargo shorts. When he arrived at the main bar, he perched himself on the stool next to Eli.

Eli snarled "It's about fucking time."

Dutch shrugged with a smile. "So fucking sue me."

Eli polished off his beer as Dutch asked, "How much have you had to drink?" Eli shrugged as Dutch asked, "Where did you go after?"

Eli curtly replied, "I don't see that you should be interested in any of my weekend after you so improperly fucked off on Friday night."

"Quit being a fucking dick Eli. It's not like I didn't look for you before I left."

"The fuck you did Dutchie."

They were both silent as Eli then mumbled, "After you left I went to the bathhouse."

Dutch saw right through that comment and said, "Okay fine…" He then asked, "You didn't see Samuel at all?"

Eli matter-of-factly lied, "Samuel's off at that manager's retreat for Wendy's this weekend. Yeah…" Eli grimaced and then added, "If it wasn't for the fact he actually still fits in his uniform, I would let Keith keep him all to himself."

"You know that Samuel is fucking beyond skinny Eli. He couldn't gain weight even if he binged for two years straight." Dutch then asked, "Are you going to ever have a relationship with someone that is not going to bring down about three others in the process?"

"Maybe, when I'm forty and dead."

"Christ, you have such a rosy outlook on life."

"Well in gay years forty is the new sixty-five."

Dutch chuckled as the bartender sat the pitcher of beer in front of him. Then just out of nowhere Dutch slid in, "I had a nice night after the Pink Bar Friday night."

Eli by this time had begun to calm down a little as he then asked the obvious. "And who did we whore ourselves out to on Friday night?" Dutch only smiled and half-nodded as Eli let out a half-smile of his own. Eli teased, "He must have been pretty good for you to just vanish like that." Dutch snickered as he sipped on his beer a little more.

Eli wasn't prepared for the next comment that had tumbled out of Dutch's mouth. "I think we're going to try hanging out again this coming week after work. The weekend with him was absolutely amazing." Eli's smile vanished as Antoine's rejection rewound and started to repeat from the beginning in the back of his mind.

Eli slowly said, "You're…fucking…kidding…me."

Dutch shrugged, "I don't see there being an issue here. I mean you thought he was a French steroid monkey so I know you aren't interested in him."

Eli coldly said, "I really don't want my best friend dating a steroid queen."

Dutch said, "Fuck off he's not a 'roid queen."

"You really know how to pick the pretentious ones don't you?"

Dutch sat up straight then pointed out, "Like you're one to fucking talk. I mean look at you. You don't fuck unless he comes out of an Abercrombie and Fitch catalogue and a six-figure bank account. Or unless there's something you so badly want at your disposal. Sometimes, I wonder how you and Samuel ever got together at all."

Eli breathed, "Sometimes I think the same thing."

Dutch then asked, "Does Keith know…?" Eli shot him a nasty glare that broadcasted, you fucking prick how could you fuck me over like that. Dutch knew that a line had been crossed as Eli ordered another drink.

Dutch finished his beer and Eli said, "When it comes to me and Samuel, what is there to know? I know he's not happy where he is right now…"

Dutch argued, "Samuel's a great guy Eli. I don't know why you don't see that."

"I guess I'm just an emotional retard."

"Better you to admit it than me."

Eli said nothing as Dutch then continued, "So the Elite team may be getting another member in the next few weeks." Dutch then said, "They've got all of us working on the Regenesis project."

Eli complained, "I don't know why I wasn't chosen for Regenesis."

Dutch explained, "Because you go to school part-time, are in fourth year and you also passed on the supervisor position."

Eli grunted and said, "It was the best move I'd ever made."

Dutch then said rolling his eyes, "If you say so…"

Eli then asked, "Can we skip shop talk for now? It's Sunday night, and I'm not up for a rehash of the Go Credit shit-show right now."

Dutch said, "Fine suit yourself…"

After a few minutes of silence and horrid karaoke Eli asked, "So what did he think of your Manic Street Preachers wall hanging?"

Dutch smiled and replied, "It definitely raised a few questions."

Eli said, "I can't believe you still fucking listen to them. I thought you were done being depressed and isolated."

Dutch spat out, "Yes Miss Spears…"

Eli frowned and said, "At least I keep my finger on the pulse."

"Or mouth on the cock of mediocrity eh?"

"Oh come on Dutch, your soundtrack wasn't always music to kill yourself to."

"Well I can tell you it wasn't ever fucking *Crossroads*."

The music became marginally louder and a jumbled announcement blared over the pub's sound system. Eli wasn't sure why he asked, other than to torture himself, or to ready the next round of ammo to unleash on Dutch. Eli then asked, "Did you two go at it the whole night?"

Dutch shook his head no and said, "We hit Factory. The music and vibe was nothing short of amazing."

Eli glared and asked, "Does that place still look sketchy?" He then said, "I don't understand that hippy raver techno shit anyhow."

Dutch moments later argued, "Well some days I don't understand you Dutch. But I don't knock it."

Eli stared blankly into his drink and finally admitted, "It was a rough weekend."

"Oh how I wish I had a heart Dorothy…"

Eli just smiled and said, "Its funny how were promised Oz and the yellow brick road and in the end it just turns out to be fucking Kansas."

Dutch shrugged and Eli added, "Sad, but true."

Dutch then asked, "So why don't you ask to become part of Regenesis? It's been definitely steady, and they're even thinking about maybe redistributing some people to Montreal and Vancouver to help out."

Eli sighed, "I really can't take on any other projects at the moment Dutch. Especially with school breathing down my ass."

Dutch asked, "How many more classes do you have?"

Eli finished his beer and said, "I have a couple more to go, then I'll have my degree and maybe then I can tell Go Credit to fuck off, good and proper."

When he sat his glass down on the bar counter Dutch said, "Well I'm going to head home. I need to find out what's up with Aimee and what time we're getting together for coffee with mom this week." He finished his beer and after a few moments of silence and nothing from Eli he said, "Sorry I'm not better company right now." He then left his money at the counter and asked, "Breakfast tomorrow?" Eli nodded as Dutch waved and hurried down the steps and back out onto Jasper Avenue towards home.

Chapter Twelve

Late Monday morning Eli walked into the customer service office as Nicholas had just walked by towards the main entrance.

Nicholas briefly waved as Eli sneered, "Are you dropping her off late again?" Nicholas shyly grinned as Eli pointed out, "You know what that means right?" Nicholas shrugged as Eli said, "It means you have to buy her immediate supervisor dinner."

Nicholas only smiled and replied, "Nice try." Eli smiled back, "Charm is one of my strong suits."

He then looked over at Dawn as she deadpanned, "You might want to steer clear of Ariel. She and Jeremiah got into another fight."

Eli asked, "How many is this now?"

She replied, "Let me see…four hundred and fifty third?"

Eli shook his head, "I don't know what she sees in him. I mean I blew him and really that was only substandard at best."

Dawns eyebrows both elevated and she then said, "Dutch said he picked up breakfast."

Eli smiled at her then walked into customer service and set his bag down on the desk. He spotted Stewart handing Daniel what looked like a huge stack of bound paper. Eli then asked, "What the fuck is this?" He plucked the book from Daniel's hand as he glanced over the cover.

Stewart replied, "It's a book I've been working on getting published." Eli's nose curled up as he said, "Get outta here. I didn't know you wrote kids fiction." Stewart's eyebrows shifted as Eli inquired, "What's it about?"

Stewart explained, "It's a coming out, coming of age story." Eli grimaced as he flipped through the pages.

"Seems a little porn-y too." Ariel said, "You can tell where Stewart's mind is in the book."

Stewart pointed out, "It's a little sexually charged in some places."

Eli handed the manual back to Daniel and said, "Enjoy." As Stewart walked away he said to Ariel, "I'll bet you any money he'll write a story about us someday." Ariel snickered as Daniel walked back up the steps towards collections. Eli said, "It'll probably be called The G Spot." Ariel shrugged as he began to walk over to the washroom.

He passed by Lance's office and he leaned in and said, "Good morning Lance."

Lance looked up and said, "Hey Eli, step into the office for a minute." Eli stepped into the office as Lance mentioned, "Close the door." Eli closed it behind him as Lance leaned back and said, "I've been hearing rumors from the floor you've been picking on Stewart. Is that true?" Eli said nothing as Lance explained, "I'm sure you understand how hard being gay is Eli. You don't need to make it harder on anyone else."

Eli calmly protested, "I'm only having a bit of harmless fun with him Lance. He knows that."

Lance asked, "Does he?"

Eli said nothing for a few moments and then said, "Look, I know where this is coming from."

Lance sat back and said, "Enlighten me"

Eli sucked back his breath and blurted out, "It's because I'm the one you can't..." when Lance held up his hand silencing him.

Lance said, "Please stop right there Eli. For the record it was the other way around."

Eli hurriedly stood up and opened the door. He turned and breathed out, "Fuck you Lance."

He slammed open the washroom door and walked to the back as he found Dutch wiping his nose and adjusting his tie.

Eli growled, "I fucking hate Lance, Dutchie."

He closed the stall door behind him as Dutch commented, "Well trying to pick him up at the company Christmas party wasn't a great idea." Dutch added, "It was also not a bright move you fucked his partner of four years in the bathroom."

Eli tapped his nose as he snorted up the rest of the residue. "They were nearly broken up anyhow."

Eli inhaled the other line as Dutch said, "Well you surely wrecked that home."

Eli wiped his nose as he asked, "Usual suspects this weekend?" Dutch shrugged as Eli asked, "What?"

Dutch explained, "I want to hang out with Antoine for a bit this weekend." Eli bit his lip as Dutch reasoned, "You should really get to know him Eli. He's actually a nice guy."

Eli said, "Let me guess, just as awesome as Daniel."

Dutch then smiled and said, "You will never guess who Daniel's running after now." Eli cocked his head to the side as they began to walk out of the washroom. Dutch smiled and explained, "He's been trying to put the moves on Ariel." Eli said, "But Ariel's fucking dumb. Plus she's in that never ending soap opera with Jeremiah."

Dutch stopped at his desk and said, "Hang out with me and Antoine this weekend Eli." Eli was silent and Dutch pleaded, "You're my best friend, and I really want this to work." Eli remained quiet as Dutch said, "You have four breakfasts to figure it out man." Eli nodded in agreement and he walked over to his desk.

He promptly sat down as he overheard Ariel explain to Stewart, "I can't believe it but I still have a thing for Daniel. Pretty sad eh?" Eli could feel the tension start to seep into the aisle as Stewart had tried to contain his frustration. She then continued, "I mean it's like me and him have this thing, this understanding." She then said, "We'll just sit there and just talk for hours. It's absolutely crazy."

Eli teased, "It's more than you'll ever get, eh Stewart?"

Stewart abruptly stood up and walked off as Ariel asked in confusion, "What was that all about?"

Eli said, "It's nothing Ariel, go back to your bubble."

She then asked, "Well what do you think?"

Eli asked, "About what?"

She said, "About Daniel?"

Eli turned to her and said, "He's a flake Ariel, and honestly has his own shit to deal with. His mother is fucked up or what not."

Ariel then beamed, "I've talked to his mother on the phone. She sounds really cute."

Eli shook his head and whispered, "Brother" as he started to work through his e-mails.

Stewart returned minutes later and Ariel asked, "Is everything okay?" Stewart was silent while he pressed his available button on his phone and took the next call. Eli smiled to himself as he knew that he had hit a very sensitive nerve on Stewart.

Later in the week Eli had walked into the lunchroom which seemed completely silent except for Daniel at the tables all by himself. Eli walked up lunch in hand as he asked, "This table free?"

Daniel swallowed his bite and offered, "Seat's all yours dude."

Eli sat down and opened the bag as he asked, "Where's your partner in crime?"

Daniel shot him a confused look. Then as if a light went off in his head suddenly, "Oh yeah right…' Daniel explained, "He's got some book stuff to take care of on his lunch break."

Eli then asked, "How's reading been so far?"

Daniel leaned back as he said, "It's really well written, a little more detailed than expected but hey, it adds to the story."

Eli asked, "Not your cup of tea?" Daniel shrugged as he explained, "I'm not used to the whole gay lifestyle or culture, so to me it's a little bit of an eye opener."

"Did you think we were all rainbows and show tune queens?"

Daniel laughed and smiled, "No not really Stewart's a gifted writer though. He's going to be a success if he continues to write." Daniel then fell silent, and took a sip of his drink. "I worry about him sometimes. He likes to jump down the rabbit hole a lot of weekends. He also has a hard time with his exes. We went to a club night at Fever for someone's birthday and he just vanished. I tried calling him on his cell a few times and so did everyone else. Eventually the next night he told me that his ex showed up there with another dude and he did everything he could to just not lose it."

Eli chuckled as he continued, "I dunno Eli. I know I'm supposed to be straight, and it's not like I'm horrible with women. It's just that I don't know how to start off on the right foot."

Eli replied, "Well what I can tell you, Daniel, is you need to stop chasing the girls who are partnered off."

Daniel then said, "I can't help it. I like the challenge and the chase."

Eli finished his lunch then smiled at him. He pointed out, "But you're still going to be a v-card carrying member if you keep it up."

Daniel said, "Fair enough" and blushed.

When Eli returned to his desk and opened his e-mails he saw one from Dutch that read ANTOINE AND I ON FRIDAY? His eyes narrowed with disgust as he sighed and leaned back in his chair. He felt a tap on his shoulder as he looked up and saw Christine standing over him. Eli smiled and said, "If it isn't the wee princess."

She asked, "How are you?"

He sighed as he shook his head and leaned back into his chair. "Fighting the good fight. How about you?"

Christine said, "If not fighting the good fight then beating up on the boy." She giggled and then said, "Me and Nick want to hit Vivid on Saturday night. Are you game?"

He waffled as he then asked, "Can I bring Dutch along?"

"Of course" she beamed as she added, "Ask him to bring along Antoine."

His facial expression soured as she asked in sudden confusion, "What?"

Eli sighed and explained, "You know what? I don't think I've been giving him a fair shake."

She asked, "You don't like Antoine?"

"It's not that I don't like him…there's just something not right about him." He reasoned.

Christine then said, "You should be happy for him. Word on the floor is that Antoine makes Dutch really happy. How long has he been single for?" She then nudged him and said, "Kinda takes the pressure off you eh?"

Eli argued, "Dutch would never be interested in someone like me." She mischievously smiled and walked away.

Eli then typed in his response to Dutch. He typed in VIVID ON SATURDAY NIGHT? YOU, ME, CHRISTINE, ANTOINE AND NICHOLAS? He pressed the send button and began to focus on inbound calls, all the while waiting for Dutch's response. Forty minutes later a SOUNDS GOOD appeared on the lower right hand side of his screen. He sighed out and blankly stared at the screen while tapping his pen against the desk.

chapter Thirteen

Tuesday afternoon and Dutch heard the phone ring, quickly picking up the handset. "It's about time you."

The female voice on the other end replied, "Never mind Dutchie! I had a tutorial this morning that lasted forever. Good thing the T.A. was hot or I would have been fucking lost."

Dutch smiled and asked, "One of those eh?"

She then sighed, "Twenty-two, fresh out of graduate school." The voice then teased, "Plus I figured you needed some comedown time after your lost weekend before visiting mother."

"Aimee, you know me too well." Dutch said with a smile

Aimee barked, "Get on your Sunday best and straighten yourself out. We have a lunch date."

He hung up the phone and darted into the shower. Aimee was right. Her being always right was one of her least attractive qualities. Aimee was Dutch's younger sister, and in all actuality was his last link to the immediate family. She escaped for Edmonton shortly after he did, electing to take her studies at the University of Alberta. More importantly, she did it to be closer to him. Aimee always thought the world of Dutch, Dutch thinking she was the only sane one in the family, he included. If Dutch could name the adhesive that held the family together, it would be, without a doubt, her.

Minutes passed and he heard, "Dutchie, your sister is in the lobby!"

He screamed back at Erin, "Well let her in already!" He flipped off the faucets and after a quick towel off, he threw on boxer briefs and an undershirt and opened the door and walked into the living room. Erin went to open her mouth as he said, "Don't you even."

She teased, "I'm just saying…" as he raced to the door and let her in. She stood a little shorter than he was and excruciatingly thin. Her brown shoulder length hair fell neatly onto her shoulders.

They hugged as she whispered in Dutch's ear, "She doesn't like me." Dutch pulled away and gave her a confused look as she said, "I'll explain in the elevator. Finish getting dressed…"

Moments later and as the elevator door closed behind them Aimee waited a few seconds and at floor ten she said, "Dutch, your roommate is a hater."

He asked, "What?"

She continued in exasperated tone, "It's true Dutch. If looks could kill…"

He laughed and brushed it off by arguing, "But you're my sis Aimee. She can't be a hater."

She argued, "Doesn't make a difference. She's a fag hag and she's jealous of our relationship." Even though Dutch was grinning he still shook his head no. Finally Aimee sighed, "Don't say I didn't warn you." Aimee then added, "She'll find a way to permanently tangle herself into your life."

The walk over to Bliss was just mere minutes as she suggested, "You know you could kick her out and let me move in."

Dutch chuckled as she said, "It would save me a shitload on res." Dutch was silent as she teased, "It's not fair that you get to live in Edmonton for free and you're even making decent money."

Dutch asked Aimee, "Do you think I enjoy being a black sheep?"

She conceded the point with, "Fair enough." Aimee added, "Just think when dad retires, you'll have to rethink your options."

He chuckled as he reasoned, "Hopefully by then I'll be somewhere else."

They arrived at Bliss's warm storefront window as she then held the door open. "Can I come too?"

He mischievously grinned as he said, "For sure." They looked around as the café was almost completely full. Dutch quickly eyed a table over by the window, "Over there?" She nodded as he walked over to the table and sat down.

Aimee quickly joined him as she explained, "Server will be over with coffee."

When Aimee sat down she said, "You know what's going to happen when mother gets here right?"

He rolled his eyes as he replied, "First she'll complain because of the gay clientele at Bliss…"

"Then she'll tell you your bleach is coming out…" Aimee continued for him

"Which she'll be elated because the roots will show…" Dutch said preemptively.

"And she'll ask how you are…"

"From there she'll remind us of how dad has just systematically run over his political nemesis…"

"And she'll point out how I'm still single…" Aimee said ringing her hands on her purse strap.

"And she'll ask me if I'm seeing anyone…"

"In which you'll reply…?" She asked curiously

"Fuck Aimee do we know our parents or what?" Dutch deadpanned.

The server came up and poured them coffee as out of the corner of his eye he saw a car slowly pass by and a dark figure glance into the window. Dutch felt a chill run through him as he looked down at his coffee. When he looked back out the window the vehicle had disappeared.

Aimee broke him from his trance as she gave Dutch a quick tap on the hand with her spoon. As he looked up he saw his mother walking into the café. She had the brown hair that ran in their family, in addition to the youthful complexion that subtracted years off her face. She was neatly dressed in a basic black dress as she looked up and promptly came to the table as she quickly hugged Aimee, then Dutch. She proudly announced, "My darling children."

Dutch smiled and said, "Hey mom."

As they sat down Aimee said, "You look really nice."

She flushed as Dutch added in agreement, "Absolutely stunning."

She explained, "There's a party function later this evening. Your father and I will be there in a few hours."

Dutch flashed a smile and asked, "Confidence vote?"

Aimee grinned as their mother asked, "Donald I don't understand what's so special about why we do coffee here. It's such a gay place."

Dutch's eyebrows rose as he explained, "Mom, you've forgotten I'm gay and I'm comfortable here…and plus their coffee is the most amazing cup you'll ever have in Edmonton."

The server returned with a slice of cheesecake as his mother shyly smiled and asked, "You did it to disarm me didn't you?" They all chuckled as she then looked over and pointed out, "Your blonde…"

Dutch then interjected, "Is coming out and the roots are beginning to show." He continued, "I'll get it touched up next week."

She then said, "I miss you with brown hair. How long has it been now?"

"Nineteen" he mumbled irritated.

She then asked, "How's school Aimee?" Aimee cleared her throat and replied, "School has been nuts for the past few weeks. I didn't think that second year was going to be so ballistic."

She then turned to Dutch and asked, "What about you? How's work?"

Dutch fidgeted with his spoon as he could start to feel his irritation grow. "Work has been really busy. We're starting this new project at work. It's mainly a loyalty boost. We're trying to stay competitive with the major players in addition to securing strategic alliances with Canadian retail icons."

Aimee shifted her eyes over as she then asked, "Any thoughts of school?"

He sighed and replied, "I've saved up some money, and I'm thinking on going into marketing."

Their mother's eyes lit up as she asked, "And what made you decide on marketing?"

Dutch smiled and said, "I like being part of the forward design process. I guess putting the gloss and glitz on the final product."

His mother then asked, "Are you seeing someone?"

Dutch remained silent momentarily and then shook his head. He said, "I'm not seeing anyone right now." He then paused and continued,

"You know it's been a little tough with work. Plus…" He then sighed, "In hindsight I guess I'm a little nervous about dad…"

She then said, "Your father is running for re-election in two years." Dutch bit his lip as she continued, "He said he's not ready to retire yet."

Dutch then deadpanned, "I saw his defense of marriage speech on television." She remained silent as he said, "I think it sucks what he said, especially on air." He point blankly continued, "It's not enough that he has a fucking queer kid that hates himself already for the simple fact that he is. But to go out on air and say something like that on television…"

She shot him a glance and spat out, "It's not like that Donald…"

"Will you please quit calling me fucking Donald already? He said hotly. "Dutch will suffice."

She looked shocked as he then asked, "Well then what is it?" She said nothing and he continued, "He's not sitting here having coffee with us. He's said nothing to me since you both shipped me up here so I would be out of sight and out of mind."

She then argued, "We'd thought you'd be more comfortable being open here than Calgary."

He glared at her and asked, "Am I supposed to thank you for that?" He grunted and said, "You know all the money that you throw at me doesn't make up for the fact that I miss you both. That I can't come home for Christmas and Thanksgiving or even for your birthday. Between Aimee and Eli, I feel like this is all the family that I have left."

She then asked, "How is that self-destructive prick anyhow?"

Dutch looked up and asked, "And who would that be?" She pierced him with her glare as he asked, "When are you going to stop blaming Eli for me being gay?" She then began to say something when he stopped her. "You know this has gotten really old, really fucking quick." He downed his coffee in one gulp and said, "If you really want to blame anyone for me being gay, why don't you blame the boy next door who fucked me bareback. Dad only caught us just as he came in my ass for the third time."

Her face resorted to anguish as Dutch continued, "I'm your gay son." He then pointed out, "Donald 'Dutch' Bryant, son to Ted and Cybil Bryant. Nothing will ever change that." He stood up and emptied his pocket, throwing his money on the table. "I'm sorry if what it's going to take for you to acknowledge me is that I have to be beaten unconscious, tied to a fencepost and left for dead in the middle of fucking nowhere.

I don't have the time for this mom." He then leaned over to kiss her on the side of her head as he pushed himself away, tears running the mascara down her face as he calmly said, "It was good to see you. Say hi for dad for me…and I love you." He then walked out of Bliss and quickly glanced to see her perfect porcelain face smudged by tears. A block away he felt his phone vibrate. When he looked down he saw that the number was hers and sent it straight to voicemail.

LOVe's sweet exile - Disc 56: three minutes, twenty five seconds

"I almost fucking hate you some days."

"It's hard enough that you both…well not so much you but he has excommunicated me from the family, all due to 'work'. That's right, work. You would think I would be happy that you've sequestered me in this wonderful apartment and every month you both throw enough money at me in the hopes that daddy's little queer secret out of sight and out of mind. What upsets me more is you continue to validate his work and his opinions by giving him your support. I know you love me but I cringe every time when some new piece of legislation is put on the table and there he is, staunchly defending family values."

"What ever happened to my value? Between you and Eli you just can't band-aid me with money in the hopes I will keep my mouth shut so you can better your interests on the political stage. I remember when dad won that seat way back when I was fourteen. I remember the four of us being up on that podium in front of that conservative blue and all those people cheered us on. I was so proud of that moment, that he was in office and that he planned to make the world a better place."

"It fucks with my head the most that the last time he won, I sat and watched it from one of the televisions that were on in the Pink Bar. People just looked at me as I unraveled as the three of you were there. There was such a gap missing on the podium in the riding that time. It broke my heart into a million little pieces. I wonder what would happen if the media really knew how he felt about family and how he treats his own."

Chapter Fourteen

"Do you hate me?"

It was those words which nearly made Eli choke on a piece of beef from his noodle box. He looked up at Samuel and gave Samuel a pained expression. Eli replied, "No..." He finished his bite and swallowed. He then asked, "Why would I hate you?"

"Because I'm still with Keith."

They were sitting in the upper floor food court at Edmonton City Centre. It was Samuel's first day at the law firm and Eli received the text to join him for lunch, to which Eli had explained to Marie that Dutch should not to wait up for lunch. Eli tried his hardest not to notice that Samuel was making a complete mess of his noodle box. Samuel said, "It's just because Keith was such a pompous, pretentious prick of misery, and I know I told you that I wasn't interested in getting back together with him again."

Eli reasoned, "Maybe there's a legitimate reason that you two got back together." Eli shoveled more food into his mouth and muffled, "Everything happens for a reason Sam."

Samuel argued, "I know Eli, but it just feels..." He spaced his arms apart and elaborated, "I love Keith. It's not like the things I fell in love with aren't there anymore." Samuel trailed off, "It's just I hate the way he treats people. It's not even polite...look at the way he treats you."

Eli only shrugged as he pointed out, "He has his reasons I'm sure."

Samuel shook his head in disagreement. "I don't know of anything other than..."

"You and I?"

Samuel put down his chopsticks and then deadpanned, "You have a point there." Eli was silent as Samuel said, "I don't know if I should tell him about us. It's not like he's cheated on me or anything."

"That you know of at least..."

Samuel only smiled and replied, "I don't think he'd lie to me about that Eli." Eli looked up at him as he explained, "He might be morally vacant, but the one thing I can vouch for is he's honest." When Eli cleaned up the last portion of his noodles Samuel continued, "When I point-blank told him he was a superficial prick, he flat out said then and there that he knew he was." Eli kept chewing, trying to stomach the rest of the lunch that was mixed in with Samuel's previous comments. Samuel then added, "That's when he told me he'd fucked someone the night before." Eli again tried not to choke as Samuel asked, "Isn't that just messed?"

Eli's eyes widened as he replied, "You're telling me."

Samuel then said, "When I asked him how many times it happened, he said four. I asked him why he never told me. He told me, 'You never asked'. Keith then proceeded to explain that it wasn't like he lied to me. He just never told me."

Eli reasoned, "Well think of it only as a silent revenge...and I think we're only at three." Samuel blushed as he leaned back against his chair. Eli asked, "So how is the firm so far?"

Samuel thought for a moment then replied, "Its okay. I don't see Keith very often because he works in another part of the office. I do see Paul a lot however."

It was at that point that Samuel shuddered. Eli chuckled as he heard, "It's not that I don't like him. It's just that he's so fake to everyone. Including Keith." Samuel stretched again after standing up. "It's strange because Keith knows."

Eli commented, "Misery loves company I guess."

He stood up as Samuel said, "Come on. I'll walk you back to the office."

They headed down the stairs as Samuel asked, "What about Dutch?"

"Hrmm?" Eli mumbled while Samuel pressed again, "How about Dutch. Is he dating anyone?"

Eli grimaced and said, "Dutch right now is seeing some steroid jock from Montreal who's working in the office."

Samuel asked, "And you're not happy with that?"

Eli replied, "I just don't want to see him get hurt by someone who's making him a bunch of empty promises."

Samuel asked, "Are you absolutely sure those promises are empty?"

Eli said nothing and Samuel said, "You're both the same age Eli. He needs to experience that for himself." Eli sighed as he continued, "When was the last time he had a boyfriend?"

Eli said, "I think about six years ago."

Samuel appeared shocked as he said, "Let me guess, if you say something it might come across as meddling."

Eli was silent as Samuel wondered aloud, "I'm kind of stuck as to why he's been single for so long."

He then looked at Eli. "You haven't been scaring them off have you?"

Eli shot him a puzzled look as Samuel chuckled while heading up the escalator. "Are you saying I...." Eli began to ask as Samuel just stood and grinned. "Fuck you Samuel."

Samuel teased back, "You wish."

Eli then spat out, "I do actually."

Samuel was suddenly silent as the grin on Eli's face disappeared.

When they reached the top of the escalator he said, "Follow me" as they walked into the hotel lobby by the lounge. Eli led him into the washroom where once inside he switched the lock on the stall door and pinned Samuel to the wall.

They began kissing as Samuel protested in a whisper, "We'll get caught."

Eli's hand undid his belt then forced open his pants as he reasoned, "As long as you're not too loud councilor we'll be okay." Samuel chuckled while Eli dislodged his shirt, his hand reaching into his briefs where he found Samuel's erect penis.

As Eli quickly dropped to his knees Samuel asked, "Does this make it number four?"

Eli briefly looked up and smiled, "Three and a half."

Samuel's chuckle was shortly replaced by a quiet moan as he could feel Eli's lips around the head and then down to the base of his shaft.

Chapter Fifteen

As Dutch shut down his computer for the day he began to walk over to customer service. Out of the corner of his eye he spotted Christine texting on her cell. Dutch walked over and slyly said, "You know you're not supposed to be texting on the floor… *right?*"

She smiled and replied, "It's either that or improper use of company resources."

He teased, "You know what Eli would say if he was on the floor right?"

She countered, "Then I would have told him he should have taken the supervisor position."

They both laughed and Dutch commented, "Touché."

He then looked around and asked, "Where's Ariel? Isn't she supposed to be in tonight?"

She quickly peered over the partition as she said, "She was here an hour ago. Ask Stewart."

He then walked over to Stewart and asked, "Hey where's Ariel?"

Stewart set a code on his phone into aftercall and sighed, "Looks like Jeremiah dumped her via text message."

Dutch then sighed, "You gotta be fucking kidding me." He looked around the cell centre and then asked, "Lunch room?"

Stewart nodded and picked up the next call as Dutch quickly called Antoine. "Hey I'm gonna be late. There's a bit of an issue here at work I gotta fix." He then hung up his cell and asked, 'Where's Daniel?"

Stewart deadpanned, "He called in sick an hour before the start of his shift."

Dutch breathed, "Fucking figures" as he quickly hopped up the steps and into the glass lounge.

When Dutch opened the door he looked and saw Ariel's face buried in her hands and Kleenex strewn all over the table beside her, spotted in black as she tried to dry her eyes. Dutch walked over cautiously and sat down across from her seat. She briefly glanced up and said, "He dumped me by text message today."

Dutch asked, "Are you okay?"

She sobbed a little more as she explained, "It was right before I got into work, and…"

Ariel completely broke down and continued to cry as Dutch reassured her, "You're gonna be okay Ariel. It doesn't look like that right now, but couples go through a rough patch like this all the time. I'm sure he just needs a little time to think it through."

She continued to sob as she said, "All of his friends hate me. They think I'm a bitch and they don't agree that I'm good for him."

Dutch swallowed the lump in his throat as he asked, "What did the text message say?"

She began, "It said that he needed some time alone and some space. He needed a chance to reevaluate things."

Dutch said, "Maybe he's right."

She replied in an irritated tone as if she had never heard anything so stupid in her life, "Dutch, when does someone suddenly reevaluate things when he's been out shopping for an engagement ring? It just doesn't happen."

She began to cry again as Dutch scratched his head. He said, "Maybe take the night off and think it out a little. Get some headspace and hopefully by that time things will start to sort themselves out."

Ariel sniffled, "Okay"

"Whatever you do, you need to give him his space Ariel. Don't push the issue. If he needs space he probably means it so don't push it. It's going to drive him further from you…" Ariel only nodded as he said, "I'll let your supervisor know you're gone."

She scurried out of the lounge and back on the floor while Stewart walked in on him picking up her Kleenex. "She seems pretty heartbroken"

Dutch nodded, "Let your supervisor know that she went home for the night. She's pretty shaken up." Stewart nodded as Dutch then asked, "Are you okay?" Stewart only shrugged as he turned around and walked out of the lounge and back to his desk.

Dutch then quickly headed out the door as his phone rang. "I'm just on my way home" he explained as he looked at his watch.

Antoine asked, "Did you want me to come and get you?"

Dutch smiled and said, "You don't drive though…"

Antoine explained, "I'll catch a cab over."

Dutch protested, "You don't have to do that."

Antoine replied, "But I want to. Plus I don't remember your apartment except what I bumped into in the dark."

Dutch laughed and said, "All right then you win. I'll see you in a bit."

When he got back to the apartment, he unlocked the door and quickly walked in. He heard from the living room, "It's about time you got home!" He walked in and smiled as he gave Erin a quick peck on the cheek as she asked, "What are you up to this evening?"

Dutch explained, "I'm out for dinner with my boss from work tonight, and gonna take him out around downtown"

Erin said, "Ohhh…" as he disappeared into his room.

He then called out, "Did you want to come with Eli and I to Vivid on Saturday night?"

She then thought for a moment and replied, "I just might have to. Who else will be there?" Dutch said, "It will be us as well as Antoine, Christine and Nicholas."

She asked, "Who's Antoine?" He returned back in the living room, towel over his shoulders clad in only his boxers.

He explained, "He's the boss from work."

Erin then said, "I left supper in the microwave, just in case…"

He peeked his head out of the washroom and said, "You didn't have to do that."

She countered, "I know Dutch, but I just wanted to."

Dutch sighed as he closed the door behind him. At that moment he heard the door knock and opened the door as he sped to the front door.

He smiled and opened it as Antoine looked in and smiled. "Am I eating in tonight?" he grinned as Dutch ushered him in. Antoine leaned in and kissed him.

When Dutch pulled away he said, "I missed you."

Antoine replied, "Likewise" as Erin walked up to them both.

She said, "Dutch I'm on my way to the station. I've got some catching up to do."

Dutch then said, "Erin this is Antoine. Antoine works in the office in Montreal."

Antoine extended his hand as she said, "Hi Antoine I'm Erin."

Dutch elaborated, "Erin works for the urban FM station downtown in the old Bay building. She's just down from the call centre."

Antoine said, "Pleased to meet you."

She then smiled and said, "See you later."

Antoine closed the door behind Erin with a suspicious look on his face. After a few seconds Dutch asked, "What?"

Antoine then replied, "She has no idea you're gay."

Dutch said, "Fuck you"

Antoine protested with a grin, "I kid you not Dutch. Either she doesn't know or she's deep in denial."

After a few second of silence Dutch smiled and said, "Come on in and make yourself comfortable."

Dutch led him into the living room as Antoine mused, "You know the last time we were here it was much darker." Dutch snickered while Antoine inspected the apartment. He asked, "How much do you rent a place like this for?"

Dutch explained, "My folks own it."

Antoine grimaced and said, "Not bad. Not bad at all."

Dutch then asked, "Do you want to surf around on the internet while I go hop in the shower?" Antoine strolled up to him as he began to kiss Dutch. Dutch then pulled away and said with a smile, "Not until after dinner."

"Tease" he said as he followed Dutch into his room. Antoine grinned and said, "Now this room looks very familiar."

Dutch said, "It'll be only a few minutes."

Antoine watched as Dutch sped into the bathroom and then let his gaze roam around Dutch's bedroom while hearing the hiss of steam. He looked at Dutch's computer tower and saw the collage of pictures, mostly those of him and Eli over the years. He plucked one from the side and let his hand run over the smooth surface on the picture. He rubbed the photo some more, as if he was trying to smudge Eli out of the picture. With a quick glance around he placed the photo back on the tower His gaze moved a little lower as he saw a small stack of minidiscs on the desk. He rubbed the shiny plastic case as read the words Love's Sweet Exile – disc forty five, scrawled on the sticker. He placed it down and then opened the bottom left drawer as Dutch called out, "Did you find your way okay?"

"The cab driver knew his way downtown" Antoine replied as he discreetly put the disc down. Antoine then began to surf around on Dutch's internet while the hissing stopped and Dutch came back into the bedroom. Antoine asked, "What's Love's Sweet Exile?"

Dutch hesitated then explained, "When I was in high school my English teacher gave us this assignment. It was to start keeping a journal. Just something that would document a part of life. So I kept an audio journal of my time with Eli." He then pulled a shirt over his head and said, "It was only to be a snapshot for a semester…but then I became completely engrossed in it."

Antoine picked it up and fidgeted with the disc as Dutch then headed back into the washroom. Dutch loudly explained, "In a way it's a bit of history since coming out. All of my thoughts, hopes and dreams when I started figuring myself out." Antoine placed the disc back down as Dutch came into the bedroom fully dressed. He said, "My sister Aimee firmly believed in the organic part of the creative process, so she bought me a minidisc recorder." He said after, "I like it. It's therapeutic in a way."

Antoine stood up and said, "I'd like to maybe read it some day when you get it published."

He smiled as Dutch said, "You might get your chance."

They kissed again and Antoine then asked, "So where am I taking you for dinner?"

Dutch said, "There's a place called Panda in the mall on the main floor. It's one of Edmonton's best grills."

"And after?" Antoine asked

Dutch suggested, "Let's play it by ear."

"Fair enough" he beamed while Dutch locked the door and they ventured back to building lobby. Dutch reasoned, "Let's walk towards downtown. We're not too far away from the mall."

Antoine agreed as they began to walk towards the towers that stood on the edge of downtown. As they walked down the street Antoine commented, "There seems like there's very little history left in downtown Edmonton. I've only seen two or three buildings that look anything like history."

Dutch shrugged and explained, "That's Edmonton for you. Our previous mayor who was a complete redneck retard, hated queers, ravers and anything that would remind him of his true age."

They laughed as Antoine then said, "You'd love Montreal, especially the village. There's tons of beautiful buildings in the village and the Plateau neighborhoods." Dutch looked at him as Antoine said, "Don't get me wrong. Progress is important, but your past and its preservation is equally important. It's a fundamental window into your soul."

The further they ventured downtown Antoine explained, "Montreal is a beautiful open city. You could transfer out there move into a cozy little apartment." Dutch chuckled as they slowed down in front of a bookstore just across from Corona train station.

"How about this?" Dutch asked as Antoine looked inside.

"We're eating here?" Antoine asked as Dutch playfully poked him.

He then said, "No I mean look at this building stupid."

"Oh" Antoine replied as he looked back and peered above the awning. Antoine grinned and tacked on, "It's a start…" while Dutch playfully pushed him while they walked down the street.

When they reached Commerce Place, they ventured up the escalator and walked down the empty halls as Antoine asked, "Is it always this quiet at night?"

Dutch nodded as he explained, "Downtown Edmonton for the most part rolls up the streets after business hours. Everyone goes down to Whyte Avenue if they want to eat, drink, and get wasted. And the gay bars are all scattered around downtown."

"Wonder why that is" Antoine mused.

Dutch replied, "It's because gay Edmonton is fragmented. No one really works together unless forced…" Antoine only nodded as they crossed the pedway into Edmonton City Centre and Dutch led him down the escalator to the main floor.

"Where are you taking me again?" Antoine teased as Dutch turned right and pointed to the small entrance that was decorated by the black and white sign that read Panda.

Dutch quickly grabbed Antoine's hand and pulled him through the entrance as a server came up and greeted them. Dutch explained, "Two for a private table please."

The dark haired girl then said, "Follow me Mr. Dutch." She maneuvered them towards the back of the restaurant, then to a curtained off area and into a private area in the back. She set down two menus as she explained, "I'll be back with your drinks. What would you like to start with?"

Dutch said, "I'll have a Stella."

Antoine then chimed in, "A Canadian." She smiled then walked away as they sat down on the black leather seats. The décor was very urban-dark concrete as Antoine looked around. He flipped open his menu as he said, "I like this place. It's very warm despite its greys and blacks."

Dutch chuckled as he said, "I'm so glad you like it. It's been awhile since I was here last." Antoine asked, "Why not?"

"Because Eli can be fickle as fuck some days, and it drives me nuts." Antoine shot a glance at him. Dutch groaned, "I know, I know." After a few minutes he said, He really helped me through my coming out period. My coming out was not a happy one."

Antoine asked, "When?"

Dutch elaborated, "I was seventeen and living in a Calgary suburb. My parents were and are, darling Conservatives."

Antoine then asked, "Why did you come to Edmonton?"

Dutch then deadpanned, "Out of sight, out of mind. I didn't have a choice." Antoine breathed, "I'm sorry."

"Don't be" Dutch replied as he said, "I kind of got the better end of the deal. My folks bought the condo and I don't put up with my father's bullshit views."

"That doesn't explain how you met Eli though."

"I'm getting to that…"

At that point the server appeared with two bottles and glasses as she asked, "Are you ready to order?"

Antoine nodded at Dutch as he ordered the meal for both of them. They handed back the menus as she smiled at them and walked away. Dutch began to pour his beer into his ice cold glass and explained, "I met Eli through youth parliament. Eli's parents are retired politicians and Eli's passion was to do political science." Dutch took a sip of his beer and then swallowed. "Things were rough for awhile. I had very few friends, and Eli would take me out to the gay bars and sneak in while underage."

Antoine suggested, "I guess that counts or something" He then poured his beer and asked, "What about the roommate?"

Dutch solemnly replied, "Somedays I think she's from outer space." They laughed as he continued, "But seriously…" He took another sip and said, "She's an old friend from a small town in Saskatchewan. She really wants to kick-start her career in broadcasting."

Antoine pointed out, "She dotes on you."

Dutch rolled his eyes as he said, "She's always been like that." He then said, "I know she knows I appreciate it immensely but…"

Antoine said, "It's sometimes too much."

Dutch added, especially the cooked dinners in Tupperware in the fridge."

Antoine then asked, "Why haven't you and Eli dated?"

A few seconds of silence passed and Dutch looked up at Antoine. He then said, "I don't have an answer for you."

Antoine reasoned, "Being how close you are I would have figured you two would have made a perfect…" when Dutch's glare shot that suggestion down before it could be completed.

Dutch then asked, "What about you? Any family at all?"

Antoine sipped his beer then explained, "Working class parents and I'm the middle child." He continued, "I have one gay brother. I haven't come out yet."

Dutch asked, "Isn't that hard? I mean not being out to your family at all?" Antoine replied, "I'm waiting for the right time. Father expects me to be the next Maurice Richard and win the Stanley Cup. And it's already one strike that the younger brother came out."

Dutch asked, "Does your brother at least know?" He shook his head no and Dutch asked, "You've had boyfriends right?"

Antoine again shook his head and explained, "I've been very, very discreet."

The server then placed down their food on the table as they continued to talk along with their meal. As Antoine sampled all of the dishes, Dutch began to realize something stirred in him as they traded stories about growing up, horrible one night stands and rave culture. It felt like the shortest meal within a time-span of two hours as they inspected the empty plates and glasses. Dutch wished that this moment wouldn't end, that this could last forever.

As Dutch finished his beer, Antoine opened the bill envelope and inserted his credit card into the pocket. Dutch looked confused as he asked, "What are you doing?"

Antoine smiled and said "You did all the grunt work. I'm covering the meal."

Dutch reddened as he breathed, "Thank you." The server came back and after promptly picking up the bill, disappeared.

Antoine asked, "Did you want to go back up to the hotel room before we go out?" She returned and he signed as she thanked the both. Antoine stashed his card away as Dutch nodded in agreement. They walked over to the lobby and they strolled into the elevator, continuing the conversation from the restaurant.

Moments after Dutch had closed the door behind them, he walked up to Antoine, and they embraced in a passionate kiss. Antoine breathed heavily, "I've missed you so much" as Dutch leaned in again and could feel Antoine's tongue press inside his mouth. Dutch's hands undid Antoine's belt and pushed his khakis down to his ankles, watching Antoine's erection poke the fabric of his underwear outward. Antoine then began to kiss Dutch's neck as he turned Dutch around so his bulge would press into him from behind. Antoine continued to kiss him while his hands unbuttoned Dutch's pants and reached into Dutch's underwear. Antoine moaned in his ear, "I've wanted you so bad Dutch. Since that first morning I laid eyes on you at the call centre." Dutch only grunted as he pressed backwards into Antoine, pushing down his underwear and feeling Antoine's warm erection nuzzle itself while Antoine's mouth kissed down the back of his neck and down his back.

He then kissed a trail upwards as he then turned Dutch back around, finding his mouth as Dutch unbuttoned Antoine's shirt and wrestled it off his arms. When Antoine inched away to pull off his undershirt, Dutch helped him pull it off and threw it on the floor. Antoine then sat back on the bed as Dutch straddled him and laid Antoine back. Dutch leaned in and kissed him some more as moments after Antoine shifted them so he was on top of Dutch. Completely naked, Dutch let his hands run the length of Antoine's penis while Antoine prodded two fingers slowly inside him. Dutch could feel that his movements were exciting him as his thumb had now began to play with Antoine's slippery head.

Dutch then took his thumb and hooked it into Antoine's mouth as Antoine let his tongue circle around it. Dutch then rolled Antoine onto his back again as he began to push into Antoine. After a few seconds Dutch sucked in his breath while Antoine's hands steadied Dutch's hips and let Antoine push swiftly inside. Dutch could feel Antoine's complete entrance and his movements began to dictate their rhythm.

Forever seemed to pass as Antoine continued to push upwards inside Dutch, eyes solely fixated on him while Dutch returned his gaze. Which each thrust upwards Dutch's breathing became heavier as Antoine would slow down just enough to lean inwards and kiss, while Antoine's sweat dripped off of his stomach and mingled with Dutch's. It was at that point Antoine's right hand rubbed the slickness of Dutch's chest, down his stomach and finally to Dutch's stiff penis. His hand moved in unison and Dutch pleaded in quick breaths, "I'm so close Antoine. I want us to come together."

Antoine slowed down just enough that when Dutch could feel him stiffen while he tightened up, Antoine's hand tightening as finally Dutch pushed down as far as he could, tightening in spasms while Antoine could feel the pulses release inside Dutch. Dutch responded by unloading all over Antoine's upper torso. Their breathing slowed down as Dutch rolled off him and onto his back. Minutes passed and Dutch nuzzled into Antoine, kissing his neck as he leaned over and continued to kiss Dutch. Dutch let his hand rub Antoine's semen-coated chest.

He asked, "Did you still want to go out tonight?"

Dutch replied, "I'd almost prefer a night in right now."

Antoine only smiled and replied, "Fair enough" as he pulled Dutch close as they started kissing all over again.

They eventually fell asleep as Antoine wrapped his strong arms around Dutch, his back pressed against his chest as the low purr of Dutch's snoring ushered them to sleep. When the beams of sunlight began to pour through the hotel room, Dutch stirred against Antoine's body as he pulled Dutch closer to him. Dutch moved around even more as Antoine mumbled, "I'm not letting you go." Dutch then opened his eyes while Antoine opened his.

Dutch mumbled, "I'm not going anywhere."

LOVE'S SWEET EXILE - DISC 56: FORTY-FIVE MINUTES, TWO SECONDS

"I wonder what he was thinking."

"I wonder why Richey chose to disappear right before the release of *The Holy Bible*. As uneven as *The Holy Bible* is as an album, it's still a hell of an amazing work that really stands on its own. It was definitely an idea that never was given its proper credit. A shame because it wasn't until *Everything Must Go* that it all came together. A lot of people dismissed *This Is My Truth Tell Me Yours*. Oddly enough its my favorite Manics album. If I was to have a soundtrack, *This Is My Truth* would be mine. Maybe because it encompasses everything I want to say to him."

"I tried to play that album to Eli. All he did was write it off as pretentious bullshit. And like nothing he ever does is pretentious bullshit. When he turns someone down because of any slight imperfection, that's categorized as pretentious. He doesn't realize how bad he gets sometimes. That or he realizes too late how he's gotten but at that point he's stopped caring."

"I wonder what Richey's motives for just disappearing were? Was he really that unhappy with life? Did he just have an epiphany and decided to vanish? I guess after a huge move like Cobain's suicide, it's really hard to top.

I guess everyone wished in a sense they were forever immortalized. Maybe he did it for love of his bandmates. The simple fact that he fought hard for the band to be heard could justify anything he could have done."

"Or maybe he thought that everything he fought for was a lie. That his scrawling of 'for real' on his arm, was in essence just a show, a fragment of entertainment for the crowd. That no matter what he did he would always be on the other side of love, and not get it back."

"I wish I could just disappear somedays."

Chapter Sixteen

For Eli, Thursday was the next best day to Friday in the work week.

Not only because this particular Thursday included dinner with some of the friends from work, but because Dutch had also picked up the weekend supplies and he was already beginning to plan their weekend. As Eli hit the log off button on the phone he leaned back as Christine approached his desk. She asked, "Are we still on for dinner?"

He smiled and said, "Let me just fire off a quick e-mail to Dutchie."

He looked at his computer and quickly typed the words as Christine added, "We're also bringing Stewart along."

Eli bit his lip and scowled. She asked, "What?"

Eli breathed in as she protested, "He's a nice guy Eli."

He countered, "Nice enough to run over" and grinned as Christine shot him a scowl in disapproval.

She said, "You know it makes me sad when you can't…"

"Get along with the less fortunate?"

Dutch came up as she said, "We'll see you shortly" and with that waltzed away. Dutch looked down and smirked as Eli briefly held his head in his hands.

Dutch said, "You look like someone just told you your favorite porn star died."

Eli sighed, "She and Nicholas are dragging fucking coppertop to dinner."

Dutch grimaced and asked, "Why do you hate him so much?"

Eli gave off a shrug as his answer. He then deadpanned, "I guess if I have to…"

Dutch said, "He's not that bad Eli. If you gave him a chance…" Eli winced as Dutch said, "Don't."

Eli asked, "What?"

Dutch then said, "Let's go cowboy. I'm fucking starved."

They walked out the main entrance and into the mall, down the escalator and towards the mall. Eli said, "I cannot believe I agree to go to dinner with that fucking redhead and them…"

Dutch then stopped and said, "Look if you really want we can go to Pink and skip dinner."

Eli hummed and said, "No fuck it we'll go…I'm in the mood for a laugh this evening."

Moments later they arrived in the parking lot while Eli pulled out his car keys and unlocked the doors. As Dutch closed his door he opened his bag and asked "Do you want appetizers?"

Eli looked over as Dutch was pulling out a small bag and replied, "Maybe a little later after we hit the club." Dutch then placed the bag inside the glove compartment in front of him while Eli maneuvered the car onto Jasper Avenue.

They had just escaped downtown when Dutch spotted Peter at a traffic intersection and pointed in his direction. Eli immediately honked the horn to get Peter's attention. As Peter looked over they both waved while Dutch mused, "That was quite diplomatic, even by your standards."

Eli said, "You can't help but feel sorry for your elders."

They light turned green and as Eli lightly hit the gas pedal Dutch asked, "Are we going to end up like that?" Eli remained silent as he looked over to the right and parked beside the restaurant. Dutch quickly glanced the parking lot and spotted Nicholas' car and breathed, "They're here."

As they got out of the car they started to walk past the glass enclosed patio and into the main entrance. They both looked around and Dutch deeply inhaled while Eli scanned the bar. Stewart came up to them and explained, "We're over at the table by the patio." He pointed to where Christine and Nicholas were seated as they waved.

When they arrived at the table Eli sat down as he asked Nicholas with a smirk, "So you finally decided to make good on buying dinner."

Nicholas sheepishly smiled and asked, "Is that the case?"

Eli explained, "It's only company policy you're required to adhere to."

Dutch then glanced at the empty seat and asked, "Who is the extra seat for?"

Christine explained, "That was for Daniel. He said he was going to come join us for dinner." Eli only grinned and shot a glare at Stewart while Dutch immediately spotted the server.

As she arrived Eli said, "I'll have a Heineken."

Stewart chimed in, "Stella please." Eli teased, "Isn't Stella a little too butch for you?"

Dutch then said, "I'll have a Jack and Coke."

Nicholas sipped his beer as Christine asked, "So Dutch what you think about the Regenesis project?"

The server placed their drinks down on the table as Dutch replied, "It's quite ambitious and also quite aggressive. I think especially because expansion into the States is quite risky, however overall smart."

Stewart then asked, "How come you weren't picked for Regenesis Eli?"

Eli only looked over, bottle in hand. "It's because I didn't suck Natasha's cock to get on it." Stewart remained silent and shocked as Eli then added, "But in all actuality it's because I've plainly stated that I don't see Go Credit as my career choice. It's why I've paid a shit load of money to go to school and…" He gulped down his beer and breathed, "Go Credit is such a hotbed of gossip. I mean they'll talk about anything, and anyone, from who you're fucking to that ridiculous unibrow on your head."

Stewart protested, "I don't have a unibrow."

Eli grinned as he said, "Stewart, you're not fooling anyone. Hence, why I call you Bert."

Dutch jabbed Eli in the side as the server came back around. Once they ordered Dutch asked, "So when are the two of you officially getting married?"

Stewart asked, "You're getting married?" She quickly held up her hand as Stewart and Dutch's eyes widened.

"Fuck that's a huge diamond" Dutch commented in amazement.

She replied in an anticipatory tone, "We're looking at next summer as the date."

Christine then teased, "You know Stewart you'd think for the fact you and I sit in reject row together you'd have noticed the ring by now."

Eli interjected, "He's got Daniel on the brain." Stewart only began to drink because Eli knew that he had touched a nerve.

"Oh come on Eli you should know better than that" Christine said.

Eli teased back, "I might, but I don't know if Bert does."

The server returned as Stewart then said as he stood up, "I'll be right back. I have an incoming call."

He quickly disappeared as Christine then asked, "So Dutch how are you and the French boy getting along?"

Dutch blushed as he commented, "He and I have hung out a few times."

She then explained, "You know ever since that meeting we had you seemed to have really caught his attention."

Eli then said, "He's not to be trusted."

Nicholas added, "I've heard that he's a pretty nice guy."

Eli argued, "He's pretty vacant, that's why."

Nicholas then asked, "Dutch, What do you think of him?"

Dutch shrugged and explained, "He's pretty cute. And he seems nice enough. But he lives in Montreal."

Just at that moment Stewart returned and explained, "I'm sorry guys but I gotta go. Something's come up."

Christine asked, "Is everything okay?"

He nodded, "I'll see you at work tomorrow."

He then turned to Dutch and said, "Good night."

As he darted away she glared at Eli. "You know…" she began as Eli started his second drink. "You could be a little nicer to him. He did fuck all to you."

Eli complained, "It's just such hard work…"

Dutch teased, "Eli's just jealous because now he's got competition for Daniel." Eli shot him a deadly glare as Dutch added, "Oh come on Eli. You know I'm just fucking with you."

At that moment Eli said, "I'm going to piss and make a call. I'll be right back."

Christine said nothing as Nicholas then said, "I'll be right back. I'm gonna follow him to the washroom."

She said, "Don't take too long" as Nicholas quickly stood up and headed to the washroom in the same direction as Eli.

She then turned to Dutch and said, "What's been up his ass lately?"

Dutch shook his head and replied, "I'm his best friend Christine and even I don't have the answer to that." Dutch then elaborated, "He's always been like that to Stewart. I really feel bad for him sometimes."

She asked, "Do you think Stewart has a thing for Daniel?"

He looked back as he shrugged, "All I know is Daniel is running after that girl in collections and she thinks he's the flakiest thing since homemade apple pie that you get at that fucking ridiculous deli in the food court near work."

She chuckled as she said, "So I'm sure the reason why you haven't said anything about Antoine in front of Eli is because of the fact that he hates him."

Dutch nodded in agreement. "Eli's kinda pissed still because I ditched him for Antoine last Friday night."

She then trumpeted, "Good for you Dutch! You deserve to be happy and I'm so happy that Antoine is treating you as an equal and not a sidekick like Eli does."

Dutch then spotted Eli coming back to the table. "Let's continue this discussion another time."

Eli asked as he sat down, "What did we miss?"

Dutch only smiled and replied, "We were discussing what type of flower girl dress you'll need to wear for the wedding."

"Fuck off" Eli snapped as they began eating. Dutch's grin vanished shortly after as he glanced up and saw Nicholas quickly dart his eyes away as Christine continued to discuss work. It was at that point that Dutch wished Stewart had stayed for dinner.

Chapter seventeen

Summer was always Dutch's favorite time of year in Edmonton as he watched the continual stream of headlights wind down Jasper Avenue from his window. Not only did the warm weather seem to make downtown come more alive than any other time of year, but it also gave him the opportunity to walk back and forth. Seeing that he didn't live too far away, he would follow the scattered reflection of the buildings and within minutes arrive at the glow of lights that punctuated the water-like colors of blue and grey that served as the skyline's backdrop. Lightning would dance behind it as Dutch passed the Pink Bar and gradually inched closer to the outer border that signaled Downtown's heart. With the smell of fresh rain around him, Dutch continued onwards while the navy darkened into black while the orange reflections from concrete, steel, and unlit windows indicated the shift from day to night.

It had been awhile since he had made the walk on his own. Usually this path had been more often traveled by him and Eli. On this particular night he had decided to travel alone and thoughts of Eli had not been apparent. There seemed to be a lot about the main road to downtown that he hadn't noticed in the time he had traveled. Whether it was the fact he was always with Eli, or that he chose to remain oblivious to the world outside his own immediate circle, Dutch felt that this particular walk was very different to prior excursions.

When he reached the corner of Jasper and 109th he looked behind him to see that the sun had retreated from its luminous position behind him replaced by pastels which were layered under darker colors. When he looked to the right, the awning that once proudly displayed Smith Funeral Homes had made multiple evolutions to what now read Globe Taphouse and Grill. Further forward sat the now empty Mayfair Hotel which was now lightly dressed with boards over the majority of its windows. When the walk light finally beckoned him across the street he passed by the neglected buildings as he could feel the light nudge of his phone. He answered, "Hello?" and shortly after, when he recognized the voice, he automatically smiled. He then explained, "I'm almost there. I'm just walking down Jasper Avenue right now."

He crossed the next set of lights as he explained, "Meet me in Commerce Place on the second level and we'll walk back to the club together." After a few more seconds he said, "All right. I'll see you soon."

He hung up the phone and again crossed the street, past the old Bay building and finally to the giant glass exterior. When he walked inside he looked around at the lights that illuminated the glass ceiling above him. It was hauntingly empty, coupled with the silent whir of the escalator gears. He gently stepped up onto the escalator and watched as he slowly moved upwards to the second level.

When Dutch could finally peer over the top, he spotted Antoine casually leaned up against the nearby pillar. He embraced him and they passionately kissed. When he pulled away, Antoine whispered, "I missed you."

Dutch replied, "I missed you too" as he leaned in and began to pin Antoine against the huge pillar while they continued to kiss.

Antoine then pulled away and asked, "Where are you taking me tonight?"

"We're going to an afterhours club called Escape. It's just south of Jasper Avenue on 105th." Dutch then explained, "It's just by a strip bar called Chez Pierre. It's an amazing little shoebox of a party spot." Antoine looked confused as Dutch reasoned, "It's small and claustrophobic, but the vibe is beyond unreal."

Antoine then said, "I thought I read online that Escape was sketchy."

Dutch rolled his eyes and teased, "Are you sure Eli didn't tell you that?" Antoine jabbed him playfully as Dutch laughed while they walked down the street.

They arrived at the corner and Dutch peered ahead to see Peter slowly shuffling in front of them. They passed him by and Dutch waved, "Howdy Pete."

Pete looked at the pair and made a face of disgust, "Who are you?"

Antoine shot him a glare as they finally arrived at the corner of 105th and Jasper Avenue.

As the walk light beckoned them across the street Antoine asked, "Who the fuck was that?"

Dutch replied, "I'll explain later."

An aqua blue sign signaled their arrival as they walked into the building and made their way down the narrow flight of stairs. With a quick turn left they descended down to the entrance where the door person stood at the window. She cordially greeted them with a smile. "Welcome to Escape Afterhours."

Dutch then started to explain, "I'm not sure but…"

She then looked at the clipboard and smiled, "Mr. Bryant." She placed a bracelet on Dutch's left arm, then one on Antoine's. She then crossed them off and said, "Enjoy your night boys."

The bouncer quickly frisked them both and ushered them into the main entrance.

Antoine asked, "How do you do that?" Dutch only shrugged as they walked into the main area.

Escape was a huge room that was evenly flanked in both sides by large monitors that boasted an amazing array of colors. Leather couches spaced out on either side of an already packed dance floor. Just at the back wall a tiny open DJ booth where a female was deep in concentration while tribal rhythms vibrated crisply from the sound system's speakers. Dutch walked over to the bar and picked up two bottles of water. He returned over to where Antoine stood, transfixed while Dutch took one of the cold bottles and pressed it into his back. Antoine jumped out of his trance and looked over. Dutch motioned him to follow as they both headed to the washroom.

Dutch checked if the coast was clear and pulled Antoine into one of the stalls as Antoine leaned Dutch back against the stall wall. He leaned in and began kissing Dutch while Dutch moaned, "Not in here."

Antoine breathed, "You have no idea how bad I want inside of you right now."

Dutch replied, "After…" Antoine chuckled while Antoine pulled out a small bag of pills and popped one of them in his mouth, quickly swallowing as he washed it down with water.

He then popped a second one in his mouth when Antoine asked, "Are you sure you want to do two right away?" Dutch then leaned Antoine back against the other wall and pressed his lips against Antoine's. Dutch pushed his tongue and the pill into Antoine's mouth. His hands wrapped around Antoine's body as he pressed himself against him. Dutch could feel Antoine stiffen as he held himself closer, still locked in their kiss.

Dutch pulled away and they smiled. Antoine took a sip of his water and asked, "Shall we go back out?" Dutch nodded while Antoine unlocked the stall and they both quickly shuffled out and back into the main hall. By that point people were streaming into the club and the dance floor became more crowded.

Dutch loudly suggested, "Did you want to just stay here and dance? Or move towards the back?"

Antoine suggested, "Let's just stay here for awhile. It's close to the booth and you can see the DJ."

Dutch said, "Fair enough" and at that moment began to dance along to the music.

After a few minutes he looked to the side and watched Antoine as he effortlessly moved along. While he admired Antoine slide around in his spot to the beat he could suddenly feel the first wave begin to stir inside him Dutch paused for a moment and inhaled deeply while he closed his eyes. He started to dance along as the music seemed to push, knead, and almost massage the sore muscles around his body. The ecstasy continued to crescendo in him as he finally said to Antoine, "I'm gonna sit down. I'm starting to get pretty high."

Antoine offered, "I'll come join you."

They retreated to the corner where they both ventured up the small flight of stairs and onto the leather couch where two girls were seated on one end. Antoine sat down in the middle while Dutch sat beside him on the end. The girls looked over and they smiled at them as Dutch asked, "How are you ladies doing?"

One of them said, "Not too bad, just hanging out waiting for our boyfriends." She was clad in fun fur that wrapped around her lower legs and matched the fuzzy wristbands and cowboy hat she also sported. The other girl on the furthest end of the couch had blonde hair and was wearing a white t-shirt and matching skirt. The girl in the cowboy hat then asked, "What about you two?"

Antoine said, "Just thought we'd come and unwind tonight."

The girl in the white outfit asked, "Where are your girlfriends?" Dutch only smiled and grabbed Antoine's hand.

"No way" the fun-fur cowgirl said as then the girl in white piped up, "That's so cool. You two make a very cute couple"

She then whispered something in the other's ear as the cowgirl explained, "We're going to meet our boyfriends at the door. You two have a good evening." Dutch nodded while they stood up and went down the flight of steps and towards the entrance.

"She thought we looked cute" Dutch mused.

Antoine replied, "Well we do look cute." Antoine then looked around and said, "Sit on the floor." Dutch gave him a confused look as he reassured him, "Trust me it will be fun." Dutch sat on the hardwood as Antoine positioned himself in front of Dutch's back. With his hands he began to rub Dutch's shoulders and moved his way down to his spine. Dutch closed his eyes as he felt Antoine un-knot him.

Antoine said, "You carry so much stress on you Dutch." Dutch moaned in agreement as Antoine's hands continued to press and knead into his back. He arched as Antoine's hands moved lower, further into the lower back as Dutch was able to loosen up. Antoine said, "You never told me who the old man was."

Dutch began to explain, "The guy on Jasper Avenue's name is Peter." He leaned back while he continued, "He used to be a regular at the Cactus Bar on 106th, just blocks down from Vivid. He was also a huge partier in the late seventies and all through the eighties. When Flashback opened, the story goes he hoovered cocaine like it was sugar." Dutch then breathed in, "Also was a huge drinker. That guy apparently had an indestructible liver and heart. He definitely was the life of the party." Antoine began to massage him again as Dutch continued, "One day after Flashbacks had closed down some of his closest friends said he just mentally and emotionally crashed. Suddenly all that youth vaporized into thin air and he went from a hard-working job to living off disability in record time."

"Some days he'll talk to you like he's your best friend, tell you you're good shit etc. Some days he'll do nothing but tell you what's wrong with the gay community and every fuckin' establishment in town like he owned them at one point. Then there's the days he doesn't recognize you for anything and doesn't give a fuck who you are. It's as if he thinks the gay community owes him something."

Antoine then suggested, "Let me guess. You're scared you're going to end up like him."

Dutch then stood up and sat back down on the couch, "I don't understand it. I sometimes don't even understand myself. I'm twenty-four, supposed to have goals, know where I'm supposed to be in life and where I'm headed. I ain't done fuck all yet."

Dutch looked over at Antoine as he asked, "Dutch, when did you realize you were gay?"

He replied, "I knew I was gay when my parents left me at home one weekend when I was fifteen. They came to Edmonton for a political party function and my best friend at the time who was my next door neighbor had come over. We went to the same high school. He was a football jock, and I played hockey." Dutch sipped his water, "I remember the first time it happened. We were downstairs in my room in the basement. I think we were watching something on TV. I don't quite remember, but at one point he pinned me down on the bed and kissed me."

"When he and I got completely naked, it was beautiful and amazing. He knew how to do everything. It became our favorite thing to do when either of our parents was gone."

Antoine asked, "What happened?" while Dutch took another sip of his water.

"We'd thought my parents had gone out after a sleepover one morning on my seventeenth birthday. Little did I know that dad came downstairs to find us in the middle of the act. It was a fucking nightmare. My dad just lost it, devastated that his hockey-jock son from Buttfuck, Alberta was a faggot." Dutch blankly stared into the crowd. "Suddenly all the love disappeared from his eyes."

He continued, "Its funny how I'm blissfully ignorant of his rampant homophobia up until that moment." Dutch could feel Antoine's hand slide into his, "Thank fuck for mom. She more than anything played peacemaker throughout the ordeal. Instead of completely disowning me and throwing me out on the street, they moved me up to an apartment in downtown Edmonton. Ironically they also wanted to use it for when they came up while Legislature was in session." He then glanced over at Antoine. "But they never did set up shop in the apartment." He sighed in defeat and aid, "I'm every disowned gay kids envy. People would kill to have money thrown at them to just go away."

Antoine argued, "But you're not happy." Dutch's face became expressionless as he nodded in agreement. Antoine asked, "What have you been doing with the money?"

Dutch said, "I've tried to give it to my parents but they won't take it. So, I've been putting it away, either for a change of scenery or to go to school, or both…" Dutch stared back out into the crowd, "I know I'm still really young and I have a whole life ahead of me, but I feel like it's already passed me by."

Antoine looked deep into Dutch's dilated pupils, "What are you waiting for?"

Dutch said nothing as Antoine explained, "You've got to make it happen Dutch. You're right it's fun to live in a non-stop party, get fucked up and spend every few days detoxing. But it's up to you to move forward. Your time is now. Does that make sense?" Antoine looked at the full dance floor, let go of Dutch's hand, and stood up. He then reached his hand back out to him and said, "The only way out is through." Antoine then smiled as Dutch grabbed his open hand and pulled himself up.

They found a space on the floor as Dutch looked around and started to move his body along to the music. At this point he fished around his pocket and opened the small baggie, and inserted another pill into his mouth while sipping his water. Within twenty minutes the pill began to supplement the first while Antoine leaned in and said, "I want to take you back to the hotel." Dutch turned around and nodded as they headed up the steps and out the front door. He looked at his cell phone as the time read 6:30. Across the street strands of orange began to illuminate the sky behind the church.

As they walked from the club they both spotted Peter sitting on a bench in the park just down from the club. Antoine nudged Dutch and they both glanced at him, Antoine mentioning, "Early start to the day." They both laughed and they continued down Jasper and into Commerce

Place. Antoine reasoned, "For someone who's not mentally there, he looked pretty peaceful."

Dutch said, "I guess self-abuse grants you serenity."

The hotel lobby appeared busy while Antoine quickly nodded at the desk clerk and led Dutch to the elevator. Once the doors closed, Dutch pinned Antoine to the wall and began kissing him, almost missing their floor.

When the hotel room door was finally closed and Antoine sure it was locked, they began to kiss again while Dutch's hands reached for his shirt and pulled it off. Dutch's mouth then traveled down Antoine's smooth, defined chest while Antoine steadied himself with one hand on Dutch's shoulder while the other cupped Dutch's head.

Dutch let his hands unbuckle Antoine's belt and urgently pulled his pants and underwear down to his ankles, Antoine's penis stiffening as Dutch quickly engulfed it. Antoine moaned as he could feel Dutch's tongue probe between his foreskin and the head of his penis. He moaned as Dutch continued to dictate their private rhythm in approval while finally Dutch finally pulled his mouth off Antoine's penis, watching the skin around the head retreat further.

Antoine then pulled Dutch to his feet while his hand fumbled with Dutch's clothing while kissing all over again. Antoine's mouth began kissing Dutch's neck, laid him down on the bed, and pulled Dutch's jeans off. His mouth continued to work on his chest and back up to Dutch's mouth. Dutch could feel Antoine's erection push up against him, Dutch finally and completely naked under Antoine's body. Dutch breathed out, "Inside me" and Antoine began to lick and suck between Dutch's legs, pushing a finger inside him while Dutch loosened to his touch. Antoine's mouth then moved away from the sac between Dutch's legs, up the underside of his shaft and up towards Dutch's mouth. With his knee he tried to nudge Dutch's legs apart as he could feel Antoine try to push inside him.

Sensing this Dutch flipped Antoine onto his back as he then began to mount Antoine. While they kissed Dutch pulled Antoine up so he was seated up on the side of the bed and Dutch reached behind, finding Antoine's erection and lowering himself all the way down. As he pulled up again Antoine's hand held them in place as he would push Dutch back down while they kissed.

Antoine focused on his eyes while Dutch returned the gaze down. He'd secretly wanted Antoine inside him forever. He knew at this moment it wasn't the ecstasy. As Dutch could feel their sweat slicken them, he began to feel Antoine's erection twitch while Antoine fondled Dutch's penis.

Dutch stammered, "I'm getting close" as Antoine tightened his grip. The first wave shot out of him and onto Antoine's chest as his muscles tightened around Antoine. Finally Antoine began to writhe as his hand pressed all the way down pushing himself all the way in as he came inside Dutch. Antoine deeply exhaled as he leaned back, his shoulders keeping him propped up part of the way. Dutch slowly collapsed on him as he pulled himself off Antoine, kissing and licking parts of his semen-coated chest.

Antoine breathed, "Dutch that was absolutely amazing."

Dutch snickered as they kissed again. When Dutch pulled away he said after a few minutes, "Antoine, I don't want you to go back to Montreal."

Antoine bit his lip as Dutch laid down beside him. He looked into Antoine's eyes as Antoine replied, "I don't want to leave you here." Antoine's thumb ran along Dutch's lips as Antoine continued, "I've learned to get to know someone very special during my time here. It's going to be hard to get back on the plane." A few moments passed then Antoine said, "I don't want to think about that right now."

Dutch then leaned in and whispered, "Then let's not," their lips again embraced in a passionate kiss.

Dutch then propped himself up with his elbow and began to let his hand fondle Antoine's penis all over again while Antoine asked, "Do you want breakfast?" Dutch said, "I wasn't thinking on breakfast...but..." Antoine wrestled him down onto the bed and pinned Dutch while Dutch let out a small chuckle.

"What were you thinking Mr. Dutch?" Dutch grinned and after a few seconds sighed out,

"I was thinking of you."

Antoine smiled and said, "Let me get into the shower. We'll go have breakfast in the restaurant." Antoine stood up and went over to his suitcase and fished for underwear as Dutch said, "I can't believe how fucking hot and built you are."

Antoine only smiled as he said, "Comes from playing hockey in high school."

Dutch then asked, "You ever do any hockey players?" Antoine grinned while Dutch's gaze traveled down Antoine's perfectly smooth and bronzed lower body.

Dutch could hear the shower hiss and he heaved his legs over the bed and inched to the edge. He looked down and saw something vibrate under his pants. He reached into his pocket and clicked on the button illuminating the screen. The first message from Eli read WHERE THE FUCK ARE YOU? Dutch sighed, "Fuck" as the next set of messages sent a chill up Dutch's spine, draining the life out of him. He could barely move as he clutched his stomach and tried to control his breathing.

At that Antoine came out from the shower and asked, "Are you okay Dutch?"

Dutch stammered, "I…I g-gotta get home Antoine. Something's wrong."

He quickly pulled on his clothes as Antoine said, "I'll get a cab."

Dutch began to protest, "You don't need to come Antoine…"

"Fuck that Dutch, I'm coming with you…"

Dutch was silent as they both escaped to the lobby and got into the nearest cab. They were silent as the buildings shrunk, signaling the end of downtown as they finally pulled up to his building. He leapt out of the cab and Antoine followed him in and up the elevator. When he walked into the apartment he heard a noise from the washroom and at that moment the rotting smell hit him. Dutch went into the washroom where Erin was, vomit crusted on the bowl as Dutch began to rub her back and kneeled down flushing the toilet. He whispered, "Come on Erin, you're okay." Tears streaked the mascara down her face as her breathing was erratic. Dutch kept reassuring her, "You're all right Erin. You don't need to be doing this."

Erin started to cough and cry as Dutch wiped her face with a cloth. Antoine peeked around the corner. Dutch asked, "Can you get her some water?" Antoine nodded and went into the fridge. He brought over a bottle as Dutch said, "Erin we need to get you into bed okay?" He then asked,

"Are you supposed to go into work?" She shook her head no and started to cry all over again as Dutch walked her through standing her up. "Now let's get you into bed...that's it Erin...now let's slowly get you into bed." Erin held onto Dutch for dear life as they walked over to the bed.

She crawled in and promptly turned her back to Dutch as she sobbed, "I'm so sorry Dutch."

He rubbed her back as he said, "It's okay Erin."

After an hour when he was sure that she was sound asleep, he walked out to the empty living room. He began to worry as he headed over to the apartment entrance. Dutch then scratched his head and headed back to his room where Antoine laid flat on the bed, eyes fixated on the ceiling. Dutch sat at the foot of the bed and leaned back and Antoine asked, "How long has this been going on for?"

Dutch sighed and replied, "Since I've known her." Dutch sighed and breathed, "She doesn't even think twice anymore when it hits her." Antoine bit his lip and just listened. "She finally realized a year ago it's a problem, but she hasn't gotten help yet."

Dutch's expression was blank as Antoine nodded and said, "You're only able to do so much. She needs to help herself, and you. I mean, look at the way you reacted." Dutch nodded silently as Antoine asked, "Do you still want to go out?"

"If you don't mind Antoine, I'm going to keep an eye on Erin for the day. Maybe get some sleep myself before we have our night out" Antoine silently nodded then sat up as Dutch embraced him. They hugged as Antoine's stare was fixated on the computer and the collage of pictures. His concentration broke when Dutch leaned in, letting his lips brush softly against Antoine's. Antoine then closed his eyes as they passionately kissed. When Dutch pulled away he whispered, "Call me later." Antoine nodded as he walked with Dutch to the door.

When he closed the door and locked it behind Antoine he walked back into his room and quietly closed the door. He turned on the computer then leaned back as he opened the top drawer on his desk He pulled out the minidisc recorder and a new disc in addition to his pipe. When he stared at the baggie, he emptied it out, making a mental note to call E after the weekend.

LOVE'S SWEET EXILE - DISC 56: SIXTY-THREE MINUTES, NINETEEN SECONDS

"I wonder what she thinks when she does it. For awhile I thought maybe she had a severe food allergy and it left her near unconscious. But I guess it was always more then that. I guess all of those years she thought she was too fat. Which is complete bullshit. She definitely looks more amazing than she herself believes. Erin had a stack of photos left on the coffee table one afternoon. I flipped through them all and she never had a visible issue when it came down to weight. But more frequently as of late... she's been getting sick to the point where she can't get out of bed...or it's near impossible to get her back in. I've told her she needs to get some help but she doesn't listen to that. And the smell has progressively gotten worse the more she gets sick."

"She left me a letter the other day...I opened it up and she completely exhumed everything that she felt about this guy at the station. She doesn't have the balls to go up and talk to him, and it's not like he's made himself completely unavailable to her. I'm sure if she talked to him, it really would help her out. It only makes sense. But she feels so inadequate and the shyness takes over, and she's back at square one."

"Part of me wonders if that's what's holding me back? Am I really that inadequate to Eli? What if I was to finally say what I'd felt to him? Would it matter? I have everything to lose here, including our friendship."

"But even now…truth be told, I'm really beginning to flow with Antoine. Antoine is the boyfriend I've never had. Which in a lot of way is why I'm so scared to open up to him. He genuinely cares so much that it fucking scares me. With him, I don't have to watch what I say. I don't need to put up a front and hide what I'm thinking. One thing is certain. I'm going to miss him when he goes back. Everything about him is too good to be true. I need to stop waiting for the other shoe to drop. It's especially not fair to him. He's been so good to me…"

"I really hope Eli can finally see past his own shit and start to actually like Antoine. Or there may be some very tough decisions to make…"

Chapter Eighteen

When Eli walked in on Monday morning, Dawn smiled and sweetly asked, "How are you this morning?"

Eli rubbed his eyes and smiled, "Long weekend."

Dawn mused, "You know, everybody I've talked to this morning so far has had that type of weekend."

Eli shrugged "All I know is I'm going to kick Dutch's ass when I see him."

Dawn said as the thought occurred to her, "Oh he's in on overtime. He and Antoine went for breakfast this morning."

Eli smugly said, "Cute."

Dawn scolded, "You're saying that you're not happy your best friend who's been terminally single for how long finally has someone who's completely into him."

Eli only shrugged and walked in as he slowly scanned the desks. When he sat down uneasiness began to creep in as he then turned to Stewart. "Hey coppertop…" he said as Stewart paid no attention. Eli again said a little louder, "Coppertop I'm talking to you…" Stewart then looked over and Eli asked, "Where's Christine?"

Stewart explained, "She's on the late shift tonight. She's actually not coming later because she's sick."

Eli smiled faintly then asked, "Where's Ariel?"

"Dunno. She's been texting all day back and forth. Probably talking to either Jeremiah or Daniel."

Eli maliciously pointed out, "It must really eat at you inside out to see Ariel talk the way she does about Daniel." Stewart was quiet as Eli continued, "It's your worst kept secret Stewart and everyone especially Daniel knows. Even if he was gay, he wouldn't be caught dead with a queen like you."

Stewart then asked nonchalantly, "Do you pride yourself on being a home-wrecker, or does that come with the coke-addicted territory?" Eli heard his extension pick up while Stewart in turn answered the next call. Eli was ready to say something, however decided at that point it was not worth the energy.

Two hours into his shift, an e-mail that read BREAK? popped up. Eli scowled and typed back WHAT KIND OF BREAK? He continued to pore through his e-mails when the words LATE BREAKFAST popped up. Eli leaned back in his chair and gazed upwards to where Antoine and Natasha were talking. He typed, SEE YOU IN FIFTEEN.

Eli walked towards the washroom, watching the floor around him teem with activity. Lance walked by him and nodded as Eli only nodded in return and grunted. When he arrived at the entrance he quickly glanced in both directions, and walked in. He returned to the familiar back stalls as Dutch said, "Sorry. The lines are a little off." Dutch opened the stall door as he was wiping his nose.

Eli said, "You should invite Antoine to breakfast sometime."

Dutch countered, "Not fucking likely Eli." Eli inhaled his first line as Dutch breathed, "I don't want him tainted."

Before Eli snorted the second line he asked, "Is that the reason you two fucking ditched on Vivid Saturday night?"

Eli then bent down and began to inhale and Dutch replied, "There was a personal emergency at the apartment."

Eli opened the door and asked, "What happened?"

Dutch said, "Erin…"

Eli groaned, "You gotta be fucking kidding me."

Dutch explained, "She's getting sicker"

Eli then said, "You gotta get her out of your apartment Dutchie."

Dutch protested, "I just can't kick her out of my place for being bulimic Eli."

Eli said, "So what Dutch, let her fucking burn a hole in her stomach on her own time and place!"

He wiped his nostrils as Dutch seethed, "Love to see you have a sense of humanity, fucker."

"The only reason she does that Dutch is because she's in love with you. Think about it. Every time she's had one of those fucking fits you've always gone running back to her. It's why she makes you dinner, does your laundry, picks out shit you never asked for."

Dutch was silent as Eli began to focus on Dutch's expressions. Eli calmly said, "She only does it to control you Dutch. And the longer she stays, the more she'll keep you wrapped around her finger."

Dutch said, "You're so full of shit Eli." He shook his head and they both started to walk out of the bathroom.

Eli then asked, "What's on the agenda this weekend?"

Dutch replied, "Katherine asked me to take her little brother out this weekend while he's in town. I guess he just came out to his sister, and she wants me to take him to Pink Bar."

Eli wasn't sure why at that moment but he asked, "Since you didn't make it out on Saturday night at Vivid, do I get a chance to get to know Antoine again?"

Dutch grinned mischievously and said, "How about Friday night?"

Eli replied, "Done...we also need to stock up for the weekend."

Dutch asked, "How did Saturday night at Vivid go anyhow?"

Eli smugly replied, "It would have been a lot more fucking fun if you were there." Dutch said nothing and Eli watched him walk away. He knew that his little empty display of interest had temporarily won Dutch over.

Later that night, Dutch was getting ready to leave when he quickly glanced out at the customer service floor. He sighed and walked to the row of desks where Ariel and Daniel sat.

Dutch asked, "How's the call volume tonight?"

Daniel leaned back and replied, "Nothin' we can't candle boss. Just been a quiet night."

Dutch smiled and asked, "You filling in a couple tonight?" He nodded as he then waved at them both. That was that moment he heard the noise.

His ears perked up as he followed the sniffling over to the desk where Christine was. A box of Kleenex had been ripped apart while she rubbed her eyes. Dutch came over and asked, "Are you okay?" She continued to cry as he sat down in the chair beside her. She was still silent while he reached over and rubbed her back, in the similar way he'd done with Erin.

She abruptly pulled away and demanded, "Where the fuck where you and Antoine on Saturday night?" Dutch could see her face. Streams of black tracked where the tears ran, her eyes looked so desperate as she repeated the question a little louder. "Dutch…where…the…fuck…were… you…on…Saturday…night?" At this point Daniel and Ariel peered over the divider as Dutch glared at them both and shooed them back.

Dutch whispered, "It's gonna be okay" while she muffled her sobs.

Christine finally pulled away as she sat back down and began to hide her face while she wiped her eyes with her sleeves. She said, "We were all waiting for you two to show up at Vivid and Nicholas and Eli fuck off somewhere. It had been twenty minutes and I'm getting more and more pissed off 'cause they're nowhere to be found. I'm fucking texting Nicholas and he's not answering." She whimpered a little, "So Stewart appears out of nowhere and by this time I'm ready to hit the fucking ceiling. I was so angry Dutch." She looked at her ring then sighed, "Stewart talked me down for an hour and finally I thought fuck it, I'm going home. I catch a cab home…" She then began to incoherently explain, "And there are lines of coke on the coffee table and I look in the bedroom and Nicholas is fucking throwing it in Eli!!" She stopped sobbing enough to hold out her ring finger and said, "I can't even fucking look at this or go home knowing he fucked Eli in our bed."

Dutch was still silent and she started crying again. Dutch then began to rub her back again as she said, "I can't even go back there. It's just so… tainted."

Dutch replied sympathetically, "I understand"

She then said hopelessly, "I don't understand Dutch. You're Eli's best friend. Does he not have any decency or consideration? Did he not remember that we were engaged?"

Dutch remained silent then breathed, "I'm sorry Christine." He then looked at her and said, "I don't have the answer for that."

Christine asked, "Can I please leave? I just can't be here right now." He nodded as she logged off her phone and put everything away.

Dutch walked her to the entrance as he asked, "What are you gonna do?"

She shrugged and wiped her eyes. "I don't know yet. All I know is honestly I don't think I can stay here anymore." Dutch only nodded and his heart sank as he watched her walk away.

Chapter Nineteen

When Eli walked into customer service, he stopped at his desk and began to open his e-mails As soon as he opened the window the first e-mail that popped up read WHAT THE FUCK WERE YOU THINKING? He breathed out, "Fucking Jesus." He closed the e-mail and proceeded straight for the washroom where he opened the door and headed to the back stalls.

Dutch immediately spotted him and said with a smile, "I figured you would have found me here"

Eli spat, "You wanna know what I was thinking? I was thinking how much of a great fuck that's been wasted all this time because he's been engaged to that…"

Dutch began, "Eli you ruined…"

"I ruined what Dutchie? That relationship's problems were the worst kept secret on the call centre floor and everyone, I mean fucking everyone knew Dutch…"

"You still fucked up a relationship Eli. Sugar-coating it does not make it fucking okay."

"And what makes you such a moral compass?"

"All I know is you don't fuck with someone's relationship like that Eli!"

"And all I know is that I gave that boy the ride of his life, and he's not fucking complaining."

Dutch then said, "If only Samuel knew eh?"

Eli pinned him to the counter and hissed, "You fucking keep Samuel out of this…"

"Right. God forbid it would hurt your chances with the A-gays." Eli let him go and glared at him while Dutch readjusted his suit and tie, and walked out.

Eli slowly walked back to his computer and he sat back down at his desk and started to finish going through his e-mails. He became quite restless and after a few minutes proceeded into the lounge where he sat down at a small table. A few more minutes passed as he glanced towards the floor and spotted Dutch in conversation with Marie and Antoine. He sighed as his stare moved back out towards the rest of the floor. As he watched Marie and Dutch leave the conversation, he shifted his focus over to Antoine who caught Eli's glance and promptly turned away in disgust. Eli leaned back in his chair and then stood up and left the lounge back onto the floor.

He sat back down and looked over to Ariel who vacantly stared at her computer screen. Eli quickly checked his screen and snapped his fingers at her as she looked over at Eli and asked, "What?"

Eli said, "You've been staring at the screen for ten minutes Ariel." She started crying as Eli rolled his eyes and asked sarcastically asked, "Now what is it?"

She explained, "I can't handle not talking to Jeremiah. I know he told me he needed space but I texted him today. And he wouldn't text me back. I got a call when I was on lunch from one of his friends who told me that he was out at the bar last night and was all over some girl who went home with him." She sobbed even harder as she said, "I don't know what to do anymore. I just can't deal with it. I love him so much." Eli said nothing as she continued, "I don't know…if I have to try to hurt myself to get his attention."

Eli snapped, "Just promise me you'll succeed and once again the world can breathe a sigh of relief that natural selection wins out every time."

It was as if that moment was in slow motion. Ariel began to loudly sob and stood up, darting past Stewart and towards the washroom as he looked at Eli in disgust. Eli sneered, "Eyes front Bert."

Stewart then said, "You're dripping Eli." He then put his headset on as Eli quickly wiped his nose and focused on the screen. An hour passed and Eli's restlessness had elevated as a small message popped up that read YOU MISSED OUT popped up on the lower right hand side of the screen. Eli thought for a moment then typed in the two words to be his reply.

FUCK YOU

He then stood up and said to Stewart, "I'm off to get a coffee Bert. Be back in twenty." He then looked up and saw Natasha walk by as he said, "Good morning Natasha."
She replied, "Staying out of trouble Eli?"
"Always" he grinned and headed out the set of doors and into the mall. Everything seemed brighter to him as he gazed up and out the windows that domed the third floor. Eli then focused forward while he watched people pass by. Eli had always been surprised by how empty the mall felt at eleven in the morning. The office lunch rush wouldn't become apparent until noon. Enough time for him to cruise.

Eli then crossed the pedway from west to east, past the Tim Horton's and to the atrium where he leaned against the railing that fenced the opening to the basement level off. He glanced around and watched people travel up and down the escalator. Two security guards traveled up to the second level and walked over to the entrance to the washrooms. Eli waited a few more minutes and then cautiously strolled over to where the guards had been before. As he neared the entrance the guards quickly left and Eli walked down the corridor.

The first door to the left creaked open and Eli went through and up the ramp as he then slowly opened the second door. To his immediate left was a row of sinks and a pillar that divided the row of urinals. On the right were the bathroom stalls. Eli cautiously walked up to the urinals, unzipped his pants as he gazed around the washroom. It was eerily silent as he then looked down and began to let a steady stream out. He then looked up, staring blankly at the wall, giving himself a quick shake once finished.

He then heard the door open and the approaching footsteps slow down while Eli quickly glanced at the door. Someone came in and pulled up to the urinal closest to the wall and unzipped while Eli discreetly glanced over. He was clean shaven and baby-faced, which was partially hidden underneath his ballcap. He seemed partially built, small traces of muscle bulged under his t-shirt from his arms. Eli reasoned that he must be a redhead by the hairs on his lower arm. Unfortunately the flap on his jeans had blocked Eli's curiosity as Eli returned back to his blank gaze towards the tile. After a few seconds Eli began to adjust himself when he casually glanced over again to find the stranger's jean flap forced back and him stroking his partially erect but extremely thick penis.

Eli's gaze remained fixated on the man's actions as he watched the stranger's penis thicken even more, the foreskin starting to pull back. Eli responded in similar fashion as after a few minutes the outside door creaked open and both of them resumed forward facing positions at their respective urinals. The person who walked in pulled up to the closest urinal to the sinks, quickly finished and left. Once the door was closed, Eli zipped up turned to the redhead who was still aroused, and with his head gestured to the stall where he locked the door behind them.

It was over within the few minutes from the moment Eli coaxed him into the stall. A quick coordination of rhythm between the redhead and him coupled with Eli's hands had made the redhead push himself all the way into Eli's mouth, Eli gagging a little. He then quickly pulled out and zipped up, fled from the stall and out the door while Eli leaned back and exhaled. After a few minutes he stood up, rotated his jaw, and walked over to the sink, adjusting his shirt and tie. Once he was sure there was no remnant of the previous few minutes, he hurried down the hallway, and back out to the main landing as he checked both directions and headed back towards the pedway.

He'd only made it a few steps up towards the office when he heard, "Eli?"

He turned around to find Samuel as he smiled and said, "Hey there stranger", quickly giving him a hug.

Samuel asked, "How goes the battle at Go Credit?" Eli rolled his eyes in complete boredom. "That good eh? Sounds like the menial work that I've been doing at the firm."

Eli asked, "Are you glad you traded the burger name badge for the suit and tie?" Samuel grinned as Eli then asked, "Do you want a coffee?" Samuel nodded as they lined up on the pedway.

As if on cue, the sun peeked out and began to warm them as Samuel looked out to the street below. He said, "You know I've never really paid attention to the traffic underneath the pedway before. I've just been so used to crossing over to the other end of the mall that it never fazed me at all."

Eli replied, "Since they did the remodel I sometimes sit at one of the tables by the windows. It's interesting to see who passes by."

Samuel teased, "Sure it wasn't for cruising?" Eli then playfully shoved him out of the line as Eli then made his way to the counter and ordered two coffees.

As the server handed them their coffees Samuel smiled after taking the first sip. "French vanilla, you remembered."

Eli shrugged and said, "I don't forget anything."

While they walked back towards the office Eli said questioningly, "I haven't seen you and Keith out as of late."

Samuel explained, "Keith has been a little overworked as of late and we've been going to Calgary a bit more as a couple. It's been a much needed change of scenery." He sighed, "It's the fucking same anywhere you go…"

Eli asked, "What do you mean?"

Samuel sipped his coffee as they headed up the escalator. "Everywhere it seems like the same empty queers at the same bar drinking the same drinks, doing the same lines of coke."

Eli then said, "Why are you dating Keith again?"

Samuel chuckled and replied softly, "It's what people don't see Eli. He really has a soft center down there. He's just so scared to let it show." They stopped at the entrance and Samuel said, "This is your stop. Text me this weekend."

El darted his eyes around then leaned in and gave Samuel a quick peck on the cheek as he nodded and walked back towards customer service. Natasha's door was closed as he grunted and headed back to his desk. He opened up his e-mail and sighed as the words I'M SORRY prominently displayed themselves on the screen. Eli only sighed and pressed the auto-in function on the phone as he decided to wait before accepting Dutch's apology.

LOVE'S SWEET EXILE - DISC 57: three minutes, fifty five seconds

"He finally accepted my apology. Because, God-fucking forbid he ever does something wrong. It makes me so fucking mental some days the way he treats people and his aggressive push to get what he wants. He acts as if the shit between him and Christine and Nicholas has nothing to do with Saturday night. I already know what to expect from Eli, but Nicholas just completely blew me out of the water. I guess when you leave a little trail of snow behind you someone's bound to follow. I just didn't think it would be him/"

"It's not like that relationship was anywhere near perfect anyhow. I mean, the day that Christine threw her cellphone at him in the call centre, narrowly missing his head however making contact with one of the glass panes between the floor and the lounge. The engagement's only been since Christmas, but the fighting hasn't been a secret. It amazes me how she passes her quality monitoring because if they would have heard some of the infighting on those calls…"

"And leave it to fucking Eli to drive a wedge in there. He's not completely innocent in this mess. Eli has a tendency to find a flaw in someone or something and get right in there. It's fucking sad and pathetic all in one that he needs to destroy everything he touches, including his friendship with me. Is it just that he wants to push the boundaries further? Or is it really because he's that empty? Christine asked me why and I couldn't come up with a fucking answer for her. Or is it I know the answer to the question and am too scared to breathe it out? Am I next on his list? I can't help but wonder sometimes when the next shoe is going to drop."

"Something's up though. It's never taken him this long to accept my apology. But why am I the one always fucking apologizing? I'm not the one who fucking ruins it for everyone else. Maybe he knows how gullible I am and knows I'll blindly sit through it no matter what? What do I need to do to give his head a shake?"

Chapter Twenty

Friday night and Eli stood outside of the entrance to the Pink Bar. He checked his watch as he hit redial on his cell. Just as the call went to voicemail, Dutch appeared around the corner from the drycleaners as Eli scowled and hung up the phone. "Well our lady of the wild rose, we finally decide to arrive."

Beside Dutch was a freckle-faced boy. Dutch glanced at the boy and said, "I'm sorry. I had to pick up tonight's party prescriptions."

The boy then said, "I'm Landon. Katherine's younger brother."

Eli said, "Fucking charmed."

The boy looked at Dutch in shock as Eli walked in Landon asked, "Is he always like that?"

Dutch rolled his eyes and explained, "He's high strung. Don't mind him." Landon smiled as Dutch said, "C'mon lets go inside."

As they walked in Dutch asked, "This is your first time at a gay club?"

Landon nodded as he explained, "Arianne's the only one who knows I'm gay."

Dutch reassured him, "Just stay close. It's a jungle in here."

As they reached the entrance the person in coat check explained, "Eli's paid your admissions. You're good to go."

He stamped their hand taking special care and attention to Landon's hand as he then said eyes fixated on him, "Enjoy your evening."

Landon said, "He was awfully nice."

Dutch then grinned, "It's already started…"

Dutch noticed that while he was used to the sights and sounds that were Edmonton's Pink Bar, Landon watched with a wonderment that reminded him of when he snuck into the bar when he was sixteen. At that time Dutch and Eli were both very much amazed at the sheer intensity of their queer surroundings. Dutch then snapped his fingers in front of Landon as he asked, "Hey you…do you want a drink?"

Landon glanced over and said, "I'll have a beer." He then added, "And a party prescription."

Dutch looked down at him and asked, "What?"

Landon shyly smiled and fidgeted. "You were talking about party prescriptions earlier, so I was wondering…"

Dutch bit his lip as he pulled Landon aside and explained, "Look Landon…I know you're just eighteen but if you're going to drink we're not letting you have drugs being this fresh."

"But I've done them before" Landon quietly protested.

"What have you all done?"

"Well…all I've done is pot…"

"Really?"

Landon said nothing as Dutch promised, "Look Landon, if you've never taken harder chemicals before, it's not a good idea to mix alcohol and drugs."

Landon spat out at him, "And you don't…"

Dutch argued back, "I'm also an informed drug user. I am very much about moderation, and not going overboard." Landon's expression sent a clear message of not buying it and Dutch promised, "Look, I'll buy you a drink, and we'll see how you feel. But you need to go back to your sister and folks in one piece."

At that point Eli crept up behind Dutch and reached into his pants pocket as he whispered, "I'm getting impatient Dutchie…" and yanked the small bag out of his front pocket, quickly stuffing them in his.

Dutch turned around and asked, "What the fuck?" as Eli leaned in close enough, just enough to give Dutch a waft of the scent of alcohol on his breath.

Eli pulled away, "I'll get the bumper bottle ready."

Dutch shook his head while Landon stood there scowling. He then said while Eli pranced away, "Eli's life is one big pretense."

Landon asked, "How did he get like that?"

Dutch shook his head and said, "This will be a discussion that you and I will have to have over drinks another night."

Landon replied, "Fair enough."

When he'd ordered a drink for himself and Landon, Dutch instructed, "Stay here. I'll be right back."

He then headed to the back washroom by the bar here he opened up the door and heard a voice exclaim, "In here!" Dutch walked over to the stall as he gently pulled the door open. He wasn't sure what to think as the door creaked and sighed while Eli stood there with a grin on his face and a small spattering of white powder under his nose.

Dutch asked, "How did you know I was here?"

Eli's grin widened and he replied, "Because I'm fucking psychic Dutchie."

He laughed as Eli handed him the small vile of cocaine. Eli asked, "Where's diapers?"

Dutch inhaled deeply, the pulling the bottle away from his nose. With his fingers he wiped the residue from his nose as he replied, "I told him to stay put outside." Eli looked confused as Dutch could suddenly feel something pull him towards the floor

Dutch laughed and said, "You fucker. You gave me the K by mistake."

Eli then said, "Oh right. Wrong vile."

Eli then handed Dutch a drink and said "Suck back on that for a bit." Dutch did as he was told as Eli asked, "So are you going to watch over kid while you're fucked up?"

Dutch then slurred as the ketamine started to surge in him, "Don't…"

Eli asked innocently, "What?"

Dutch replied, "I know what you're trying to do…really Eli?" Eli laughed as Dutch could only smile in disapproval. When part of the drug's grip had finally started to loosen Dutch admitted, "Plus Antoine will be here soon so in case I'm too fucked…" Eli's smile vanished as Dutch asked, "What?" Dutch then snickered and leaned in a little too close into Eli. Shortly after, Eli shoved him into the wall where Dutch landed with a thud. Eli shouted, "What the fuck did you do that for?!" and with that he stormed out of the washroom leaving Dutch propped up against the toilet bowl on the floor.

When Eli looked around, the cocaine and traces of ketamine began to ripple through his body. Where the Pink Bar had not been busy when Dutch had found him in the washroom, there had been an explosion of men on the dance floor, fag hags in tow. He spotted Landon, still anchored at the side of the main bar, then nasally ingested another small pile of coke and made his way over. Landon glanced over then gazed back over to the entrance as Eli smiled and said, "Hey."

Landon looked at him and shyly smiled as he asked, "Where's Dutch?"

Eli smugly replied, "On the bathroom floor, K-tarded out of his fucking tree." Landon mmm-hmmed as Eli explained, "It's what happens when you mix ketamine and alcohol."

Eli then asked, "How's your first trip to the bar?"

Landon shrugged and said, "It's all right." Landon then looked back out to the sea of people.

Eli put his arm around Landon's shoulders and said, "Welcome to Oz."

Landon chuckled as he then said, "In a way it's different than what I expected."

Eli said, "Oh?"

Landon took a sip of his drink and explained, "I expected it to be a little more…"

Eli asked, "Flamboyant?" Landon continued sipping his drink as he felt Eli press something into his hand.

"We still have a long way to go between Edmonton and San Francisco Landon. I mean coming from Calmar to Edmonton is one thing…" Eli then popped a tab of ecstasy into his mouth and said, "This is fucking Alberta. We still have a lot to fight for." He then watched Landon pop his pill as Eli reassured him, "Dutchie and I will take care of you tonight kid."

"So why aren't you two together?" Landon asked as he turned to see Eli wince in pain. Eli then shrugged as he watched Dutch saunter up to Antoine, kissing their hellos.

Eli seethed, "I'm not his type."

Landon said, "I dunno about that…you two look like you would make an amazing couple." He then smiled and added, "You should see the look he gives you when you two are together." Eli shot him a dirty look as Landon polished off the rest of his drink.

Eli asked, "You want another drink?"

"Why?"

Eli replied, "So you won't ask any more awkward questions about me and Dutch."

At that moment Dutch and Antoine appeared as Eli mused, "Speak of the devil…"

Landon joked, "And he looks mighty pissed."

Neither of them appeared very happy as Antoine breathed, "Eli."

Eli snorted as Landon extended his hand to Antoine. "Hi I'm Landon" he said as Antoine shook it and replied with a smile, "Antoine."

Dutch explained, "Antoine is an immediate supervisor at work. He focuses mainly on collections." Dutch glared at Eli as he continued, "He's based out of the Montreal office, but he's here helping with virtuality between the offices."

Landon asked, "How are you enjoying Edmonton?"

Before Antoine could respond Eli barked, "He's not…"

Dutch asked, "Antoine, can you grab us drinks over at the shooter bar?"

Antoine nodded, "Landon follow me and you can help me with the drinks." Landon nodded and followed him across the bar.

The moment they left Dutch glared at Eli. Eli groaned, "And you had to invite him out…"

"What did you feed him?"

"Feed who?"

"Landon you dumbfuck…"

"I was about to feed him a drink if that's what you're asking."

Dutch replied, "Nice fucking try asshole."

Eli argued, "I fed him a pill Dutchie. That should kick in about anytime now."

He started to gaze at his watch as Dutch seethed "What the fuck were you thinking Eli?"

Eli shot back, "I thought it was time to validate his point of view on queer life in Edmonton."

Dutch rolled his eyes as Landon reappeared with a drink for Dutch, followed by Antoine who forced a drink into Eli's hand. He explained, "Dutch tells me you drink this."

Eli at first grunted. After a few minutes he replied, "Thank you Antoine." Antoine only nodded as Eli noticed Landon's facial expression change while Eli's pill started to ripple through him. Landon's eyes widened as his pupils darkened.

Eli asked, "How are you feeling?"

Landon weakly smiled as he said, "I feel fucking amazing…"

Antoine turned to Dutch and asked, "Did he take something?" Eli only watched as Dutch leaned in and whispered something into his ear, Antoine smiling shortly afterwards.

Eli suggested, "I think we better take him out to the dance floor and show him what he's missing." Dutch grinned in approval as the four of them made their way to the tiny, crowded area.

Eli's high began to surge as the mix of chemicals rode the waves of bass vibrations that bounced through the packed crowd. Eli watched as the group seemed to follow along. It was at that point he stopped caring about Antoine's presence and focused solely on the high he was experiencing. He finished his drink while he danced, mainly focused on himself while occasionally glancing over to both Dutch and Antoine, then to Landon. Landon looked like he was thoroughly enjoying himself as Landon would move along with the beat and which ever diva's vocals soared over it.

After what seemed like forever, Landon stepped off the dance floor and headed to where Eli, Dutch, and Antoine were all seated. He first heard, "Eli, how long have you been with the company?" With that question Antoine quickly snorted some coke from the small vile and saw Landon.

He asked, "Did you want some?"

Landon cocked his head to the side and asked, "What is it?"

Eli replied, "Its a little white powder that will make your heart race."

Antoine let his hand slip under the table as Dutch instructed, "Landon, put your hand under the table." Landon did as he was told and Antoine passed it to him. As Landon went to pull it up to his nose he glanced around.

Eli whispered in his ear, "Be discreet about it kid" as Landon held it to his nose and inhaled.

When he put his hand down with the vile Eli announced, "I've been with the company for about…five, six years now." He then placed his hand inside Landon's, at first searching for the vile as he continued, "I started off in customer service, then made my way into retention." While Eli talked about company tenure and his hand found the vile, it slyly made his way onto Landon's crotch as Eli found Landon's penis with ease, letting his hand run along its contours through Landon's jeans, then back across his leg as Eli brought the vile to his nose.

Antoine asked, "Is that where you and Dutch met?"

Eli chuckled and replied, "Fuck no. We met at Youth Parliament when we were both sixteen. Dutch's family was in for session and I was just another face that eventually corrupted him."

Antoine asked, "Session?"

Eli then beamed, "You mean he hadn't told you?"

He passed the vile under the table as he explained, "Dutch's daddy is a hardcore Progressive Conservative from good ol' Calgary." He grinned as Dutch shyly smiled and said nothing.

Antoine asked him, "That's where your family's from?"

Dutch mumbled a "Yeah." Eli continued in his best John Wayne accent, "His father gone done and disowned him for being a buttfuckin' queer. Sent him to Edmonton to shut him up."

"Fucking Christ Eli!" Dutch spat as Eli crowed, "It darn true dere Dutchie. Aint no room for buttfuckin quers in dem dere Klein government."

Antoine asked, "And you?" Eli said nothing for a few seconds.

He then explained, "I have two sisters. I'm gay, my older sis is a dyke, and my younger sister's straight."

Antoine asked, "How do your parents feel about that?"

Eli replied, "My parents are thankful for at least one straight child." Dutch took a sip of his drink as Eli then blurted, "But she's dating a darkie so I guess it evens out…" Dutch spit out his beverage as the table laughed.

Antoine then asked, "Anyone up for one more before we go back out onto the floor?"

Eli said, "I'll have another." the server quickly approached Dutch then looked at Landon and asked, "Now are you going to be okay to have one more?"

Eli barked in response, "Of course he's fucking okay…" He then said, "He's fucking fabulous. He's with us."

Antoine then said, "Landon?"

Landon was silent for a few moments then replied, "Yeah I'm okay for one more."

Eli slapped him playfully on the back as Antoine said, "Four tequilas and water."

Eli grinned as he let his hand wander down to Landon's crotch again. This time he could feel Landon's penis was fully erect as he asked Antoine, "How long have you been with Go Credit for?"

Antoine thought for a moment then replied, "I started off three years ago in customer service and I found I could make more money in collections. They made me a junior supervisor just this summer."

Eli then asked, "So what was the big reason to ship you out other than to do your office tour?"

He replied, "They made me a project manager for the Regenesis project. So I get to float around between the offices right now, making sure process is aligned, all the little shit…"

Eli grinned and asked, "So do you fuck anyone you see in any office at any given time?"

Antoine only smiled and he started to explain, "Very few have caught my attention." He then looked at Dutch and said, "I'm lucky. I get to be in Edmonton for at least a good few weeks."

Eli spat back, "Enough to make your way through Edmonton post Dutch?"

Dutch suddenly knocked his glass over, the ice cubes sliding off the table and into Eli's lap.

"Fucking Christ!" Eli shouted as the cubes began to melt. As he stood up Dutch began to shove Antoine out of the booth and stormed away while Antoine watched him in disbelief.

Eli chuckled, an evil grin across his face as Antoine glared at him. Antoine held his drink up and shot at him, "Some of us are not morally bankrupt, like yourself." And with that he left to find Dutch.

Landon looked over at Eli and asked, "What the fuck did you do that for?" Eli suddenly leaned in and kissed him passionately, slipping his tongue in as Landon at first tried to pull away. However after a few seconds he let himself lean into Eli.

The kiss only lasted a few moments more as Eli pulled away. "This party's been crashed, and I need to clean up." They both exited the booth and Eli grabbed Landon's hand circling around the bar. Landon asked, "Where are we going?"

Eli said, "The party's somewhere else. Follow me, it'll be fun."

Eli led him up the steps and out to the first available cab where they both hopped in. Eli said, "To Lockers on west Jasper and 122nd Street please." The driver nodded as he circled the block and turned left onto Jasper Avenue, all the while Eli's hand firmly on Landon's crotch.

Eli could feel him harden all over again as the driver asked, "Front, or back?"

Eli said, "Front is fine." The cab stopped as Eli tossed him a twenty and they fell out of the taxi on to the sidewalk. Eli pressed him against the brick wall and started kissing Landon as horns and homophobic epithets were shouted from a couple of trucks as Eli finally pulled away and they both smiled. Eli then shoved a vile under his nose and he said, "Have a bump." Landon paused as Eli then explained, "It'll help you fly…" Landon inhaled deeply as he pulled the vile away from Landon and reached for his hand as Eli opened the glass door and dragged Landon down the steps.

They reached the bottom of the steps and the attendant said, "Eli." He smiled and then looked over at Landon. He then asked, "Is he old enough?" Eli smiled as he handed the clerk his credit card and he swiped it through the machine. The clerk then buzzed them both in and Eli pulled the door open, dragging Landon in as Landon looked around.

Immediately six men clad in only towels and of all shapes and sizes hungrily eyed them both. Eli then took a towel and shoved it into Landon's chest as the smile vanished from Eli's face and he motioned Landon to follow. Eli turned to the right and Landon followed him into the room as Eli closed the door behind him.

He pressed Landon against the door as Eli again pushed the vile under Landon's nose, letting him again deeply inhale. Landon finished snorting as a small trail of powder was still under his nose. Eli took his thumb, wiped Landon's nose and snorted. Landon snickered as Eli began to undress him. Within seconds he let his mouth travel down Landon's chest and down his stomach as Eli's hands opened his jeans. Landon tried to undo his shirt while Eli was able to wrestle Landon's pants down, his boxers shortly after. Landon's erection flopped out as Eli began to engulf it, all the while Eli's hands pulled off Landon's shoes and socks.

His hands finally crept up Landon's legs, one of them steadying him while the other hand moved between Landon's legs, a finger pushing inside as Landon yelped.

Eli let his mouth move up him again as Landon groaned, "I'm…" Eli kissed him and pushed him back against the door as Landon began to let his mouth travel downwards, unbuttoning Eli's shirt. Landon did the same as he tried to take Eli's penis completely in his mouth. Eli hardened while Landon stopped for a moment, then continued sucking him while Eli moaned.

Eli then pulled Landon up as he again pushed a vile under his nose and said, "Take a deep breath kid." Landon inhaled as Eli then placed it under the other nostril while Landon inhaled deeper.

Eli then pulled away as he watched Landon lean back against the door. Landon exhaled deeply as Eli slyly put the vile into his pants and reached in to the other pocket. Landon tried to move as he wobbled, one step forward slowly as Eli chuckled, taking a snort of the new vile as Landon said, "I…don't…feel…good." Landon started to fall forward as Eli haphazardly caught him. He started kissing Landon again as he laid him down on the thin mattress, Eli mounting him as Landon wrapped his arms around Eli.

Eli's fingers started to push inside Landon while Landon said in a half whisper, "I'm not…I'm not…" as Eli pushed his fingers deeper into Landon. He writhed as Eli turned on the T.V. , Landon's expression becoming more and more glazed as Eli reached back into his pants and pulled out the vile, opening it and sprinkling some more of the powder into Landon's nostrils as he protested, "I don't need…" Landon then snorted, his eyes fixated on the television as Eli took one of the packets of lube and ripped it open with his teeth.

He applied some to his fingers, then forced the cold substance inside Landon as he grunted, his expression becoming more and more blank. Eli then opened a condom and rolled it down his erection to the base while he pulled Landon's legs over his shoulders as he began to push himself in. Eli then thrust in all the way as Landon at first tried to tighten up, to resist him while Eli continued to push. Eli was able to finally push back in as Landon tried to formulate sentences telling Eli to stop. Eli continued to thrust in as he looked down at Landon's empty expression gazing back at Eli as his thrusts became rougher, Eli becoming more turned on with each thrust back inside Landon.

Minutes continued to pass by as Eli became enwrapped with Landon. He was so engrossed that he did not hear the door open ever so slightly. Eli sensed he was close and looked out to the doorway where he recognized a bleach blonde face that was just as detached and as empty as Landon's expression that now fell to the doorway. Eli's gaze shifted from the doorway and back to Landon as Eli pushed in all the way, his body jerking as the door slammed shut.

LOVE'S SWEET EXILE - DISC 57: thirty-four minutes, twelve seconds

"This is the end."

"This is the final chapter between me and you. For the past few years since we met I've let you tear me open systematically piece by piece. I watched as you went off with them, begged for your acceptance. Let you cover up your emptiness after all this time, and my sacrifice has been all for you and you still don't give a fuck about me."

"It's about how you place me below your tricks, your empty conquests. How you've used the funnel fund that my parents have allocated me all of these years because I'm daddy's shame. It's about how you find your way into everything and carelessly damage it for the sake of your own personal edification."

"I never thought I would ever get to the point where I would have to write myself out of this story and trust me it's killing me on the inside. I've loved you for so long and I don't know what to do anymore to make you see that. If all our relationship is going to ever be is you fucking some K-tarded kid and not cleaning up the mess, I don't want to be a part of it anymore."

"I hope some day you see how bad the hurt was. And maybe then you'll finally realize how much I've loved you this whole time."

"There will be no sequel."

Chapter Twenty-one

Saturday night at Vivid was much busier than its standard weekend. By ten the line was already forming as Dutch decided that he would meet Eli there eventually. The bouncer at the door moved him through the line as they said, "Eli's not here yet."

Dutch replied, "Not a problem," as he made his way through the entrance and down the steps into the Playground.

He hadn't returned Antoine's calls since last night. After storming out of the Pink Bar, Antoine had tried to talk him down from the headspace that was written all over his face. For the most part it had been successful. If he had trusted his gut instinct, he should have gone home with Antoine. Pleading exhaustion, instead he subconsciously headed over to the bathhouse where in his altered state had stumbled upon Eli taking his sexual frustration out on a visibly intoxicated Landon. It didn't happen at that point, but once the drugs had worn off Dutch began the terrifying comedown that seemed to gouge out whatever hope he had left to win Eli's heart.

This was nothing new for Dutch, however the memory of Eli and Landon had made it much worse and much different than his other conquests. Dutch could not stop the auto-replay that repeated in his head. He wanted it to stop. He wanted the emptiness that came along with it to just go away. Eli had left Dutch a voicemail in the afternoon, something Dutch instantly erased as he lay curled up in the fetal position on his bed, staring at his cell phone, then up at the wall. He could not avoid it this time. This time it hurt more than every time before it. This was the final straw for Dutch. There would be no healing from the night before.

He scanned the Playground as the dance floor began to fill. As the light cut through the darkness, he went over to the side bar where the bartender was talking with Keith. He breathed in and walked over to the bar as Keith casually mentioned, "You're not leashed tonight Dutch. What gives?"

"Fuck off Keith" he snapped.

Keith then said, "He still has you bark on command when he's not around though." Dutch ordered a drink as he then turned to Keith and leaned against the counter. Keith's sarcasm disappeared from his facial expression as he said, "Look Dutch, it's not that we don't like you. It's that we don't like him…"

Keith sipped his drink, "Dutch, he's morally empty and if you really opened your eyes to what he's doing to himself and everyone around him, you would walk away too if you had that clear-headedness."

Dutch handed the bartender money as he asked, "What the fuck is your biggest issue with Eli? He's really not that bad. I swear to god."

Keith shook his head and then asked, "Then tell me what Eli did with that barely legal kid that you two dragged out to the bar." Dutch was silent as Keith said, "I'll tell you what happened. If it wasn't for the fact that I got to Lockers when I did, I found him being used by an obese troll without a condom while people were lining up to take their turn." A look of worry swept over Dutch's face as he quickly forgot to ask why Keith was there in the first place. Keith continued, "Eli was nowhere to be found Dutch." Keith then took a sip of his beer. "That is not the way you introduce someone to the gay life in Edmonton Dutch. It's wrong."

Even though Dutch knew this he still blurted out, "And you're telling me you didn't fuck him."

A wave of anger swept over Keith as he spit out at Dutch, "If you want to be an accessory to fucking up someone else's life then go right ahead. But keep in mind Dutch he will never love you the way you so desperately want him to." Keith set down his bottle. "I hope you get the sense to walk away before you get dragged down in his self-destruction."

As Keith walked away Dutch scowled and tears began to run down his flushed cheeks as he walked over to a lone table and leaned against it while watching the crowd. He felt his phone vibrate as he then sat on the stool and flipped it open. The message read, YOU ENJOYED WATCHING? Dutch erased it immediately as he downed his drink within seconds. He then fished out the vile of ketamine and began to inhale deeply as the feeling of vertigo kicked in. Dutch sighed and shyly smiled as he sauntered back to the bar and ordered a second drink. As the drink arrived Dutch began to sip it as he noticed that everything seemingly began to melt together. The music wrapped itself around Dutch as he sat back down at the table and fixed his eyes on the lights that now began to simply pierce through the darkness.

He felt a tap on his shoulder as he looked over and spotted Stewart standing at the table next to him. Stewart asked, "How are you doing this evening?"

Dutch replied, "I could be better. How are you?"

Stewart shrugged, "I'm pretty tired. I just finished work and am having a drink with some friends."

Dutch asked, "Anyone I know?"

Stewart smiled shyly and shook his head as Dutch continued, "So what's the story with you and Daniel?"

Stewart was silent for a few moments then explained, "There's nothing. We're just amazing friends and that's it."

Dutch thought for a moment and then half-pleaded, "Stewart, don't fall in love with Daniel." He took a sip of his drink and continued, "Despite what you probably think, I don't hate you and I really think when it comes to Daniel you really need to be careful."

Stewart then protested, "I don't know, but he's said a few things that have made me question that." Dutch looked confused as he continued, "Daniel told me one night that if he was gay…"

Dutch interrupted and said, "See that's the problem Stewart. He wants something. And I don't want him to lead you to somewhere its not."

Stewart reassured him, "I'm good Dutch. Thanks for your concern." Stewart then changed the subject, "Where's Eli?"

Dutch only shrugged, "Probably at home in recovery from last night."

Stewart asked, "Is everything okay?"

Dutch only sighed and sugar coated his response. "It's just a bit of best friend tension. Nothing major."

Stewart asked, "Does he always treat you second class?"

Dutch said nothing as Stewart pointed out, "It's just what everyone says on the floor."

Dutch only smiled and said, "Don't believe everything you hear."

Stewart then asked, "Even from Eli?"

Dutch said, "Especially from Eli."

Stewart nodded then said, "Come up to the lounge in a bit for a few beverages."

Dutch smiled and said, "Will do" and with that Stewart headed to the exit and up the stairs.

As Dutch finished his second drink he spotted Paul coming into the lower area. He saw Dutch and quickly made his way over. "Hey Dutch how are you?"

Dutch scowled and replied sarcastically, "Fucking fantastic Paul." He then looked over at him and asked, "Are you here to reach out to me after Keith?"

Paul shrugged and then replied, "The A-gays and I are going out to Heaven tonight. Do you want to come?" Dutch's eyes briefly lit up as Paul added, "There is one string attached." Dutch appeared confused as Paul smiled and replied, "We need to get you more fuckered than you already are."

Dutch then asked, "And how pray tell do you plan to accomplish that?"

Paul grinned as he sat another drink down on the table. Paul said "Take a quick sip." Dutch did a quick suck through the straw and shrugged and said, "Okay…" Paul glanced around to see if anyone was watching when Paul pulled out a small bottle full of clear fluid. He then unscrewed the cap and asked, "How much?"

Dutch said, "I don't understand."

Paul explained, "This shit will let you melt into the floor. You're gonna love it." Dutch watched as Paul poured in the liquid from the cap into the drink. Dutch only stared as Paul used the straw to mix the drink. Paul then took a sip and said, "Not enough." He poured a little from the bottle into the glass. He took another sip then smiled. "Just right."

Dutch picked it up and began to drink. The first gulp caused a pained expression to surface while Paul chuckled. Dutch then said, "It's got kick"

Paul said, "Come up into the lounge when you're ready."

Dutch held up his drink and said, "Cheers" as he swallowed some more.

Within minutes Dutch had completely ingested the drink and he stood up from the stool. He began to feel claustrophobic as he reached into his pocket and tried to grab for his cell phone. It vibrated as he noticed Eli's number on the display screen. As he answered he began to wobble as Eli screamed, "I'm at fucking Vivid! Where the fuck are you?!"

Dutch could feel his body being pulled to the floor as Dutch said, "I…I…"

Dutch's feet suddenly gave out from under him as a crowd watched him knock his table over while his cell phone split against the wall. A few minutes later Eli sped down the stairs, finding Dutch facedown on the floor.

He raced over and screamed, "Call 911!" Eli tried to move Dutch as Stewart watched from the staircase along with his friends.

Eli shook Dutch as he said, "Come on come on Dutchie…don't fucking give up on me…" Eli screamed, "HAS SOMEONE CALLED A FUCKING AMBULANCE?!"

Eli began to panic and cry as two paramedics came down with a stretcher. Eli quickly fumbled in Dutch's pocket and hid the vile of ketamine on him while the first paramedic asked, "Does anyone know what he's taken?" Out of the mumbling nothing was decipherable to Eli as the paramedics lifted Dutch. The second paramedic opened his eyelids and shone into them with a miniature flashlight. He said, "He's G'ed out. We need to get him to emergency…"

The paramedics lifted Dutch up the stairs as the third one asked Eli, "Do you need to come along?"

Eli said nothing then mumbled, "I need to collect his phone." Eli watched as they pulled Dutch away on a stretcher, shortly after spotting the two pieces that comprised of Dutch's cell phone. As he picked it up he looked around. By this point the crowd had dispersed except for Stewart who was still on the stairs.

Eli began up the steps and just as Stewart was about to say something Eli shot out, "Not a fucking word." Stewart tried again to say something when Eli then said, "You fuck right off. You do not breathe this to anyone, or I will put you through fucking hell…"

Chapter Twenty-Two

Dutch woke up to the sounds of beeping. His eyes stung as he saw the heart monitor, breathed in and turned his head forward. That's when he noticed what was either a holy apparition, or real life seated comfortably at the foot of the bed. Eli sat at the foot of the bed across from Dutch. His black suit accented the clinically pale white room. Dutch moaned as he struggled to position his head up. Only silence was lodged between them, Eli perched on the back and of a wooden chair, his feet firmly planted on its seat. A crucifix hung at the top of the wall over Eli. Dutch breathed slowly as he now began to move his arms slowly, feeling the tubes almost holding his arms down as he finally managed to move his head to his left. When Dutch discovered nothing but stained curtains, a familiar voice uttered the words that were not only cold but calculated.

"You.Fucking.Selfish.Asshole."

Dutch winced in pain as he tried his best to focus on his best friend sitting at the foot of the bed. Eli hung his head down as he wiped his forehead. Dutch remained silent as he then tried, in his head, to formulate the sentence he was going to breathe out. He knew he wanted to say aloud "The fuck you know about selfish…" The words he wanted to say were beginning to formulate in his head, it would only be a case of getting them out.

Instead the words that tumbled out of his mouth were, "I wasn't think…"

Eli said, "The fuck you weren't Dutchie." He began to raise his voice. "Did you really mean to put that much GHB in your fucking drink?"

Dutch began to explain, "I didn't think it was that highly concentrated…"

Eli said, "You didn't think Dutch. That's the problem."

Dutch sighed as he said, "I'm sorry that it put you in such a difficult position…so how long were you planning to hover over me like a fucking vulture? Why didn't you just pull the plug?"

Eli asked, "Why would you want me to do that?"

Dutch spat at him, "Because in my last will and testament you are designated plug puller."

Eli loosened his tie, "Why me?"

Dutch replied coldly, "Because you're fucking heartless enough to finish it."

Eli looked up at him and could only look frightened for a moment, then hung his head back down as he grunted and loosened his tie some more while Dutch's stare pierced right through him. Dutch sighed and asked, "Does Aimee know I'm here?"

"I called her the moment you went into the ambulance."

"Fuck" Dutch moaned.

Eli sneered, "What are you worried about? You pretty much have this hospital stay paid for."

Dutch asked, "What is that supposed to mean?"

Eli replied, "Your parents paid for this visit. You got a three day vacation away from work. Your folks will throw more money at you because they want the problem to go away. Antoine will fuck you senseless when you get out of the hospital, and you will live happily ever after."

Dutch suddenly felt a wave of anger as he shot at Eli, "You really think I had this sorted out didn't you?" Eli remained silent as Dutch raised his voice even louder. "You think I fucking staged this Eli?" He said, "You think I really enjoy being disowned by my family and having money thrown at me because they can't accept me?"

Eli reasoned, "You don't know how good you have it Dutchie."

Dutch argued, "You have no idea how much it hurts. Especially since you seem to work oh so hard at alienating yourself from your family." Eli looked up and Dutch yelled, "You always get what you fucking want Eli!

And no matter who you hurt, how many you fuck over to get it, you get it. Have you ever thought about where you're going to be in ten years?"

Eli growled, "I don't plan to be here if that's what you're asking."

Dutch stared deep into Eli's eyes and said, "Really Eli, when are you going to let anyone in? So you're telling me you'll still be raping barely legal teens whacked out on K in ten years?"

With that comment Eli could feel a snap and chill down his spine, his senses suddenly heightened as a surge of adrenaline ripped through him. It was something no amount of cocaine or ecstasy had ever come close to giving him. He knew Dutch had nearly disarmed him by this admission alone. Dutch had never intentionally done this before.

When Eli finally dismounted from the chair, he met Dutch's icy gaze. Silence with the exception of the heart monitor enveloped them both. Finally Eli said, "Text me when you're ready to leave."

Dutch let his head rest back as Eli's shoes signaled his departure. Tears began to flood his eyes as he sniffled and leaned back, head then cocked to the side. He was at a complete loss for words.

Chapter Twenty-Three

Eli sauntered into Lime Salon, enclosed in a corner on the main floor of Edmonton Centre. As he walked into the ivory encased marble entry, the sounds of house music casually poured from the salon on his right. The owner passed by him and smiled while Eli nodded and forced a brief smile back.

The receptionist at the counter smiled sweetly at him and said, "She'll be out to get you shortly." He sat down and reached over to the nearest magazine which was neatly piled on the table as he casually flipped through its worn pages.

She then asked, "What are you having done?"

Eli replied, "I'm thinking on having it all cut off."

She said, "Maybe you should bleach it, make it blonde."

He smiled and argued, "Nah. My friend is blonde enough for both of us." After a few more minutes of flipping through the magazine he heard thunderous steps and the words, "I cannot believe how messy this bleach is…" almost matching the rhythm of the music.

Chelsea looked over and said, "Get in the chair Mister."

He asked, "Which one?" She cocked her hear, motioning into the salon area, then asked, "Shampoo as well?" He nodded silently.

Eli loved it when he came to visit her at the salon. The whole area was bright as five black sinks accented the off white and beige colors of the area. The salon chairs were fortressed by the glass windows which offered a birds-eye view out into the mall and the escalator that traveled up to the second and third floors. He sat in the leather chair that was in front of one of the sinks and leaned back as Chelsea came back and started to turn on the warm spray of water.

Eli asked, "Are you ever planning to quit Go Credit?"

As she ran the water through her fingers she replied, "Not when I have to go back to school and rent is due." She started to run it through Eli's hair as she explained, "Not all of us have a money tree growing in our apartments."

Eli said, "Jealous…"

She looked down and said, "Be careful before I waterboard you."

Eli smiled and said, "You wouldn't…" Chelsea argued, "Be careful, because I know for a fact there's enough people in the call centre who want to see that."

"Fuck 'em, they're just jealous" Eli snapped as he continued, "Half of them wanna be me while half of them want to fuck me."

"Don't be so sure" she said as she stopped the water and whipped out a towel. "If you keep taunting Stewart the way you've been, it might come back to you and fuck you in the ass."

Eli then said, "Nice analogy Chelsea."

He sat up and walked over to her chair as she asked, "And what are we doing today?" He replied as he glared at the mirror and sighed dramatically, "Army."

Her eyes widened as she said, "What?" As she started to ready a razor he then said, "Okay maybe not completely off. Leave a little on the top and sides. Stewart can really go fuck himself if he can't take a joke."

She asked, "So what category does Stewart fall under?"

He replied, "Definitely not column A cause he could never be as fabulous or as amazing as me and he won't fall under B cause he's a huge nelly bottom. And that trumps any chance of him fucking me."

Chelsea then asked, "So then what category does Dutch fall under?" Eli was silent for a few seconds as she paused for a moment and then asked, "Is everything okay?"

Eli replied, "Dutch is in the hospital right now. He apparently had an overdose of GHB in his drink."

"Fuck…is he all right?"

"He's been preoccupied lately."

She then said, "When are you going back to the hospital?" Eli looked up at her as she began to press the razor into his head.

He explained, "I'm not too sure."

Chelsea then asked, "What the fuck is going on with you two anyhow? I've heard that you've been treating him quite badly as of late." He grunted as she said, "You know what? You need to be there for him Eli. You're pretty much all he's got." Eli only shook his head as in frustration Chelsea then pushed the razor a little harder.

Eli let out an, "Ouch. Fuck…"

She looked sternly at him and said accusatorily, "If you didn't move your head it wouldn't have fucking tugged at your skin." Eli grunted again as she said, "Mom told me that's how you were when you were a kid at the barber's."

"Ahh, the voice of experience…"

"Well it's true Eli. I remember that Supercuts barber nearly took your ear off."

Eli instinctively reached up and felt his right earlobe as he said, "The only thing my younger sister remembers about me is when I'm at the hairstylist."

She smiled and teased, "If you were around more I might have better memories. They complain they never see you anymore. That you stop in once in awhile, you don't bring Dutch with you and it's like you're this completely different person." She then put the razor away and pulled out her scissors while she snipped on what was left of Eli's hair while she continued, "You don't have a reason to feel repressed yet for whatever reason you make a lot of fucking excuses to be." Eli rolled his eyes and hmmphed as she continued to snip away at his hair. "So what prompted the new do?" she asked as his eyes darted around the mirror and out to the people that crisscrossed the window in front of him.

Eli smugly replied, "Hair felt heavy…"

Chelsea breathed, "Can't see why…"

He then asked, "What?"

She lied, "You could use a lighter dye on your hair." Eli smiled and said, "Liar."

When the scissors went down she then asked, "So what are your thoughts on the supervisor from Montreal?"

Eli said, "The separatist steroid monkey?"

Chelsea grabbed the duster and started to wipe away at his neck. "I guess you haven't gotten to know him better yet…"

Eli said, "He's vacant."

She then said, "If the shoe fits…"

It was at that moment he stood up and glared at her, "Are you done?"

She said nothing for thirty seconds, then finally commented, "All done Mister."

Eli said, "Thanks" and abruptly left.

Behind him he heard the comment, "Don't worry he'll square up with me later" echoed with the music.

He never understood why she could be such a brutally honest bitch who was absolutely right. Apart from the whole raging for no reason, he thought for someone who was younger than him she had a hell of a lot to say about what went down in the call centre.

The escalator could not get him back up to the office fast enough as he walked back into the main call center area. When he looked over to see Stewart and Daniel talking he immediately sat down and sifted through his e-mails.

Ariel said as she glanced over, "You really got rid of it didn't you?"

He looked over and asked, "Excuse me?"

She said, "The hair…" He looked up and then forced out a smile as Stewart then sat down and glanced over.

He blurted, "Wow, not only are you a thug, but you now look the part too."

"Fuck off coppertop…"

"I'm just saying…"

"My sister could set you up with someone who could take care of that fucking rug on your forehead…"

"Do you ever get tired of being so empty?"

"Fuck Stewart, you are such a nelly little queen."

Stewart huffed and replied, "You're more of a queen then I am Eli."

Eli grinned as he leaned back in his chair and threatened, "Don't play this game with me Stewart cause you'll lose."

Stewart then shot at him, "At least I'm not the one who has a fucking rainbow come out every time he open his mouth."

Stewart snickered as Eli continued, "Maybe in terms of style and taste yeah, I might be gay. But when it comes to how I act, unlike you I am not a dead giveaway."

Ariel snickered and said, "Actually, Eli the glass slipper fits better on you than it does Stewart."

Eli was quiet for a moment then seethed, "It might fit me better Ariel but at least that particular glass slipper in actuality was shaped around Jeremiah's foot."

She scowled and Eli went to say something when Stewart raised his middle finger and said, "Thank you for calling Go Credit customer service. My name is Stewart..." Eli turned around as he heard the tone in his earpiece and answered the line. During the call he mentally began to construct ways to torture Stewart. Shortly after, he made the decision to leave it alone and logged out, making his way out of the office, and back to Royal Alex hospital.

Chapter Twenty-Four

He'd woken up again to the beeping, almost thinking that he would also spot Eli perched on the chair across from him. He sighed when he only saw the crucifix hanging on the wall. The sun had finally crept out and began to pour through the window. It warmed Dutch as he began to move a little more. The pain of the previous day had been reduced to manageable as the nurse shuffled in and began to read his chart as she looked at him and smiled.

She said, "Dutch, its good to see you awake."

He smiled back as he asked, "Do you really mean that?"

She asked, "Why wouldn't I?"

He teased, "You're union. You have to say that."

They both chuckled as she said, "Your sister was here. She dropped some chocolate off, and a pen and notebook." The nurse then continued, "You've been out like a light the past twenty-four hours."

Dutch asked, "Anyone else?"

It was that moment he heard, "I hope you're not ready to leave just yet." He looked over to the doorway and saw Antoine with a bouquet of flowers. Dutch smiled as he handed the flowers to the nurse to briefly hold and once bedside, leaned in and kissed Dutch on the forehead. Antoine then pulled away and gazed down at Dutch as Antoine let his hand brush against his cheek.

Dutch breathed, "I'm so sorry Antoine."

Antoine replied, "I was scared I lost you."

Dutch breathed, "I'm so sorry Antoine" as he felt himself flush while Antoine sat down on the bed beside him.

Antoine asked, "Do they know what it was?"

Dutch replied, "Someone spiked my drink with GHB." He then added in a subdued voice, "Eli found me at the Playground at Vivid and called an ambulance." Antoine was silent as Dutch explained, "He made sure I was okay."

Antoine said, "I'm glad he managed that for you."

Dutch lied to himself as much as to Antoine, "He's really not that bad of a guy Antoine. Once you get to know him he's great."

Antoine only nodded as they heard, "He's right Antoine. You really should get to know me better before you snap judgment." They looked over and saw Eli leaned against the doorway, box of chocolates in hand as Dutch's smile widened a little more. Antoine's eyes widened as Eli placed the box with Antoine's gift on the nightstand.

He sat on the chair across from the bed and Eli said, "I just dropped by to see if you'll be ready to check out tomorrow."

Dutch replied, "Yeah I should be okay to be picked up. The doctor's going to give me a once over before he releases me."

Antoine then asked, "Are you going to be okay to come back to work?"

Dutch nodded as Eli then said, "I'll see you tomorrow then."

He then looked over, sneered, "Antoine…" and then walked out of the room and into the hall.

Eli had only made it down the hall a few feet when he heard, "Eli!" shouted from Dutch's room.

He turned and saw Antoine catching up to him as he slowed down and began to explain, "Hey Antoine, I'm really sorry if…"

Antoine checked to make sure if the coast was clear and grabbed Eli by the suit jacket, throwing him against the concrete wall with such force that they both could hear snaps coming from Eli's body.

Eli yelped in pain as Antoine seethed, "Look you fucking piece of shit. I don't like you. I don't like what you've done to Dutch and what you're doing to him now."

Eli snapped, "Fuck off!" trying to break free of Antoine's grasp.

Antoine slammed him into the wall again. He said, "You're not going to drag him down with you when you decide you're going to drown do you understand me?" By now Antoine's face had reddened while Eli tried to break free. Antoine continued, "You are the most vile, empty, ruthless person I have ever met. You want to kill yourself? Fine! Just don't drag Dutch down with you."

Antoine finally let Eli go as he then lunged forward at Antoine. Antoine backed away and said, "Dutch deserves a better best friend than you."

Eli sneered, "Fuck you French boy you know nothing." He started to walk away as Antoine stood centered in the hallway, gaze fixated on Eli as he watched him storm into the elevator.

Antoine walked back into the hospital room as he sat down on the chair at the foot of the bed. He leaned back as Dutch said, "I feel like shit."

Antoine smiled and said, "It's from the legal drugs they've been feeding you." He then asked, "Are you okay to leave the hospital tomorrow?" Dutch nodded, "I'm about to go mental in here. I need to get back to work."

Antoine then said, "If you need anything…"

That very moment Dutch patted the space beside him as Antoine asked, "Are you sure there's enough room?" Dutch then nudged over a little as again he patted the space beside the bed. Antoine crawled onto the bed and laid down on his side as he whispered, "You mean the world to me Dutch. I don't ever want to lose you." He then leaned in and began kissing Dutch's neck while Dutch shifted around the bed and pulled Antoine close behind him. He trembled as Antoine's hands slowly caressed Dutch while Dutch nuzzled back into him. For a moment Dutch forgot where he was as he could feel Antoine's arms wrap around him. Dutch felt weightless, like his body was ready to float out of the bed and back into the open world.

They were both asleep holding each other when the nurse walked in and playfully slapped Antoine with her clipboard. She said, "As much as I would love to have you sleep over…" Antoine groaned as she finished, "Visiting hours are over."

He stood up and slipped into his shoes as he said to Dutch, "Call me when you get out." Dutch half nodded as Antoine leaned in and kissed him one more time before leaving into the hallway. The nurse then asked, "Are you planning on picking him up tomorrow?" Antoine shook his head no. She said, "That's too bad because the other friend is a real cocksucker."

He said, "You don't know the half of it…"

The next day when Dutch was released from the hospital desk he looked at his phone to see if Eli had called or sent a text message. He then sent Eli a message making him aware that he was still waiting at the hospital. He stood outside and watched the grey float by as he cracked his neck and stretched. He rifled through his bag that Aimee had left him at the hospital and sighed as he leaned back on the bench.

An hour passed and he sighed one final time and said to no one in particular, "Fuck this." He dialed the number for a cab and hopped in upon its arrival. The ride home seemed like the longest ten dollars Dutch had ever spent. As the taxi finally pulled up in front of his building, he headed up the elevator and finally into his suite. When he walked into the living room he noticed that all of Erin's furniture was missing. Everything in the living with the exception of the television was gone. Dutch shook his head and promptly went to her room where he had found everything had been emptied. He leaned back against the wall and after a few minutes completely scoured the apartment as he struggled to find a note or something, anything that would have announced her departure.

Dutch checked the phone once more to see if any messages were left, text or otherwise. He opened up his room and checked to see if anything was out of place. Nothing. When he set everything down on the floor, he then laid back on the bed and dialed Antoine's number.

Antoine answered as Dutch said, "I should have had you come get me. That useless motherfucker didn't pick me up from the hospital."

Antoine said, "You're kidding me right?"

Dutch said, "Ahh whatever. Hey do you know anyone that needs to rent a room here in Edmonton?"

Antoine replied, "Not off the top of my head. Why?"

Dutch returned to an empty living room and said, "My roommate fucked off. At least she didn't steal anything."

Antoine then asked, "Are you going to be coming in tomorrow?"

Dutch replied, "As long as nothing else happens today?"

Antoine said, "Did you want me to come stay the night?"

"I think I will be okay unless something else fucked up happens."

Antoine then suggested, "Get some sleep then. And we'll see you tomorrow."

Dutch then hung up his cell as he heard the door unlock. He looked up as Erin closed the door and walked in. She spotted him then stopped, her eyes sporting huge black rings as she remained silent. Dutch returned her gaze as tears began to stream down her face. He looked down to her hand that clutched the suicide note that Dutch had written to Eli. It was the note in his top drawer, on top of the audio journal.

She squeezed it tighter as after a few minutes she asked, "How long has this been going on?" Dutch said nothing as she inched a little closer. "When...were...you...going...to...tell me?" Her mouth quivered as Dutch moved up to her and stretched out his arms.

He said, "Erin…"

She clutched the note tighter and screamed, "Fuck you!!" pushing Dutch back as he fell onto the floor. She wildly started hitting Dutch as he shielded his face with his arms.

"Fuck you! After all I've fucking done for you!"

She continued to hit him as he screamed, "Fucking stop!!"

She kept screaming, "After all I've fucking done!" Dutch then lowered his hands for just a moment as one of the apartment keys in her fist had dislodged itself and poked out from her clenched fingers. When her hand made contact with his face, the key dug into his cheek and tore it open as he screamed in pain, finally standing up as she then stood back and watched Dutch nurse his bruised face.

She said almost scared, "I'm sorry Dutch let me…"

He then screamed at her, "I never fucking asked you to do anything for me Erin!" Erin could see the blood trickling down between his fingers and she dropped the keys onto the floor.

She then stepped back as she tried again to plead, "Dutch I'm so sorry. Please let me mend…"

"Get the fuck away from me!"

He then looked at his hand and the blood as he then screamed, "I've never asked for any of this. I never asked for you to love me. I never hid myself from you. You can't tell me after all of this time you never fucking knew…"

"Please Dutch I'm so sorry…"

"Erin don't you fucking dare…"

"Dutch I love…"

"Get the fuck out of my house you crazy fucking bitch! I would never love you!!"

Erin looked at him and asked, "Is it because you can't?"

Dutch coldly breathed out, "It's because I won't…"

She started to cry as she ran out, slamming the door shut as Dutch picked up his cell phone and dialed Aimee's number. As she answered the phone he said, "Aimee you need to come over right fucking now…"

She asked, "Is everything okay?"

His voice started to waiver as he said, "No not everything is okay." He then pleaded, "Please Aimee just get here."

Dutch then hung up the phone and sat back down as he began to cry. He threw his cell against the wall as it snapped to a million pieces all over the living room while he sobbed. After a few minutes he finally had regained his composure and got up to lock the door.

LOVE'S SWEET EXILE - DISC 57: fifty minutes, fifty-nine seconds

"Sometimes in the back of mind, I feel like I've failed her. I understand why she's upset with me. I can't believe I was oblivious to it the whole time. It explains a lot. A lot which seems to have fallen into place. Could she not have waited till I was out of the hospital? Has she felt like this for the whole time we lived together? I know I couldn't just pretend that it's not been there for this long. But at the same time I couldn't just pretend it didn't exist. Now I know why my cell phone bills disappeared. I know why there were those meals that were made for me in neat containers in the fridge."

"Everything in my room has always been in its right place. Maybe she didn't think that she was going to ever get the answers that she was so badly looking for. Maybe she thought 'This is it, it's completely catching up.' And just for that reason alone her search for the truth would lead her to fuck with the lock on my door and rife through my desk drawer, finding the discs and the note."

"Instead of just being brokenhearted that I died, she opted to be brokenhearted because of the truth. I don't know which was more damaging. I shattered out pretty little portrait. The little girl from St.

Brieux, Saskatchewan's world nearly came crashing down, all because she was oblivious to the simple fact I am gay."

"Maybe she was hoping her and I would write our own happy ending, that I would remain unpartnered to Eli and that instead of him, I would realize where my heart was, and from there she and I would write the last chapter. We'd look back on it and I would laugh because really, isn't that how the formula's supposed to work? It's what society expects. Maybe some right-wing fuckhead organization could run it and my parents would be elated and welcome me back into the family. We'd get married and it would be a happily ever after all around."

"No, fuck that. I would not give them that victory. It's best she knew now instead of much later."

Chapter Twenty-Five

Dutch woke up beside Antoine and draped his arm over him as he moved closer. He'd pleaded with Antoine to spend the night shortly after Erin had left Dutch in an injured condition, physically and emotionally. When he opened the door he literally pinned Antoine to the door and began kissing him. The next hours were a blur as it began on the living room floor, the moonlight pouring in as Dutch would gaze at Antoine in that same light. Eventually they found their way to Dutch's bed, blurred between the point they stopped and when Dutch finally awoke. There was an urgency that had never appeared before in their lovemaking, something that Dutch sensed immediately as a light blue glow bathed the room and Antoine stirred a little while Dutch lay awake.

Antoine's eyes opened as he asked, "Is everything okay?"

Dutch breathed, "I'm so thankful you're here."

Antoine mused, "Your apartment is a lot emptier than it was before."

Dutch explained "She moved out."

Antoine asked "Really?"

Dutch silently nodded then explained, "She went into my room, went through my audio journal and fucking flipped." He looked up at the ceiling and sighed out, "I guess I should have seen the warning signs all along."

Antoine tightly embraced him as he continued, "Eli was right though. She really did a lot more than she really should have as a roommate and a friend."

Antoine sighed, "It's not your fault. She didn't want to see it and because of that she got hurt."

"Your biggest issue is that you beat yourself up far too much Dutch." Dutch propped his head up as Antoine reasoned, "You're an amazing person Dutch, but sometimes you don't see it. And I think that's what you lose sight of." He then looked down at him and continued, "Eli… as much as he's your best friend Dutch, is not that great of a person to be around. He really doesn't seem, or want to give back to a relationship that's teetering on collapse." Dutch was silent and Antoine reasoned, "At least it's what I see."

"As painful as it was for me to hear that…" Dutch breathed in, "You're right." Antoine let his fingers run up and down Dutch's body as Dutch twitched and giggled.

Antoine apologized as Dutch said, "I don't want you to go." Antoine then kissed him on the forehead. Dutch leaned in reaching his neck upwards and positioning himself to find Antoine's mouth.

He wrapped his arms around Antoine and Antoine briefly pulled away and said, "You've made me feel something I haven't felt in a long time." Dutch only nodded as he leaned in and they kissed again while Dutch rolled Antoine on top of him.

The next time Dutch stirred awake was the sound of a key turning in a lock. He opened his eyes as the blue had been replaced by the brightness of the sunlight that augmented the room colors. He crawled out of bed and pulled on his boxer-briefs as he walked out to the living room and to the door that Aimee had propped open. She hugged him tightly as Dutch said, "I'm so glad you're doing this."

Aimee replied with a smile, "I know hon. Some guys from school are helping me move stuff up. You might want to get dressed." She then looked behind him and smiled as she then exclaimed, "So that's who you've been hiding in your bed…"

Dutch blushed as Antoine extended his hand. "You must be Aimee. I'm Antoine."

She shook his hand and she asked, "Are you sure he's not straight?" Antoine blushed when Dutch turned to him and explained, "She was just saying we should get dressed. Her movers are bringing stuff in."

She then teased, "I changed my mind about Antoine. He can stay in his underwear."

Antoine grinned, "I'll get dressed." He leaned in and kissed Dutch and then strolled back into the bedroom.

Aimee leaned over and whispered, "I'm sorry Dutch, but at this moment in time I'm extremely jealous."

He only grinned as she then said, "Thank you for freeing up a room in the condo. I'm sure mom and dad will be happy they now don't have to pay rent twice."

Dutch added, "Even though they didn't have to..." She then asked, "What do you do with the extra money anyhow?" he said nothing as Antoine came back out dressed.

"I'll see you later at work?" He said to Dutch. Dutch nodded as he leaned in and kissed Antoine. Antoine then said, "Nice to finally meet you Aimee."

When he disappeared she said, "Damn you for being gay." They laughed and she then grinned, "And what's with the finally bit?"

Dutch smiled and replied, "I talk about you all of the time." He paused for a moment. "I brag that you're the only normal one in the family." She snickered as he said, "I gotta get ready for work. Please don't fuck up the flow of my living room."

She teased, "What flow? There's only the television here," while the first of her friends arrived with the boxes.

Dutch walked into the call centre an hour after Antoine had left the apartment. It had been nearly a week since the overdose at Vivid. Given four days in the hospital and an extra two days trying to organize his living situation since Erin's abrupt move, it also meant a quick stop at Etienne's for another two bags of crystal for himself in addition to the regular party prescriptions.

After the readjustment and detoxification from legal hospital medication, he finally strolled into work and looked around. He noticed a few people turned their heads and saw him while he headed over to his desk. He immediately spotted the flowers, the cards all decorated as he turned on his computer and sat in his chair. Marie walked up as Dutch sat down. "Dutch!"

He stood up and smiled, hugging her tight and replied, "Hey…"

She said worriedly, "I was so scared we almost lost you…How are you feeling?"

Dutch shrugged as he explained, "I'm fine Marie, just something was poured into my drink.

She sighed and said, "I'm glad you made it through okay. We were all quite worried about you."

Marie then asked, "Who are the flowers from?"

He opened the little card and began to flush as he grinned and said nothing.

She quietly asked, "Antoine?"

He held his finger to his mouth as she stopped and said, "Ahh."

Dutch asked, "Did you see Eli today?"

She flatly replied, "He was in earlier, haven't seen him since."

Dutch quietly nodded, "I better say hi to Antoine."

She then asked, "How is that going anyways?" He only smiled as he walked through customer service. He noticed Eli's empty seat and made a mental note of where to go visit after his visit to Antoine's desk.

Dutch quickly walked past the lounge and up the steps as he glanced out at the row of desks. He spotted him pointing out something to Natasha when she looked up and smiled. "Dutch how are you feeling?"

He smiled, "Much better thank you"

Antoine smiled and continued, "I'll finish these documents with you later." She nodded as she headed down the stairs.

Antoine said, "Welcome back to the office."

"Thank you so much for the flowers."

"I'm really glad you like them."

Dutch then teased "My sister has a crush on you. I think we may have to set her up with one of your brothers."

Antoine blushed, "Are we hanging out this weekend?"

Dutch nodded, "Call me tonight after you're done work and we can talk more about that." Antoine nodded as Dutch then headed down the stairs past Eli's desk and towards the men's washroom.

When he passed the second door he headed towards the back stalls. Dutch opened the door at the back where Eli stood hunched over the back of the toilet seat. He stood up as Dutch asked, "Where the fuck were you when I checked out of the hospital this past week?"

Eli wiped his nose and replied, "I was tied up."

Dutch sneered, "Or were you busy fucking someone into a K hole?"

Eli spat out, "Fuck you Dutch it was never like that."

Dutch mumbled, "Looked pretty crystal fucking clear to me..." Eli then stepped out of the stall and said, "Breakfast is getting cold."

Dutch stepped in the stall and closed it behind him as Eli explained through the door, "I have been pretty tied up with work and school. It's been fucking nuts." Dutch finished his first line as Eli leaned back against the mirror. He continued as Dutch held together one of his nostrils, "It was great of Antoine to stop by the hospital and visit you."

Dutch mumbled, "A far better gesture than some."

Eli asked, "What?"

Dutch finished his second line and replied, "It was Eli. I didn't expect it at all."

Dutch then opened the door as Eli asked, "Are you?"

Dutch replied, "I'm fine, Eli." He wiped his nose and said, "Let's go back into the call centre okay?"

Eli looked irritated as they walked back out to the floor. Dutch immediately spotted Lance as he was talking to Christine, a pained expression on her face. Dutch immediately knew as they watched Eli conveniently disappear across the call centre. Christine handed Lance her lanyard and badge as he then walked her out of the call centre. Marie handed Dutch a coffee as she said, "You know she blames him for the dissolution of the relationship and her engagement." She then pointed out, "He wrecked their engagement Dutch."

Dutch turned to her and argued, "It was ruined long before Eli ever got there Marie. I mean, did you listen to the calls between those two on the phone at any given time? And do you remember when she shattered the window in the lounge when she launched her cell at Nicholas?" Marie was silent as Dutch said, "I don't discount that Eli went somewhere that he shouldn't have. But that fucking relationship was a train wreck for longer than anyone let on, especially Christine."

Marie walked away as Dutch sighed and sat down at his desk. He started to chew on the pen at his desk while he wished he'd not returned to work so quickly. Daniel walked by him and said, "Hey dude. Good to see you back at work again."

Dutch replied, "Thanks Daniel." Dutch thought for a moment, and just when Daniel was about to leave he said, "Hey Daniel…"

Daniel stopped in his tracks and asked, "Yeah dude?"

"Please Daniel, do not break Stewart's heart. Please treat him well. He deserves it." Daniel was silent as he walked away back to his desk. Dutch opened his e-mail and typed in the words, DANIEL HE THINKS THE WORLD OF YOU…

Chapter Twenty-six

This was not how Eli envisioned his Friday night.

Restlessness had begun to stir in Eli. While he continued to cruise online in his apartment, he sighed and checked his cell phone, hoping that Dutch would have texted by this point. However the last text he'd received from him was when he had left the weekend's supplies in his desk drawer at work so Eli didn't have to worry about him picking up from E while he spent the weekend with Antoine. He didn't take Dutch's admission that he was hanging out with Antoine too well, and the fact that Dutch had left Eli a small supply of drugs in his desk at work seemed to only rub more salt in the wound. This would be the first Friday since the incident at Vivid that Eli would be without a sidekick and he felt at a loss for what he wanted to do.

Part of him wanted to see Samuel...badly. He knew that at that moment he would most probably be with Keith, faking coupledom as Eli saw it. When Samuel and Eli had sex the very first time, Samuel in point detail laid out all of the reasons that Keith was not worth the effort or energy anymore. Now all of those fine point details pricked Eli each time he remembered them. It was that piercing feeling that would haunt Eli every time he fished for Samuel's number. In a sick, twisted way Eli reasoned the secret arm's length relationship was a jittery link between him and the A-list gays that he's been systematically excluded from all this time. He knew what he'd been doing was wrong for so many reasons, but for every prick of brutal honesty when it came down to Samuel and Keith, there would be another of indifference that pointed out to Eli that if he didn't keep Samuel at an arms distance that Samuel would think of him as a carbon copy of Keith.

Another hour and a couple more lines of coke, Eli decided to abandon his apartment and proceed to the Pink Bar. After a quick shower he threw on a pair of jeans, and t-shirt, then made his way out the door. It was unusually muggy on his block, considering how the weather had already been quite indifferent over the summer. As the high rises gave way to Jasper Avenue, he quickly glanced over at Dutch's building then began to walk in the direction of the Pink Bar.

Once he'd arrived at the bar's entrance, he'd decided to make his way upstairs. Karaoke had been replaced by top forty dance music and Queer As Folk reruns, as he decided to sit at the open windows and gaze out onto Jasper Avenue from above. While he nursed his beer his gaze was divided between the outside world, the main door where people shuffled in and out and the television screen, then back out to the sidewalk below, and then back to the entrance. This was the given time that he and Dutch reenacted a colorful play by play as the majority of the patrons would clumsily make their way though the doors. Except tonight it would be just Eli. Dutch was nowhere to be found.

After the fourth beer Eli's gaze returned to where he'd spotted Lance and his partner, along with a set of friends by the makeshift stage all enjoying a drink. Lance caught his glance and icily glared back at him, shaking his head. At first Eli did nothing and just grimaced. A few minutes later he quickly disappeared to the washroom, pulled out the vile of cocaine from his pocket and applied a small mountain onto his hand, shortly after snorting it completely off. He quickly looked in the mirror to check for any possible residue. He then walked back to the bar and ordered two beers, beginning to drink one of them while he walked over to Lance, second beer in hand.

Lance looked up at him and asked, "Can I help you?" It was an icy greeting as Eli showed him the second beer and sat it down on the table.
Eli said, "I remember your favorite beer from…"
"When you tried to fuck my partner?"

Eli said nothing as Lance asked, "Eli, what do you want?"

Eli paused, his facial expression becoming one of deep thought. He then said, "Lance, I'd really like for us to start over again. I mean, I don't think you and I started on the right foot."

Lance asked, "What are we starting over?"

Eli replied, "This. I don't understand why you fucking hate me so much. You look at me and treat me like I've got the word cunt written on my forehead."

Lance took another sip of his beer and said, "Now let's just examine that for a moment shall we?" Lance began, "I hate you because when I met you, I could see right through your pretentious and petty bullshit on and off the call centre floor. I hate you because really Eli, you put on this huge fucking act, and nothing about you is authentic or real."

Lance then seethed, "You know I might have been able to overlook the fact that you did try to fuck both myself and Cory on two separate occasions, if you had any shred of remorse, authenticity, or integrity. Eli you have none of that." Eli was beginning to feel the urge to punch Lance while he continued, "It really begs the question Eli, how has Dutch really been able to play wingman all this time?"

Eli snapped, "Fuck you Lance."

Lance replied, "If I didn't have morals I might have let you." Lance then asked, "Speaking of your wingman where is he?"

Eli replied, "He's out with his friend tonight."

Lance then said, "So when do you plan to fuck that up too?"

Eli asked, "What?"

Lance then pointed out, "You need to leave Dutch and Antoine alone Eli. Dutch is finally happy and I'll be damned to sit back and watch you try and destroy that, like you've swiftly done with everything else he's ever had." Eli still remained silent as he then explained, "It's too bad he's not here with you tonight." He then handed Eli the full bottle of beer and said, "I was going to give him this and see what you put in it."

Eli scowled and asked, "You fucking hate me that much eh?"

Eli turned to leave as Lance said, "Something to think on Eli. If you were in my shoes and it was Stewart who asked that exact same question you asked me, what would your reply be? By the way, do you ever worry what Samuel would ever think if he knew what you were really like?" That comment made Eli stop dead in his tracks. He slowly turned around, walked back up to Lance, and stared deep into his eyes. After a few seconds Eli said, "You have nothing on me Lance. Absolutely nothing."

It took all he had not to take the peace offering and smash it in Lance's face. Instead he snatched the bottle and began to drink from it, slamming the empty down on the table beside him. He stormed away and down the steps as he pulled out his cell and texted   Dutch WHERE THE FUCK ARE YOU? As much as he'd hoped, he knew that he wouldn't be getting a text back until Monday.

chapter Twenty-seven

When Dutch arrived at work Monday afternoon, he quickly stopped into Natasha's office and she said, "Hey Dutch have you got a moment?" He nodded as she said, "I need someone to fill in on Saturday just to be on hand for help with any questions in regards to things on the floor." She then added, "Maybe if you get a chance you can work on the Regenesis project as well."

Dutch smiled and replied, "Fair enough."

He then walked over to his desk as Marie greeted him with a quick pat on the back. She asked, "How are you this morning?"

Dutch sighed as he leaned back and started to swivel in his chair.

Marie asked, "Are you okay?"

Dutch shrugged as he gazed briefly down to the floor, then back at Marie. "Just got a lot of stuff on my mind is all…"

Marie asked, "Do you wanna talk?"

Dutch replied, "I don't know if there's anything you can do on your end."

Marie then asked, "Is it Antoine?"

Dutch shook his head no as he explained, "I…just can't…put my finger on it right now…"

Marie replied sympathetically, "When you're ready to talk Dutch let me know okay?" He silently nodded as she explained, "I'm off to a meeting in an hour or so. I know that you've been back for a few days, but it's good to have you here Dutch." He then turned to his desk as he opened his e-mail. The most recent item came from Antoine as he opened it up and across it in large font read, I LOVE YOU.

While Dutch had heard the words the night before his eyes widened and he smiled as he stared at the e-mail. When he exhaled suddenly he heard, "How was your weekend?"

He quickly closed the e-mail and looked up while Eli stood over him. "It was really good Eli," Dutch said.

Eli asked, "What did you two end up doing?"

Dutch shrugged and explained, "Not much really." He added, "And it's not like you care anyways Eli. You practically hate Antoine, and really why would I want to tell you something to just wind you up?"

Eli was silent and he then said, "Sorry, I was genuinely interested in your weekend."

Dutch only smiled and replied sarcastically, "Riiight…"

Eli then asked, "So what is on our agenda this weekend?" He was silent as Eli prodded, "Something up?"

Dutch shook his head no. "Actually Erin moved out abruptly this past week."

Eli said, "Good fucking riddance Dutchie. She was starting to imagine happily ever after with you and plan the two-point five fucking children."

Dutch shrugged and replied, "It just means no more dinners in Tupperware for awhile."

An awkward laugh ensued them both as Eli pointed out, "Just think. Maybe it's a signal for change."

Dutch nodded and said, "Maybe…Antoine and I are going to hang out this weekend. Probably do a quiet night in."

Eli asked already expecting disappointment, "You didn't want to do the Pink Bar on Friday?"

Dutch then pointed out with a grin, "I have to work on Saturday morning and make sure customer service doesn't implode."

Eli reasoned, "You can do it. Work has never stopped you before…"

Dutch shook his head and asked, "What are you doing Eli?"

He said, "I don't understand."

Dutch said almost fearfully, "Please don't Eli. Don't fuck this up for me."

"Oh…" Eli replied, "If you change your mind…"

"I'll be in touch."

Eli then hurried off as Dutch shook his head. He knew he'd partially lied to him. While he knew that more than likely he would be spending it with Antoine, Dutch had felt a reassurance that he knew Eli would not be checking on Antoine's schedule as Eli hated him enough as is. His mind then returned to the e-mail as he sighed and smiled. Dutch had never been told those words before, and here Antoine was. Dutch stood up and walked over to Antoine's desk as he quickly glanced over at Eli's desk which now sat empty. He shook his head and as he hopped up the steps walked over to where Antoine had just gotten off a call. He spotted Dutch looking at him and smiled.

Dutch said, "He wanted to do Pink on Friday."

Antoine asked him, "What did you tell him?"

Dutch ginned mischievously as he replied, "Not a chance."

Antoine then asked, "Did you want to spend the night at the hotel on Friday night? We can have breakfast and you're only steps away from work."

Dutch nodded and Antoine smiled even wider as he stood up and said, "I have a meeting with Natasha right now. Dinner later?"

Dutch leaned in and whispered, "Thank you for the e-mail."

Antoine thought for a moment then said, "You're the first person I've felt like this for in a long time. I'm just glad I finally was able to say them to someone who is more than worth it." Dutch blushed and as Antoine walked away he said, "I'll see you after my meeting." It was that moment Dutch couldn't help feel his heart skip little at the thought of Friday night with Antoine and without Eli.

Chapter Twenty-Eight

Saturday morning found Eli leaning against the escalator, still high from the night before as he peered through his sunglasses. When he arrived at the entrance of Go Credit he swiped his badge, the small light changing color on the swipe pad, an indication that he could enter, as he pulled the door open.

The office seemed very different as what was normally lit up was now darkened. He pulled himself through the double doors and looked around to see who was all in the office. The last time he worked on a weekend was forever ago, but this weekend he had decided to come in to tie up some loose ends. As he sat down, he glanced to see Daniel, Stewart, and two other reps.

Daniel looked over and asked "Hey dude, what's with the shades?" Eli was silent as he turned on his computer and began opening the applications to start his shift.

Stewart noticed him and advised, "Eli, Dutch is at his desk if you need to see him."

Eli sourly shot back, "Thanks fucker" as he then stood up and walked over to Dutch's desk.

Dutch had just finished a phone call as he looked up and quickly smiled as he removed his ear piece. Dutch teased, "Wow, you sure you really should be in this early?"

Eli asked, "Night out with Antoine?"

Dutch asked, "What?"

Eli shook his head, removed his sunglasses and said, "Fuck you Dutch."

He walked back to his desk as Dutch breathed, "Fucking Christ Eli."

When Eli sat back down he started to sort through his e-mails when he noticed that Daniel abruptly stood up to fish for his cell phone that was vibrating in his pocket. When Daniel snickered to himself Stewart asked, "Who is it?"

Eli then shot out at him, "Mind your fucking business Bert."

Daniel replied, "It's just Ariel. She's been having a real rough go of things."

Stewart said, "Don't tell me…"

Daniel replied, "Nah dude. She flirts with me, so I flirt back."

Eli said, "For someone who's still a virgin Daniel, you sure haven't aimed very high."

Daniel shrugged as he picked up the next call. Stewart glared at Eli, Eli not paying any attention.

A couple of hours passed by as Daniel again stood up and quickly walked over to the washroom. Eli looked over, watched him walk away, and then glanced over at Stewart. Eli then pressed the button to show he was in post-call work, glanced once more at Stewart then followed Daniel towards the washroom. After spotting Dutch on the phone with a customer he gently pushed open the door and walked in, finding Daniel standing at a urinal. Eli walked in and to the sink and looked over at Daniel as he turned on the water. Daniel's eyes were still fixed on the tiles in front of him as he said, "Thanks dude. Nothing like a leaky faucet to help get it flowing."

Eli couldn't help but notice the length and thickness of Daniel's penis as Eli then said, "And you still have your v card with that?"

Daniel chuckled as he began to quickly give it a shake and pulled up his underwear and cargos. Daniel then walked over to the sink as Eli walked up and let his hand reach over to the zipper on Daniel's pants. Daniel froze as Eli then pulled it down and then began to reach in.

Daniel swallowed and said, "Dude, you know I…"

Eli intercepted, "There's only one way to find out."

He then reasoned, "It will be just the two of us, in the back stall. I won't breathe a word of this to anyone, especially Stewart." He then started to reach in as he breathed, "It's a shame this hasn't been put to use Daniel." He then reached down and added, "It would be an honor to be the first." Daniel then straightened up as Eli removed his hand from inside Daniel's cargos and motioned him to follow.

The stall was all too familiar to Eli as Daniel walked in and closed the door behind him. Eli began to undo Daniel's belt and open his pants while he dropped to his knees. By this point Daniel's penis had considerably stiffened as Eli slowly engulfed the head, letting his tongue push the skin back while Daniel shuddered with every flick of his tongue as Eli's mouth continued to push further down on Daniel's erection. Daniel moaned as Eli slowly pulled back, then began again while his hands guided Daniel back in from behind. "That's it dude" Daniel sighed as Eli continued to work on his erection. Daniel continued to twitch and moan as he thrust into Eli's mouth.

Eli wasn't sure if it was the sound of either the door opening, or the footsteps that cautiously approached out side the stall. He moved Daniel over as his cargos fell around to his ankles while Daniel leaned back against the wall. Eli continued his sucking rhythm while out of the corner of his eye he spotted a pair of shoes that stood silently outside the stall door. Eli made sure whoever it was had a clear view through the gaps between the door and wall when Daniel grunted, "Dude, I'm so close" as Eli moved quicker and sucked harder.

Daniel suddenly shook as he groaned out, "Dude…" as Eli could feel him pulse into his mouth. Eli held there as Daniel's orgasm finally weakened. He released Daniel from his mouth and stood up, as Daniel breathed, "Haven't pulled the goalie in awhile." It was that moment that the feet on the other side disappeared and the footsteps hurried, the entrance door slamming open as Eli said, "I'll let you clean up."

When Eli stepped out of the stall, he proceeded to the sink and splashed some water on his face as he sighed and he readjusted himself. When he arrived back in customer service, he noticed that both Stewart and Daniel's desks were empty. He turned to Dutch who had just abandoned his own desk. Eli asked, "Where's Daniel?"

Dutch replied, "Had a family emergency. Mom fainted at bingo."

Eli mumbled, "Figures…"

Dutch then asked, "Where did Stewart take off to?"

Eli mischievously grinned as Dutch's expression changed from concerned to disbelief. "You fucking didn't…"

Eli then said while logging out of his phone and positioning the bag strap over his shoulder, "I'm done for the day Dutchie. I'll see you on Monday morning."

Love's sweet exile - Disc 57: sixty-seven minutes, fourteen seconds

He pressed play on the CD player, then repeat as he opened the top drawer of his desk, fumbling for the cloth in the drawer as he opened a smaller box with his pipe and a small bag of crystal. The guitars began to pluck at the silence while Dutch opened the bag and deposited a small amount into the bottom of the pipe.

As he watched the shards disappear at the bottom of the pipe, he quickly pressed his lips against the end and upon the formation of smoke began to suck back on it. He watched the smoke effortlessly travel up the glass pipe and felt it enter him. Once he'd felt the glass start to burn his lips he pulled the pipe back and exhaled, a small plume of smoke escaping from him. He leaned back and started to stare at the ceiling, feeling nothing. He then set up the minidisc recorder and microphone, shortly after lighting the bottom of the pipe again and sucking back for a shorter period of time.

For some reason Johnny Cash stood out to him as when he arrived home in a drunken mess he just ran his fingers through Aimee's CD collection and randomly stopped at Mr. Cash. It was *American Recordings Volume Four: The Man Comes Around*. He quickly glanced through the tracklisting and promptly retreated to his room, closing the door and getting out of his work clothes.

He began, "So Eli finally did it. He's finally gotten under Stewart's skin by giving that knobhead Daniel a blowjob." He looked at the picture of him and Eli then went back to focusing on the microphone. "Its funny be because Eli would never admit to having any sort of attraction to Daniel because Daniel lives with his mother, who in a socially acceptable way is a drug addict…" He trailed off and then began again while the pipe was cool enough for him to fidget with in his hands. "…And has too many health problems to consider."

"But even Stewart himself tried to swear up and down that he never had any interest in Daniel. And I mean really, why would he. Daniel is someone who will remain in the closet until he's in his forties. But Eli's persistence, as will all things, has become the point of aggravation for Stewart because deep down Stewart and Eli both know that Stewart likes Daniel. Of course no one is vocal about this except Eli, who gossips like a little bitch on the customer service floor and blows it way out of proportion. Then Stewart has nothing to defend himself…"

Silence ensued for a few seconds. Then Dutch began again, with a tone angrier than previously.

"Everyone also knows that in the interim Eli feels fucking threatened by Stewart. It's because Stewart is immediately likeable and doesn't have to intimidate anyone into liking him. And even if Daniel is completely straight after that blowjob, it wont matter because the illusion's been shattered and Eli has set off a chain reaction that has changed everything forever."

"It's fucking times like this I hate Eli, because now he's made two more enemies in the office. One because he's no longer clearly marked as straight, the other because Eli's been riding his ass non-stop this whole time. If the battle lines weren't drawn clearly before, they definitely are now."

"Fucking Eli needs to give his fucking head a shake because soon, very soon his world is going to unravel, and it won't be a pleasant experience. He won't be able to come crawling back to me for friendship. It's not that he would anyhow. Since we've been friends he's only done it once and months later he admitted he was forced to..."

Dutch fell silent for a few moments and then began again, the voice of longing starting to resonate from within. "Eli will never seem to understand the value of real affection and real love because the only person he seems to care about is himself. And even then...I think he fucking hates himself more than he hates the rest of us. But the person he's been damaging the most right now is me. The one real person who's ever been a friend to him. The only person who's ever loved him."

He paused right there, listened to Mr. Cash haunt him some more, then as if a light had gone off in his head, sighed as he put the lighter under the pipe and watched while the shards melted into smoke. Dutch inhaled again as this time he took the hot bulb of the pipe and after mumbling something incoherent began to let the glass burn his skin. He winced and sucked in his breath as he heated up the glass again and after pressed t back into the forearm just above his wrist. The second time hurt that much more as he made minor grunts of pain. The more he continued to blister his skin, the more noise he'd make. He was relieved Aimee had been gone out for the evening.

Chapter Twenty-Nine

Dutch didn't walk over to the men's washroom that following Monday morning. He walked into the office, adorning a black short sleeved shirt and tie to match his Dockers khakis. When he was greeted at reception Dawn beamed, "Top of the morning to ya…" and suddenly her smile vanished as soon as she spotted the huge blister on his forearm, in addition to his tiredness. Dutch faintly smiled and his eyes shifted forward towards the floor, through customer service and towards Elite where Marie was sifting through a stack of papers.

Dutch pulled his chair back and noticed a steaming coffee beside his computer. He smiled and said nothing as Marie looked over and smiled, "Well good morning there sunshine."

She then turned around and when she spotted Dutch's right arm she made a face of disgust and said, "What the fuck happened to your arm Dutch?"

Dutch asked, "Doesn't look like a cross?"

Marie replied, "It does but it looks like you were branded. Have you put anything on this so it doesn't get infected?"

"It's fine Marie trust me."

"No Dutch that does not look fine to me…"

"Don't push the issue Marie…"

"Dutch, Marie…can I see you both in my office please?"

They both looked over and saw both Lance and Natasha. Lance had a file in his hand and both looked quite concerned as Dutch and Marie followed them into the office. When everyone sat down, Lance began to explain while Marie closed the door, "Dutch, how well do you know Stewart?"

Dutch asked, "The new representative in customer service?" Lance nodded and Dutch explained, "He's a nice enough guy, really outgoing. Really friendly." No one said anything as he then explained, "At least that's what I hear from everyone on the floor."

Natasha then asked, "Did he talk to you about anything that might be causing him any stress?" Dutch was silent as then he realized that suddenly all eyes were on him.

"No, not to my knowledge."

Natasha then asked, "Dutch, does Stewart get along with Eli at all? Did you notice anything out of the ordinary between the two?"

Dutch glanced over at Marie and shook his head no as Lance began, "Not from what I've seen."

Natasha interjected, "Dutch, I need you be completely honest with me. Is there any conflict going on between Eli and anyone on the customer service team?"

Dutch shook his head again as Lance explained, "Dutch, we're in prime position to become a major credit player across North America. We're looking to open new offices. New offices as well as partner with a major U.S. bank." Lance continued, "I want Go Credit to be a healthy work environment."

Natasha chimed in, "Dutch, I respect that some of my employees are excellent performers, but let me remind you that means nothing, and I mean NOTHING, when some of those employees are poisoning my work environment." Natasha sighed and asked, "What's with the bruise on your arm?"

He breathed in and bit his lip. Marie piped in, "Dutch had a horrific tattoo experience yesterday. He's been under the weather the past few hours."

Lance scanned over Dutch's arm and said, "You need to get that checked. That doesn't look healthy."

Dutch stood up and left as Marie followed him out. Halfway down the hall she asked, "When are you going to stop defending him Dutch?" He turned around and she said, "Dutch, Stewart called in sick today. Everyone is speculating and some people know what's going on."

Dutch argued, "Let them speculate Marie. There's nothing left for me to tell." Marie pointed out, "Dutch I know you love him."

He froze as she said, "I know why you protect him and it needs to stop because it's slowly killing you, and everyone can see it." He appeared shaken by her revelation, partially because he knew deep down she was right.

He continued his silence for a long moment and then said, "I'm going to start work on Regenesis."

When he got to his desk he sat down and when he opened his e-mail he scanned the inbox. The first message was from Eli. In caps he read, THE BITCH KNOWS NOTHING.

Dutch grunted as he sighed and began to work on his e-mails. When Antoine appeared beside his cubicle he asked, "How are you feeling? I haven't heard from you since Saturday."

Dutch sighed, "I'm pretty exhausted. How are you?"

Antoine shrugged, "I've been worried about you."

Dutch looked down at the floor and back into Antoine's eyes. "I heard about what happened on Saturday morning with Eli and Daniel, and..." Antoine then breathed, "I may have to cut my stay short here in Edmonton. There's an opening for intern supervisor in Montreal as they're just about done moving the offices from Langelier to Centre-Ville."

Dutch reasoned, "You'll be closer to the Village and all of those cute French boys downtown."

Antoine blushed, "You know that doesn't catch me." He then asked, "You got a minute?"

He turned to Marie who just reappeared as she said, "Dutch, Regenesis can wait" and shooed them away.

They left the office and headed into the mall and down the escalator as Antoine explained, "The company's really pushing for me to come back as soon as everything is done here so they can get me started."

Dutch looked at him, "Don't let me stop you." Antoine glared at him as Dutch said, "I'm sorry I didn't mean ..."

Antoine then forced his hand over Dutch's mouth and held it there as Antoine said, "Dutch.I.Want.You.To.Transfer.To.Montreal.With.Me."

Ten seconds elapsed as Antoine asked, "Can I remove my hand now?" Dutch only nodded as he continued, "I love you and I want you to have a clean start. I want you to see more than what you see in life right now."

Dutch stammered out a, "W-wow, I don't know what to say about that."

Antoine pleaded, "Just say you will Dutch." They stood on the pedway over 101ˢᵗ Street as he continued, "I want to have a future with you. And I think if we're to have any shot at this, maybe we need to be in Montreal. Somewhere other than here…"

Dutch sighed as it began to all process and make sense. The thought of leaving Edmonton and Eli behind was terrifying. But at the same time he knew that eventually he would visit those crossroads, and that a thrilling proposition would be waiting for him. Maybe Marie was right, maybe he needed to stop protecting Eli. Then suddenly he realized the greater significance and began to smile. This realization also made Antoine smile.

"Is that a yes?"

Dutch replied, "Let me give it some thought. Just whatever you do…" He looked around and then said, "Not a word to anyone."

Antoine nodded with a smile as Dutch said, "Let's discuss it over the next couple of days."

"Deal."

When they got back into the office Antoine said, "I'll call you later." Dutch nodded as he looked forward and saw Eli standing at his cubicle wall, a look of disappointment on his face.

He said as soon as Dutch sat down, "You missed breakfast this morning."

Dutch shrugged as he said, "I'm not hungry."

Eli deadpanned, "Yeah, you definitely don't look it. And what the fuck happened to your arm?"

He grabbed Dutch's arm as Dutch howled, "Fuck Eli that fucking hurts!" Eli glared at his arm then glared at him.

He then said, "When did you become a fucking martyr?" Eli let go as he snidely commented, "You found a roommate for your apartment?"

"Aimee's moved in as of last week."

"Great, just what you need. The fucking dyke..."

"Eli if you have a better plan then share it right now or shut the fuck up."

Eli huffed and said, "See you at the end of your shift."

Dutch then said, "Don't fucking bother" as he stormed off and Marie returned back to the cubicle.

She asked, "What was that all about?"

Dutch sighed, "Eli being Eli..." Marie sat down and handed him a small stack of forms.

"What's this?" he asked.

Marie advised, "These are the transfer forms for when you're ready to go to Montreal."

Dutch asked, "Were you in on this as well?"

She leaned in and said, "Dutch, you're one of my top Elite members and they'll need a strong rep out in Montreal."

"How many fucking people know about this?" Dutch panicked, "No one can know about this, especially..."

"Eli" Marie finished. "It's really that much of a deal to you?" Dutch nodded as she said, "I'll keep it mum."

He replied, "Thanks" as he shoved them underneath a pile of papers.

When Eli made it back to his desk he could feel a burst of anger and confusion as he'd felt that Dutch had completely written him off. What was more disturbing was the badly done and blistered mark on his arm. He'd never seen those kind of marks on Dutch before, even before the overdose at the club. When he sat down he looked over and spotted Ariel, head in hand while poring over the text messages on her cell phone.

He said, "You know you're not supposed to have your cell on the floor right?"

She said, "I'm sorry Eli but it's just...I'm waiting for a text message from Jeremiah." He said nothing as she continued, "I talked to a psychic on the phone last night and she explained to me that Jeremiah was going to come back and we'd get back together."

He asked, "And how much did you get ripped off for that?"

She quietly replied, "It came to about two hundred dollars."

"You're fucking kidding me right?"

She shrugged, "It's all I got left right now. It's a hope I'm hanging on to."

Eli then half-sneered, "What about Daniel?"

"Daniel and I were supposed to have hung out night last night but he didn't show or call."

"So Ariel, what you're telling me is you're willing to trade one certified fuck-up for another. Am I hearing this correctly?"

"Daniel's not that bad. He just misses things cause of his mother."

"Who likes to keep her little boy on a short leash, cause he's mommy's little boy."

"Christ Eli you know nothing."

"I know a hell of a lot more than you'll ever know. And fucking get over Jeremiah already. He's not coming back."

Ariel began to water up as she took a Kleenex and started to pat her eyes. This was the routine with her over the past few weeks. Her bombardment with her epic novel e-mails got to the point where Eli would just instantly delete them because they absorbed so much time and sucked the life out of him. It didn't seem to matter though as Ariel had continuously rehashed the contents that became an uncontrollable diarrhea that sprayed in any willing person's distance. And Eli had definitely had enough by this point.

The quick tears had only worsened as she quickly stood up and stormed to the washroom, sobs trailing behind her. Eli only let out a half smile as Daniel was almost run over by Ariel's quick movements to the washroom. He then looked down at Eli and cautiously approached him as Eli began to sift through his messages. When he arrived he said, "Hey dude" as Eli looked up and nodded. Daniel then explained, "I need to talk to you off of the floor for a second if you don't mind."

Eli asked, "About what?"

Daniel explained, "You know…Saturday."

Eli's facial expression signaled that of understanding as he said, "Follow me."

Eli let him into a smaller conference room where he closed the glass door. Daniel began to sweat as he explained, "Look dude…what happened between us, the knob polish was okay, but I'm not down like that."

Eli then teased, "Funny that wasn't the expression on your face the other day."

Daniel cut him off, "Dude don't fucking even start with that. You wanted suck me off and I let you, okay? Now a friendship's been fucked because of it and I've given my v-card to a friend turned douche all for the sake of a blowjob." Daniel raised his voice and continued, "Dude I never used to think you were as shallow and empty as everyone said…"

He sucked in his breath as Eli shot back, "The pot smoke finally de-clouded from your brain eh?"

Daniel said, "Dude…" and walked right by him as Eli was silent and watched him leave. He then walked back to the floor as he watched Daniel escape back to his workstation. He briefly glanced back at Stewart's desk, only to see it was still empty, then focused back on his e-mails.

Chapter Thirty

Eli checked his cell phone as he walked up the remaining escalator steps and into customer service. It had been a week since Eli had last sent a text message to Samuel, and he was beginning to worry about what was going on with him. It was not like Samuel to not respond. He reasoned that Samuel and Keith had probably been faking the couple thing in Calgary, but Samuel should have been back by this time. It was beginning to wear on Eli as again he sent yet another text message while walking through customer service.

When he opened the lounge door he spotted Antoine on his cell phone. Eli placed his lunch in the fridge as he heard, "Are you sure?" A few moments of silence later and Antoine said, "I'll get it done right away. There has to be one downtown I can go to." Eli's ears perked up a little as he then heard, "I'm sure I have nothing to worry about. But I just want to be one-hundred percent." Eli then heard, "I'm sure it's nothing." He then heard, "I'll talk to you later. I'll call when I find out." And with that Antoine hung up his cell.
He then turned to Antoine and asked, "Is everything okay?"
Antoine spat back, "That's none of your fucking business pal."
Antoine stood up and was ready to leave when Eli said, "Antoine…"
Antoine looked at him, "What?"
"I know you and I got off to a rocky start…"
"And?"

Eli grew quiet as Antoine continued, Eli this is not Los Angeles and you're not living in an Bret Easton Ellis novel."

As he opened the door back out into customer service when Eli said, "Hey Antoine…" Antoine glared at him and Eli said, "Don't you wish you were dead like me?"

Antoine left the room as Eli walked back into customer service, down the steps and back towards his desk. He sighed as he pulled a vile out of his pocket, thought for a moment then mumbled, "Maybe later."

He then walked to the main hallway as he noticed Natasha's door closed and Lance standing outside talking to Samuel. He smiled and he began to approach them as Samuel then spotted Eli and began to leave, Eli following him.

"Samuel…Samuel!" Eli shouted as Samuel suddenly turned around and knocked Eli to the ground.

"Fuck you Eli!!" Samuel screamed in an angry posture.

Eli quickly propped himself back up and said, "What the fuck Samuel?!"

By this time a small crowd began to form outside the office that consisted of Dutch, Antoine, Lance and a few other co-workers. Samuel screamed at Eli, "What the fuck is wrong with you Eli?!" Before he could say anything Samuel continued, "I used to think you were better than Keith. And you've fucked all of that to hell in a handbasket!!"

More people began to appear from the office as Eli said, "I'm not like that Samuel, I swear to God…"

"You fucking raped a kid on K at the fucking bathhouse Eli!"

It was at that moment that Eli couldn't say anything. Eli had the words, the right phrases he wanted to say to Samuel at that point. His mouth opened, but nothing came out. It was as if Samuel had completely taken that away from him. All Eli wanted to do was prove him wrong, to cover his tracks. But Samuel's lone sentence sucked all of the words out of him. Eli was at a loss as Samuel explicitly said, "You are nothing but a fucking…selfish…empty…faggot Eli. I never, NEVER WANT TO SEE YOU AGAIN!!"

"Samuel, I…"

"Fuck you Eli we're done!"

Samuel quickly stormed off as Eli stood there, completely in shock. He played the last three minutes over and over in his mind as everyone dispersed back into the office. After a few moments his temperature rose as he started to seethe with rage. He inhaled deeply as he slowly turned around and walked back into the office. He looked to his right and saw Lance and Antoine in conversation. He then picked up his bag at his desk as Marie asked him, "Where are you going Eli?" He was quiet as he stormed out of the office, and towards the mall.

The last words from Samuel resonated in his head, repeating over and over while he cut a path through the mall. He tuned the world out as his eyes focused forward on the double doors that led into the parkade. Once at his vehicle, he threw his bag onto the backseat. He slammed the door once inside and leaned back against the seat. After a few minutes he pulled the vile of cocaine out of his suit jacket pocket, opened it and placed it in his nostril, inhaled, and then wiped his nose. Samuel's lone public confession seemed to amplify as the cocaine started to work through him. In the back of his mind it echoed while Eli closed his eyes, his entire face scrunching together as he wanted it to stop. When he opened the eyes he glanced around, then started the car.

It was at that point he knew.

Chapter Thirty-one

It had almost been a week since the washroom incident. The air of tension that hovered over customer service began to thicken. Stewart had been missing for a few days while Daniel had decided to stay put in his own department. Dutch's arrival on Monday with his newly etched tattoo on his forearm had begun a circulation of rumors and conversations on the floor. Dutch by this point had stopped caring about who said what and focused more on the crossroads he was at.

He'd woken up early the particular morning that he watched Stewart dissolve on the floor. His first instinct was to rejoin Eli for breakfast, however it was Stewart's very public breakdown that made him reconsider and once again pore over the transfer forms that have been set aside for him.

Montreal was a huge jump for him. While he had nothing really holding him down in Edmonton, he knew if he'd said anything to anyone it would bring a long string of pleads to stay. For the first time he had really begun to take into consideration the gut feeling that Eli might try to sabotage his decision. While any other circumstances may have prompted him to announce it to everyone, these were no ordinary circumstances. Over the past few years after high school, with his parents still hurtling money at him, he'd saved enough money that when he went to Montreal he could look at maybe purchasing a condo, maybe even enroll in classes there. Inadvertently Antoine had unlocked a door that Dutch thought could never be opened by anyone else. And while deep down inside he knew his relationship with Eli was unraveling, he was now thinking on the new beginnings that this new relationship with Antoine had sewn together.

His concentration was broken by a light tap on the shoulder. When he turned around he saw Antoine grin and whisper, "Just sign on the dotted line."

Dutch chuckled and said, "It's not that easy Antoine. Montreal is a big step."

Antoine reasoned, "Fair enough. Did you want to go out and have coffee tonight?"

Dutch mischievously grinned, "Only coffee?"

Antoine blushed, "The rest is up to you."

Dutch looked at the computer, to his watch. "You know work owes me half a day off. We could go right now."

They both looked over at Marie as she looked up at both of them. She asked, "Where are you two going?"

Dutch explained, "I think it was time I took him to Bliss."

"I'll sign off on one condition then." Dutch looked confused as she said, "Bring me back some cheesecake."

Dutch and Antoine looked at each other as Antoine asked, "You're on the late shift tonight?"

Marie nodded and explained, "You need to literally pry him out of the office Antoine." She then glared at him, "This boy has only been sick once..." She then teased, "He never takes holidays, he's always here."

Dutch advised, "I'll take this as a yes then."

She grinned as Antoine smiled and said, "I promise to bring him back in one piece." Dutch then put on his jacket as they both began to walk out of the call centre.

Antoine asked, "Where are you taking me again?"

"Its a little café called Bliss on the end of Jasper Avenue just before 124th. It's this little gay café that's been around forever. It used to be a hole in the wall, until this partnership bought it and made some massive changes."

"Do you go there often?"

"Not often. I really like the place. I just..." When they reached the hotel lobby Dutch flagged down a cab. "Its just I've been so joined at the hip with Eli that I haven't really gone anywhere else."

Antoine added, "Let me guess if Eli doesn't go you don't." Dutch remained silent as Antoine said to the driver, "Bliss Café?"

Dutch nodded as he finally admitted, "It's a habit that I'm trying to get out of."

Antoine said, "Understood." The cab went down 102nd Avenue as Dutch pointed out some of the odd homes that gracefully positioned themselves on each side of the canopy of trees. Antoine was amazed at the sheer beauty that they passed through. Finally the trees opened up and the cab turned left. Antoine gazed around as to his left was the video store and a neglected Dairy Queen. To the right sat Bliss.

Antoine tipped the driver and they both got out. Bliss' front window invited them both in as Dutch opened the door, ushering Antoine inside. Antoine's jaw dropped as he scanned the entire café. To the right was the counter and bakery display case where the barista was furiously working. To the left sat a wide open seating area. Dutch explained, "Usually they have a DJ on Friday night and then live music on Saturday night."

Just as Antoine was about to comment they both heard, "Lad! Where you been at?"

They both looked over and saw a figure walk up and hug them both as Dutch said, "Hey Ryan."

In a thick English accent Ryan asked, "Where's Eli?"

Dutch shrugged and smiled, "Not too sure. Where's your bloke?"

Ryan grinned, "The guvnor's out doing the beans run."

Dutch then snapped out of his trance and explained, "Ryan, this is Antoine. Antoine is one of my supervisors from work out from Montreal."

Ryan shook his hand as Antoine said, "Pleased to meet you."

Dutch then said, "Ryan is the part owner of Bliss."

Antoine said, "Very nice. It's a beautiful place."

Ryan suggested, "Let me get you lads two coffees on the house." He then pointed them to a table and said, "Help yourselves. Be right out…"

They sat at a table on the makeshift stage. As Antoine sat down Dutch asked, "Has Daniel been at work as of late?"

Antoine shook his head no and replied, "I've only seen him in one day this week. He's called in sick every other day. I've checked his attendance records and he's missed a lot of work."

"That's not surprising in the least." Dutch sighed as he blurted out, "Stewart caught Eli giving Daniel a blowjob in the men's washroom on Saturday."

"You've gotta be fucking kidding me." Antoine then asked, "Is that why…" Dutch silently nodded as Antoine shook his head.

Dutch explained, "Stewart had wanted Daniel for a long time. And Daniel said he was…"

"Straight?" Antoine added as Dutch took a sip on his coffee and nodded in agreement. Antoine asked, "What's the whole point to that?"

Dutch somberly replied, "It's because Eli takes what he wants. He did it just to fuck with Stewart's head."

As Antoine fidgeted with his coffee cup Dutch asked, "Do you think Richey is dead? Or do you think he's still alive?"

Antoine stopped then asked, 'What do you think?"

Dutch surmised, "I think Richey is still alive and well. Maybe he's in a small tour bus traveling across the States with Kurt Cobain, Elvis, and Layne Stanley."

Antoine laughed as he then teased, "Let me guess Lennon's driving the bus." They both chuckled and noticing Dutch's facial expression Antoine asked, "What?"

Dutch then replied, "Maybe he did because he knew *The Holy Bible* was the best work they'd ever achieved. Maybe it took his disappearance to forever solidify them in British rock history."

"Maybe" Antoine began to theorize, "He'd had enough of everything and everyone because he felt trapped. Pressure can do that to a person."

Dutch then added, "Maybe he did it out of love, to keep that last frame in his mind forever. To walk away before it all crumbled."

The door to the café opened as they saw Stewart walk in. Dutch felt a wave of tension waft through as Stewart looked up at Antoine and Dutch, then quickly turned his head.

Dutch told Antoine, "I'll be right back."

He stood up and walked over to Stewart as he said, "Hey Stewart are you okay?" Stewart shook his head and sighed, "I haven't eaten in a few days. I haven't slept very well either."

Dutch asked, "When are you coming back to work?" Stewart gazed up at Dutch as the tears began to well up in his eyes. "I don't know Dutch. It still hurts so bad…"

He didn't understand why but Dutch reached out and embraced Stewart tight. He said, "We're not all like him Stewart. Remember that."

After a few minutes Stewart pulled away and began to wipe his eyes. He said, "I'll be coming back to work soon. I just need some time to sort myself out."

Dutch offered, "When you come back we'll see if we can push your transition date to Elite."

Stewart replied, "Thanks Dutch. But he's not gonna stop. Eli is hell-bent on seeing me fail spectacularly." Stewart's eyes began to well up again as he said, "I am never going to be good enough for anyone, especially Daniel." Stewart then turned away and left as Dutch sucked in his breath and let out a sigh. When he walked back to the table he sat down and leaned his head against the wall while the overhead jazz was the only sound between Dutch and Antoine.

"Is he okay?" Antoine asked.

Dutch shook his head, "No. He's far from okay. He looked…dead."

Antoine rubbed his hand over his face, "I know I've asked this time and time again but it bears repeating. Why are you still friends with him?"

Dutch said, "I don't understand…"

"You know damn well what I'm talking about Dutch. You demonize Eli every second sentence but at the same time you condone his actions." Dutch was silent as Antoine continued, "You can't go crucifying yourself for him."

Dutch paused and replied, "I know." He then looked around and breathed, "It's just not that easy."

Antoine nodded and sighed, "I know Dutch." He rubbed Dutch's knee with one hand and repeated, "I know."

Before they left the café Dutch ensured to order a cheesecake. When Antoine looked over at Dutch in astonishment he said, "Some for you and me, some for Aimee later."

The sky had become a beautiful orange as they began to walk towards Dutch's building. Dutch asked, "Are you ever going to come out to your family?"

Antoine replied as they crossed Jasper Avenue, "I'm beginning to think I should. If you come to Montreal there's no sense in hiding you from the family anymore… is there?"

When they arrived at the entrance Antoine smiled, "Thanks for coffee. It was a lot of fun?" Dutch cocked his head to the side as he opened the door and asked, "Who said the day was over?"

Antoine replied, "I should get back to the office. Marie will be upset if I don't…"

Dutch leaned in and started to kiss Antoine as he pulled away and pleaded in a half whisper, "I don't want you to go."

Antoine bit his lip and Dutch explained, "Right now you're all I want to think about. You're the only one I want to be with." Antoine leaned in and they began to kiss again as Dutch then took his hand and guided him into the elevator.

Hours later he stirred awake to the sounds of Antoine moving around beside him. His eyes widened as he looked over at the alarm clock, then up to the ceiling. Antoine was fast asleep beside him, arm draped over his chest. A few more minutes passed and from under the door he could see a glow from out in the living room. As he slowly sat up he looked around as Antoine's hand slipped from Dutch's chest down to his crotch. Dutch smiled and silently chuckled as he slid out of bed and dug into the pile of clothes on the floor. When he found a pair of boxers he also grabbed a t-shirt and pulled them both on. He briefly glanced back and for a moment smiled, admiring Antoine's naked body intertwined with his bed sheets.

He closed the bedroom door behind him as he looked out into the living room. Aimee was seated at the end of the couch with remote in hand, sporting pajamas and her glasses as she looked up and explained, "Sorry if I woke you with the volume." She then looked at him in the one size too big underwear and shirt and said, "Those don't fit you kid."

Dutch stopped stretching and blushed as he then asked, "What are you still doing up?"

She adjusted her glasses and explained, "Was studying, but now I can't sleep. Think I drank one coffee too many…and you?"

Dutch shrugged as she then teased, "If I were in your position I wouldn't be sleeping either. I'd be busy letting Antoine fuck my brains out."

Dutch blushed again as he then sat down. "I'm glad you moved in."

"Dutchie I'm glad to be here too." She then put the remote down in frustration and said, "You know what's missing?"

As she escaped to the kitchen, Dutch flipped through the channels and said, "I don't know why I subscribe to cable. Erin's the only one who ever watched it anyhow." After finally settling on a channel, Dutch heard the beep of the microwave and Aimee returned shortly after with a bowl of fresh popcorn, a bag of cookies and a bag of chips. She sat them all down on the coffee table as he smiled and she ran away again. The second time she returned with a tub of chocolate ice cream and to bowls as Dutch started to laugh. She sweetly said, "Now when as the last time we did this?"

Dutch replied, "Fuck it was years ago." Dutch grabbed a cookie and dug it into the ice cream. Aimee explained, "I remember when we did this at the hotel when we came up here with mom and dad." Dutch made noises of approval as she said, "Fuck it's been forever."

Dutch said, "I remember we also pretty much did this every Saturday when we were home in Calgary."

She finished chewing and said, "I'm really surprised we didn't gain weight. We still look good."

Dutch reasoned, "Its genetics, the only good thing we got from our parents."

She laughed and as the junk food was slowly whittled down she said, "I miss those days." He weakly smiled as she asked, "So when does Antoine go back?"

Dutch explained, "He's supposed to be here for another four weeks, then off to Vancouver for two."

Dutch then trailed off, "Then back to Montreal…" He then pointed out, "He may have to go back in two though because they're doing a complete relocation of the call centre in Montreal. He's been offered an intern position." He grabbed a cookie from the bag and said, "It would be stupid for him to stay with that kind of offer. Regenesis can wait."

Aimee then pried the tub of ice cream from his hands and she asked, "So what happens when he goes back?" Dutch only shrugged as she began to eat the ice cream from the tub. He then reached over with a cookie and scooped some of the ice cream. She watched him as he started to ingest another cookie. She asked, "There's something you're not telling me."

He slowly ate the rest of the cookie as he said, "There's something I need to tell you. And I can't tell you how important it is to not repeat this to anyone…" She scooped some more ice cream into her mouth as he explained, "I've been made an offer to move out to Montreal." He was silent while she held the spoon in her mouth. Just when he thought it was safe he gulped, "Go Credit would pick up for the move."

Aimee was silent at first. She then said, "You little shit. Just as soon as I move in, you move out on me." She then sighed and asked, "What's stopping you?" Dutch then plucked the ice cream from her hands as she read it all over his face. "You didn't tell him did you?"

Dutch then said, "I don't understand Aimee. Here I have Antoine in front of me, who loves me more than I could ever imagine. Aside from the shit with mom and dad, everything's almost perfect. What's wrong with me?"

Aimee sat down right beside him and dug her spoon in and fed Dutch a scoop. She was silent again.

As he swallowed she said, "You need to let him go Dutch. Eli's drowning himself, and you're drowning with him…" He could feel a rush of tears streak down his face and she continued, "I love you Dutch and I've seen the damage he's done to you. It's been close to seven years, and I've only seen it tear you apart more and more as the years go by."

She continued, "I know it's the cross you've had to bear for the past seven years. But Dutch you can't bear that weight anymore. It's killing you. When I saw you mention Antoine for the first time…it was like there was a light in your eyes. I hadn't seen that light since…"

"Denny?" It was a name that he hadn't mumbled in a long time. The boy next door that had been Dutch's first love in suburban Calgary. It had taken him years to even mention the name, a name he was finally able to admit after all of this time.

Aimee continued, "When I see you and Antoine together…I know that it's real between you two."

"I really want to go Aimee. I'm just…"

Aimee grabbed Dutch's hand and interjected, "You can't follow him around forever Dutch. He's never going to love you."

Dutch nodded in agreement as Aimee asked, "Do you love Antoine?"

Dutch nodded as he then wiped his eyes. She scooped some ice cream out and fed it to him as he quickly caught it before it falling on his shirt. Aimee asked, "There's something I need to know Dutch all of these years…" He looked into her eyes and she asked, "Do you regret having sex with Denny?"

Dutch thought for a moment then shook his head. "It would have happened with someone else. I would have been gay, Denny or not."

He then glanced at all of the half eaten junk food as Aimee said, "I'll clean up. You go back to bed."

He stood up, kissed her on the forehead goodnight and said, "Please remember Aimee. Not a word to anyone." She nodded and Dutch made his way back to his bedroom, closing the door behind him.

Antoine was now lying flat on his back, the sheets now only covering his lower right leg as he stirred awake. Dutch pulled off the shirt as he then crawled back into bed. Antoine mumbled, "Are you okay?" His right hand reached over and caressed Dutch's cheek.

Dutch replied, "I couldn't sleep."

Antoine then propped himself up with his elbow. "Do you want to talk?" Dutch leaned in and kissed him while Antoine's hand slid into the underwear. Antoine smiled, "That's not your underwear you're wearing sir." Dutch snickered as Antoine pointed out, "You have chocolate ice cream on your chin."

Antoine then leaned in and started kissing him as Dutch then said, "You're so perfect Antoine."

He then breathed out, "I want to go back to Montreal with you."

Antoine breathed, "I love you Dutch. Don't ever forget that." Antoine's hand then pulled down Dutch's underwear as he positioned himself underneath Antoine. It was that moment that Dutch wished he could freeze forever.

Chapter Thirty-Two

Friday evening and customer service was quiet. As some lighting flickered overhead, Eli was leaned against the window that gazed out to downtown Edmonton. Both arms propped against the window, he was leaned in and glared out to the traffic below him. He watched as people streamed in ad out of the mall below, others trickling in and out of the Boardwalk building across from him. He inhaled deeply while his eyes continued to move between both visible ends of the street. His gaze then wandered upwards to the windows across from him. All of them were blackened by internal darkness, which left his focus back towards the street below.

He tried his hardest not to think of Stewart, not to think of the devastated expression that was swept across his face as he made the chilling discovery in the men's washroom. Eli tried to avoid thoughts of Arianne who broke down on the floor after finding out that Eli had sex with Landon, while high on ketamine. He definitely did not think about Daniel, who had only just returned back to work after their tryst in the washroom. Amongst everything that he neatly avoided, what he couldn't was the moment Samuel made him vulnerable in front of those people that had, apart from Dutch, never seen him embarrassed or hurt. Sometimes his gaze would only catch his expression whenever Samuel crossed his mind. That pained expression would sometimes change into hatred and anger, until he saw past the glass reflection and back out to the street.

Eli's thought pattern was suddenly broken by the vibration of his cell phone. He looked at the number and answered, "It's about fucking time you called." He stretched as he said, "Meet me inside of the department store in men's fragrances." He then asked, "Did you get the extra?" He then slowly walked down to the customer service as he said, "See you shortly." Eli then quickly glanced in customer service and walked out the main entrance and down the escalator. Soon the pastel grey and whites revealed gold and lighter shades of brown as he descended onto the second floor of the department store. It was always quiet in the evenings as the banker, government and corporate employees had deserted the towers for the quiet refuge of suburban Edmonton.

As he looked at the various fragrances, he felt a tap on his shoulder and he looked over to see Etienne standing there holding an envelope wearing a neglected jacket. Eli said, "You're looking more unfed than usual."

E grunted and explained, "Let's go for a walk. I got arrested here two years ago for lifting."

As Eli followed him into the mall he asked, "Did you get it?"

"I had her pull the file and everything checked out. He's not sick." Eli glared and stopped as E continued, "I had my girl doctor up a new report."

E handed him the envelope so that Eli could open and check it over. "White, clean, and neat."

He grinned as E yanked it from his hands. "Three hundred" he hissed and Eli then asked, "And what about the oxycontin?"

E produced a vile as Eli pulled out a stack of fifty dollar bills. "Anything else?" E asked.

Eli replied, pointing to the envelope into E's chest, "Not a fucking word of this to anyone, especially Dutch."

"That'll be another hundred."

"Fuck you."

"I dial the numbers right now and I poison your investment. Your choice."

Eli grunted and pulled out another hundred dollars and seethed, "Get out of my fucking sight E."

E pocketed the money as he said, "Pleasure doing business with you. Tell your boy to give me a call some time Eli" as Eli waved up his middle finger and snapped, "Tell him yourself you fucking crackhead."

When he reached the office he looked over to his right and saw that Ariel had disappeared. When she finally returned to her desk she sat down, looking visibly shaken as she remained silent. He then asked, "What's up your ass?"

She sighed in response, "You wouldn't care Eli."

"Try me."

"I'm pregnant. And I think its Jeremiah's."

Eli looked over at her as she stumbled on the next sentence. "I mean I haven't been with anyone since him."

Eli asked annoyed, "So what are you going to do about it?"

She explained, "I think I'm going to get an abortion."

He looked at his screen. "That's a good choice."

She said, "Really? I thought you'd pass…"

"It's good because either it would be stupid like its father, or suffering from fetal alcohol syndrome cause of its mother." Her sobs began as he spat out, "And I wouldn't worry about who he did at the bar a few weeks ago, but who he did behind your back, and trust me if he was any good he would know where to stick it."

She abruptly stood up and ran for the lounge as he chuckled to himself and opened the envelope, checking its contents again. He'd decided at that point that now would be as good a time as any for a quick snack as he walked into that men's washroom, leaving the unmarked envelope on Dutch's desk.

LOVE'S SWEET EXILE - DISC 58: SIX MINUTES, NINETEEN SECONDS

"I never thought I would make it to a crossroads…."

"For the first time since my exodus from Calgary I've been presented with an opportunity and a different direction. I thought there would be more and more chapters in this story that I would be forced to write. I always thought that the story of Eli and Dutch would have many more twists, and this cross would get heavier the further I went."

"I know that the hurt is crippling me inside out. The cracks are beginning to show. For every fissure I've tried to patch up, another appears. For the first time in seven years, I'm getting the chance to rewrite the ending. I have the chance to still turn this into one of the greatest love stories that could ever be told. Antoine appearing from stage left. I would never have expected him to come from out of nowhere the way that he has. And it in itself is amazing."

"All of the signs have been there. I finally had the chance to reevaluate them all the other night in bed with him as he was asleep. I then knew that he was the one I wanted to be with for the rest of my life, that everything before was just a test."

"After seven years, there will be a happy ending after all. I will have finally finished it. I finally have the chance to breathe…"

Chapter Thirty-Three

The more that Dutch thought of it, the more weight seemed to lift off his shoulders. That Monday morning as he made the first steps onto the escalator and up, he began to notice a warmth despite the fact that he'd been wide awake and twitchy the last forty eight hours. More and more where he thought the walls were closing in, he'd begun to see them torn down. His realization was becoming more apparent on the way to Go Credit. He realized soon he would transfer to Montreal, and he would start life again in another call centre office located in Centre-Ville Montreal. The village would only be blocks away, and Eli would only fade into random e-mails, longing for his return back to Edmonton.

He would attempt to lure him back to weekends of following him around in bathhouses and bars, watching on repeat his string of empty conquests, week after week disemboweling Stewart and shredding any self-esteem he had left. Dutch would smoke more crystal to mask the pain, continue the cycle of hurt, and still record the journal that would be endless and repetitive, the tragic tale of unrequited love that would eventually drive him to a fate embodied by Peter, an accelerated case of disco burnout.

Back to the continual disownment by his father and half-hearted attempts by his mother to keep the peace. The continual financial blackmail of what was the beautiful condo just west of downtown Edmonton. Back to years of regret that Dutch did not carve out his own identity, and finally rewrite the otherwise decided ending.

Eli would attempt to beckon him back via e-mail, and all Dutch would need to do was to simply hit delete.

The forms were signed on Friday morning and signed off on by both Marie and Natasha. Dutch decided after this Monday morning after the comedown that he would take a few days to pack and dry himself out, to finally work the meth out of his system. He'd thought of going back to the gym once relocated, and saving the party pharmaceuticals for special occasions decided by himself and Antoine. He would convince Aimee to spend spring breaks with him. The more and more his over stimulated brain thought about it, the more he was realizing this would be the last chapter he would ever have to write.

It was that thought that helped him mask the clear signs that he was coming down to Dawn in the reception area.

He smiled at Dawn as she said, "Antoine is in the office with Natasha right now."

Dutch was silent and she then pointed out, "And I'm supposed to tell you breakfast is served."

He winced as Dawn asked, "Do I need to kick Eli in the junk for you Dutch?"

Dutch replied, "About as much as he needs to kick his cocaine habit."

Dawn's jaw dropped as he swiped his badge and smiled, "See you later Dawn" and walked into customer service.

As he looked around he walked over to his desk Marie said, "Good morning Dutch."

Dutch grinned as he asked, "How are you?"

She nodded over to a brown envelope that was sitting between Dutch's screens. Dutch went to pick up the envelope when she said, "Don't open it yet."

She handed him a coffee as he asked, "Did you see Eli this morning?"

She shook her head no and said, "Have your coffee. We have a meeting closer to noon."

"Is Lance in the office today?"

"Lance is in a meeting this morning."

"I have to do something before I leave. It's really important I get this done."

"I'll leave you to do what you need to do. Make sure you see Natasha this morning."

She walked away as Dutch then started to focus on the computer. He typed in his login, and opened his e-mail and clicked on the folder that read Eli's Inbox. When the box opened there was close to over one thousand e-mails in there. As he clicked on Select All, he set it up that the entire inbox would be sent out to Lance and Natasha on Thursday. They were all of Eli's greatest hits, most of the venom directed at Stewart via e-mail. Dutch was ever so careful to ensure that they would be redirected to his own personal inbox and make sure to leave no trace of evidence behind so that Eli would ever suspect. Dutch never knew for sure, but always reasoned someday that he would need those e-mails. He decided this act alone would be the long awaited favor he felt he'd owed Stewart. Dutch would ensure that he would be long out of the call centre, and Edmonton for that matter.

Once completed he strolled back over to customer service where he noticed Eli's bag was seated on his chair. He then heard a, "Dutch!" from across the other end of the call center. It was Ariel, who had just finished a call and stood up while Dutch looked up and smiled.

She enthused, "You'll never guess what happened!" He was silent as she explained, "Jeremiah came back last night. He came to my door last night and apologized and said he was done thinking." He cracked a faint smile, "He explained he knew I was the right one and wanted us to start over again."

"Good for you Ariel. I'm glad you and Jeremiah sorted things out."

"How are you and Antoine doing?"

He teased, "My my, aren't you a little nosy…"

She blushed, "Blame it on Daniel. He talks about you two all the time." She then pointed out, "He's happy, you're happy."

"What about him?"

She scowled a little and sighed out, "I guess him and Celine in Elite have a thing now."

"But you got Jeremiah back."

She grinned, "True enough" and Dutch walked up the steps and into the lounge.

When he opened the door he saw Stewart sitting by the window staring out towards North Edmonton. Dutch went up to him and said, "Hey Stewart, it's good to have you back."

Stewart faintly smiled as he breathed, "Thank you."

Dutch asked, "Have you been doing all right?"

Stewart's eyes shifted around. "I've been seeing a therapist over the past couple of weeks I'm trying to figure myself out."

Dutch offered, "If you need anything…" Stewart nodded and after a sip of his coffee looked around and walked back out onto the customer service floor.

Dutch began to feel that something wasn't right on the floor. While the tension appeared to have been broken on the floor, something tugged at him. It seemed everything was in a delicate balance, ready to unravel at the slightest movement. Dutch asked Ariel, "Hey Ariel, where's Eli been?" She shrugged, and continued to focus back on the screen and as he walked by Eli's desk, he stopped Natasha who was just walking into the conference room.

Natasha asked, "Hey Dutch are you ready for the Regenesis meeting?"

Dutch nodded and asked, "You seen Eli?"

She shrugged as she replied, "I think he headed to the mall for coffee."

When he walked back to his desk, his discomfort was clearly evident as Marie asked, "Are you okay?"

Dutch sat down and said, "Something doesn't feel right Marie."

She asked, "What do you mean?"

He breathed, "He knows Marie. He knows I'm transferring out to Montreal. He's not going to…"

Marie cut him off. "Dutch" she calmly said, "We kept this on the down low. We told no one Dutch." He began to relax a little as she reassured him, "We really kept quiet on this one."

He looked at the envelope behind him and he asked, "For sure?"

Marie said, "Dutch, I care about you and there's no one right now that wants to see you and Antoine live happily ever after more than I do."

Dutch chuckled as he opened the envelope and slipped the papers out.

Whatever smile that remained on Dutch's face quickly vanished as he began to nervously shake. Marie asked, "What's wrong Dutch?"

Dutch's eyes began to well up as he tried to stand. He stammered, "I...I...th-think I'm going to be sick..." Marie watched as he started to weakly make his way to the aisle. Lance stepped out of his office as sweat began to pour down Dutch's face.

Marie pleaded, "Dutch, please tell me what's..." yanked the papers out of his hands and glanced them over.

She blurted, "Oh fuck" as he quickly rushed to the washroom.

He pushed open the door and ran to the stalls in the back where he barely made it into the stall. Dutch could feel his whole heart being yanked out of him as he threw up in the toilet. He started to sob while he continued vomiting,

Antoine rushed into the stall asking in a panic, "Dutch are you okay?" Do you need water or anything?" Antoine leaned in and started to rub Dutch's back while Dutch continued to be sick. Antoine said, "It's going to be okay Dutch."

Dutch said brokenly, "It's not going to be okay Antoine."

Antoine asked, "What?"

Dutch said, "Get off me Antoine..."

Antoine argued, "I'm not going anywhere Dutch, I..."

"Get the fuck off me!!"

Dutch propped himself up as he leaned into the stall. Dutch turned around and wiped his mouth as he asked, "When were you going to tell me?"

Antoine replied dumbstruck, "Dutch I don't..."

"When were you going to fucking tell me?!"

Antoine said, "What?! That fucking piece of paper in Marie's hand?! Dutch that's not even a cleared test result! It hasn't even been seen by me or signed by a fucking doctor!"

"Antoine this isn't the time to lie to me..."

"I'm not fucking lying to you!"

"I let you fuck me without a condom Antoine!!"

"I'm clean Dutch I swear!!" he screamed at Dutch as by this point Dutch had been able to feel the strength in his legs again. "You wanna know the test results Dutch?! I've got the test results and I'm clean! I'm negative!!" Antoine looked at the mirror, then back at Dutch. "What else have you heard?"

"That you aggressively tried to pursue and fuck every guy that worked in the Montreal office..."

Antoine's anger flared more, "I had one high profile fuck in customer service Dutch and most of the girls hate me because he was the one they couldn't have!"

Dutch was silent as Antoine spat out, "You know, everyone warned me about what I was getting into Dutch when I first met you. But I never expected this…"

"What?"

"You set me up to fucking fail this whole time!!"

It was as if the light bulb went off in Dutch's head as he realized what was happening between them. This was what Eli had planned all along. Dutch's facial expression suddenly changed as he pleaded, "No Antoine that's not true…" Dutch continued, "Please, I'm sorry I…"

Antoine said, "You know what?" Dutch said nothing as he continued, "Fuck it, I've been with a lot of guys Dutch. But what I can tell you, is I got tested because I love you. Because I didn't want to be with anyone else but you. Because out of everyone I've ever met this had been so different." Antoine then breathed in and said, "I can't believe I was set up to fail right from hello…"

"It's not true Antoine, I swear to God."

"Don't lie to me Dutch! You've been in love with Eli since day one!"

Dutch found this admission especially painful coming from Antoine's lips. He remained silent as Antoine continued, "I hope true love finally comes around." With those words Antoine rushed out of the washroom, slamming the door open as Dutch slammed his fist into the stall door. When the echo quickly dissipated he looked around as silence now wrapped around him. He wiped his nose after feeling something drip onto his lip. When he looked at his hands he saw where the blood painted his hand.

He glanced in the mirror and wiped his nose again as Eli appeared from out of nowhere. Eli cracked his neck and reasoned, "It was for the best Dutchie. He made his way through a hell of a lot of dick in Montreal."

"Fuck you Eli…"

"He was never good enough for you Dutchie you deserve better."

"Fuck…you…Eli…"

"Maybe it will teach you to not fuck without a condom…"

"FUCK YOU ELI!! FUCK YOU!!"

Dutch snatched Eli in one swift grab and pinned him to the mirror with such ferocity that not only did he hear the glass spider behind the weight of Eli's body, but he heard snaps and a loud crack from Eli's body. Eli's head had imprinted a cracked halo around him as he slid to the floor. Dutch watched in horror as blood trickled down Eli's forehead, Eli remained motionless as suddenly he began laughing. It was then he realized how much of a mistake he had just made. He wiped his eyes and ran for the door, Eli still laughing as he rubbed his forehead and carefully picked himself up.

Chapter Thirty-Four

It took a couple of fidgets of the key in the lock. Once he was able to open the door he violently pushed it open, dripping in sweat as he ran over to the bathroom and promptly threw up. Each spasm jerked his body as he could feel the remnants of previous meals and fluid gingerly mixed with stomach acid exhaled into the toilet, all over his shirt and onto the floor. He continued to shake as tears started to run down his face, mixing with the sweat and vomit. Within a few moments his erratic breathing started to calm itself down. Just when he thought he would be able to stand up again, the cycle repeated itself all over, crippling Dutch almost to the point that he would not be able to get up right away to project back into the toilet.

The last bout had become the worst as Dutch had nothing else to bring up except blood. He sobbed as dizziness took over. Blood dripped from the corner of his mouth as he pressed the lever down to flush the toilet, his head resting down on the seat as he continued to sob uncontrollably. His entire body hurt. The sobbing continued as he again tried to prop himself up, making it to the edge of the tub where he seated himself. With his head leaned against the bathroom wall he waited, arm pressed against his stomach. Dutch waited a few minutes then began to unbutton his shirt as he stood up, slowly removing the soiled garment and putting it in the bathtub.

It would take only a few minutes to complete he reasoned as he walked over to the fridge, carefully ensuring his dizziness wouldn't make him topple over. He opened the door and pulled out a bottle of vodka in addition to a bottle of coke. Shoving a pizza pretzel into his mouth he began to fix himself a drink and closed the fridge door. With one hand he took the bottles with him to his room while he carried his drink with the other.

Upon arriving in his room Dutch neatly placed the vodka with mix beside the monitor on his desk while he chewed on the pizza pretzel. Each chewed portion felt like sandpaper down his throat, but his stomach wholly embraced the food as slowly the emptiness coupled with dizziness from the bathroom slowly disappeared. By this time his sobbing was also under control as he finished off his drink and walked back to the bathroom. He viewed the mess that he left behind and began to clean it up while mentally piecing together what had just happened.

Once he finished cleaning the bathroom he quickly walked over to the door and pulled out his hastily forgotten keys, sniffling while he locked the door behind him. He then headed back to the bathroom to collect his glass, finally sitting back in the familiar chair at his computer desk. He pulled out the recorder and the pipe as he aimlessly searched around his room. He opened a small baggie as he pressed play on the CD player. The longing wail of a cello crescendoed out of the speakers as he filled the pipe with more crystal. The cello then took its place with the layering of a drum machine and the lone plunking of piano keys. Dutch began to cry all over again as he pressed record on the minidisc player, the words falling out of his mouth one by one in between sobs.

"I...can't...do...this...anymore..."
He sucked back the haze from the pipe, holding it even longer than he normally would, then exhaled in between coughs and crying. He then sobbed into the microphone,

"I can't...love you anymore."

He inhaled more smoke from the lit pipe and exhaled again as he sobbed harder. Finally over the music he screamed,

"WHY CAN'T YOU FUCKING LOVE ME?!!"

Dutch kept crying as he wiped his eyes with his arm, and emptiness beginning to emotionally gouge him as he sobbed, "I loved you so much. I fucking did EVERYHING FOR YOU..." He screamed, "So WHY CAN'T YOU LOVE ME?" He continued crying, filled the pipe again, and deeply inhaled once lit this time exhaling slower. He shoved what was left in the baggie into the pipe and against better judgment inhaled as deep as he could. He held it for thirty seconds slowly after and whatever was left in his lungs he exhaled. He then said, "I. Fucking. Hate. You. Eli. I. Will. Not. Do. This. Anymore." At that point the crying stopped and once again he punctuated, "This. Is. The. End." Dutch screamed out,

"I FUCKING HATE YOU! I HATE YOU ELI!! I HATE YOU!!"

Whether it was sheer will or hatred, Dutch's pipe became detached from his hand and made contact with the wall. He watched it shatter into pieces as he exhaled, his heart almost tearing out of his chest. He exhaled again then one by one took each photograph of him and Eli from the computer and tore them to shreds. He jittered as he then reached for the vodka and downed the remainder of the half full bottle in just under five gulps. It soothed his throat while he twitched in his chair. A few more minutes passed and finally Dutch removed the disk from the player and slipped it back into its proper case. He opened the drawer and placed it in the box where the others sat numbered, and filed.

Dutch shut down his computer and stored away the minidisc recorder after placing the bottles in the kitchen, the Coke returning to the fridge. He remembered his shirt was in the bathtub and quickly retrieved it, stuffing it promptly in the garbage. He vacuumed the bits of shattered glass on the carpet in his room, one piece in particular that he had picked up was still huge in comparison to the others. Dutch stared at it briefly before throwing it into the garbage on top of the shirt.

After showering and changing into a clean t-shirt and pants, he scanned the room once more. He then put his cell phone into the top desk drawer on top of the recorded minidiscs then carefully closed the drawer. He emptied his wallet and shredded the majority of his cards including his identification. After tossing the wallet on the bed he took whatever was left, looked at the bag of crystal between his fingers and pocketed it on the way out the door.

LOVE'S SWEET EXILE – DISC 47: nine minutes

"I promise you Eli, if you ever fuck with my life in the same way that you fuck with everyone else's, I guarantee you I will unleash hell on you and you will know that it would be the worst mistake you could ever have made."

chapter Thirty-Five

Eli called into work sick on Wednesday morning, citing flu-like symptoms. The manager on duty seemed all too happy to let him have the day off. As he lay back in his bed he checked his cell phone for any text messages from Dutch. Nothing had appeared as he tossed the phone over to the foot of the bed, then pulled on a pair of underwear and walked into the living room, turning on his laptop and the television. When he opened his e-mails, nothing appeared from work. He opened his e-mail and clicked onto Dutch's work address. He typed ARE YOU AT WORK? then hit the send button, then walked back to the bedroom. He returned after thirty seconds shaking the small vile of cocaine as he sat back down. The e-mail reply from Dutch was absent.

He then ran back to his room and plucked his phone from the bed. He scanned his text messages again. Still nothing. He then sent WHERE THE FUCK ARE YOU? to Dutch's cell phone and then opened the vile and inhaled. As he flipped through the channels he waited patiently for a response from Dutch. His patience however, deteriorated after three minutes. After no sign of life, Eli stood up and jumped into the shower as he stood under the rush of water, letting the cocaine start to work through his system.

Once dressed, he hopped into the car and began the drive towards Go Credit. On the way downtown Eli began to deconstruct Dutch's absence and checked his phone yet again. Despite the fact that Eli had just single-handedly turned Dutch into a single man again, it was still unlike him to not text, or e-mail. Usually whenever they had gotten into a disagreement as such Dutch would always message a couple of days later, if not the next day. The fight would be forgotten and life moved on. However even Eli understood this was not the usual spat they'd had. Dutch had managed to destroy a complete mirror in the men's washroom, which shocked Eli despite the knee-jerk reaction of laughter he had made.

When he pulled into the parkade he quickly walked into the mall and up the escalator when he spotted Samuel in the food court. His expression looked mildly pained as he and Keith ordered from the noodle box restaurant that he and Eli used to order from when they spent lunches together. Eli only stood there long enough to see Samuel quickly glance over in Eli's direction. He shot a deathly glare as Eli then turned around and headed towards the Shoppers Drug Mart, following the pedway to the west part of Edmonton City Centre. He saw Dawn at the tea house by the up escalator and quickly made his way over.

She looked over and faintly smiled as he said, "Hey Dawn."
She then asked, "Aren't you supposed to be sick today?"
He explained, "Personal day."
"Ahh"
"Did you see Dutch come in today?"
She shook her head no. "It looks like your little spat in the washroom was the cause for much conversation on the floor."

Eli said, "It's because everyone's fucking bored there and have nothing else to talk about." He then reasoned, "I'm going to try and talk to Antoine when I come into work next, get them to talk."
Dawn then explained as she plucked her tea from the counter, "I can promise you that won't ever happen. Antoine fucked back off to Montreal last night. He looked pretty heartbroken."
Eli bit his lip as he said, "Part of this is my fault. I need to help fix it."
Dawn sipped her tea. "You think?" She then looked around, "I have to go. Get better."

As she walked up the escalator and towards the office, he stayed put for a few minutes until he was sure that she was far enough that he could proceed up the escalator. He stopped by the salon and the receptionist said, "Chelsea's just in the back, she'll be right…" when she looked over at Chelsea who quickly stormed up to Eli.

"You fucking piece of shit how could you do that to him?"

Eli faked confusion. "I have no idea of what you're talking about."

She then pointed out to the mall. "Outside right fucking now."

They walked out to the parkade by the entrance to the hotel as Chelsea said, "What the fuck did you do that for Eli?"

Eli sneered, "What business is it of yours since you barely fucking work there."

She snapped back, "Dutch is my business Eli, especially because he's like family to not only me but mom and dad!"

Eli shrugged and she continued, "You need to leave Antoine alone Eli. He treats Dutch like gold unlike some other people."

Eli stood arms stretched and said, "So this is all about Eli being an absolute shitty friend to Dutch now is it? What difference does it make to you Chelsea?"

She asked, "Do I really have to explain it Eli?"

He exclaimed, "Yes, please do!"

She stood there for a moment and then asked, "Do you remember when we had to take Dutch to the hospital shortly after his eighteenth birthday?"

Eli said, "How can I forget that, the fucker doused his hair in laundry bleach so he could avoid having to pay for it being professionally done."

She said, "That's not the real reason Eli."

Eli stopped and grew silent. "What else?" he asked.

She then said as a few tears escaped down her cheek, "Eli, Dutch swallowed a cup of that bleach. Not only was he burning his scalp, but he was trying burn himself from the inside out."

Eli said, "So what the fuck does that have to do with me Chelsea?"

Chelsea swallowed, "Do you remember what you missed a few days before?"

Eli wouldn't admit it but he knew all too well what he had skipped out on that year. What was supposed to be a birthday dinner for Dutch and misadventure with his best friend had ended up with Eli not showing as he was busy having sex with the biology teachers assistant at school. Two days later Eli had promised Dutch he would take him out when he and

Chelsea discovered a panicked Erin, Dutch on the bathroom floor in the fetal position. A few days in the hospital had for the most part adjusted Dutch back to normalcy however Dutch had not mentioned the incident since. It would become another memory that Eli would not be required to confront.

Chelsea pointed out, "Eli, every time you fuck with Dutch's life, something like this happens. I honestly thought the bleach incident was just an accident. But the GHB overdose…now this…"

Eli argued, "Someone spiked his drink Chelsea, end of story."

She then asked, "Why hasn't he called or texted you Eli?" He froze and Chelsea continued, "He's been missing since Monday morning. It's not like him to just disappear."

Eli let out a deep sigh, "He's probably just fucked off to clear his head. I'm sure he'll be back at any point."

Chelsea walked up to him and said, "I really hope so for your sake Eli. Because unlike every other mess you've made, there will be no one around to clean this one up." Eli only grunted as she walked back into the mall. As he stood there surrounded by the cold grey and black of the concrete, he swore to himself that Dutch would reappear soon, and that it would only be a matter of time before he came around, and Chelsea would be wrong…

Chapter Thirty-Six

Eli received his second indication that something was wrong that Friday evening as he stumbled into his apartment, the ketamine sucking him down to the floor. He collapsed and made inaudible sounds which eventually turned into laughter as his cell phone began to vibrate and chime. The first two attempts he was unable to reach for it. Finally on attempt three he fished it out of his pocket and hit talk. "Helllo….." he slowly said as a female voice snapped, "Eli, what the fuck is wrong with you? What's going on over there?"

Eli could only giggle as he slowly tried to stammer out the words, "I've f-f-fallen in a K hole and I c-can't get up."

The voice on the other end barked, "Eli where the fuck is Dutch?" Eli only snickered as she continued, "What the fuck is wrong with you?!"

He slowly explained, "Dutch is at home. Probably packing his bags and f-fucking off to Montreal."

Eli started to laugh as the voice on the other end sighed and asked, "Eli…do you even know who this fucking is?"

Suddenly all of Eli's vertigo disappeared and the floating incoherency stopped. It was as if pieces of his mind locked together and the world which was spinning had ground to a halt.

What once was clouded suddenly snapped clear into focus as Eli took a deep breath and asked, "Aimee what do you mean?"

Her voice quivered as she began to explain, "Eli, Dutch has been gone for four days. All his shit is still here."

Eli sat up and reasoned, "Maybe he's drying himself out at a bathhouse or something. He can't really be that far away.

Aimee argued, "Eli, he's always left me a message letting me know where he's gone."

He stretched and said, "All right Aimee, I'll go snoop around and see where he is."

He tried to prop himself up as he could feel the ketamine begin to wear off. As he finally stood up, he reached to the counter and out of his pocket pulled out a yellow baggie. He opened it up and spilled the contents onto a small mirror as he rolled up a bill and said aloud, "This better be coke, or else I'm back down the rabbit hole." He grabbed a card from his wallet and centered it until it was one line, then with the bill began to inhale until the powder disappeared. He grabbed the little inhaler beside the mirror and began to sniff, clearing up not only his sinuses but any residue left from the cocaine. He then took a deep breath then exhaled, "That would be the coke."

As he flipped open his sunglasses and carefully placed them on, he slowly moved out the door and strolled out in the sunlight to the parking lot of his apartment complex. He leaned against the side of his car, wondering where Dutch had vanished to. He used the voice recognition to dial Dutch's cell number, it went straight to voicemail. As soon as Dutch's voice came on, Eli would hang up. It was not like him to disappear for anything longer than twenty-four hours. This was not something that Eli had bargained for. Maybe Dutch really did take off to Montreal right behind Antoine after all. Eli had the sinking feeling that something wasn't right in Dutchland.

He finally began to drive towards downtown while in the back of his mind he tried to piece together everything that happened prior to Dutch's disappearance. He knew that Dutch's erratic behavior over the past few days had been eating at Eli. The major schism that blew him and Antoine apart caused a tidal wave of eccentricity that could not be reversed. As the coke moved from clouded K hole to synaptic overdrive, he tried to meld together the most possible places where Dutch could have disappeared to.

His drive took him down through the river valley from 99th Street, through the underpasses and up the hill back towards the outer reaches of downtown. The street climbed upwards and finally careened to the left as he zoomed past the McDonald Hotel. As he turned onto Jasper Avenue he could feel a breeze start to move around inside the car. He let out a huge sigh as he rubbed his face. In the stretch of a few blocks he managed to pull over down from the grocery store and walked over to the intersection down from the Pink Bar. He could feel the cocaine's effects ebb as he walked towards the back entrance to the bathhouse and up the stairs.

When he reached the entrance he removed his sunglasses as the clerk glanced up at him. "Aren't you a little early for happy hour?" he smiled
Eli dryly asked, "Dutchie, have you seen him at all?"
The clerk shook his head. "Last time I saw him here was with you." He added, "And that my friend was weeks ago."

Eli's heart sank as he treaded down the stairs and out the entrance. He'd decided to walk up to the lounge just above Pink to check with the bartender. The sounds of horrible karaoke trickled down the stairs, inviting him up. Eli made a mental note to do another line of coke in the washroom before he left the lounge.

As he looked around he cautiously circled around the main bar towards where he and Dutch would normally sit, discovering him to be nowhere in sight. He ordered a drink and began to sip on it when the comment, "Out looking for your lost puppy Eli?" stung him from the side.
When Eli looked over he'd spotted Keith along with Samuel and some other random people standing at the table nearest pool table. Eli finished his drink and stood up, making his way over as Keith continued to drink his beverage.
When Eli arrived he asked, "You seen him?"
Keith only leered, "Not at all Eli. I haven't seen him. Then again…"
He finished his drink and set the glass down on the table, "Dutch is hardly recognizable without his collar and leash."
Eli spat, "Fuck you"
Keith exclaimed with a giggle, "Eli I'm sure he'll come back shortly. Just leave him a trail of crystal to follow and he'll come running back…"

It was that moment that the glass that Eli launched in Keith's direction hit Keith above his eye and shattered, a shower of rye, ice cubes and glass soiling Keith's suit.

Keith began to lunge as Eli ran towards him, the bartender jumping over the counter and pushing Eli back screamed, "That's enough you guys!"

Eli began to scream, "Fuck you Keith, you fucking coke whore!"

"Don't go blaming me for your fuck-ups Eli! At least I leave them in better shape than you do!"

"You know nothing about my friendship with Dutch!"

"I've seen and heard enough!!"

"Who the fuck asked you?! You're nothing but a cunt in a suit!"

One of the guys holding back Keith said, "Come on Keith. The douche isn't worth it…"

Eli could see through the blood smeared on Keith's face that he was all too ready to tear Eli apart.

The person repeated, "Keith he's not fucking worth it…"

Keith snarled as soon as Eli began to walk towards the exit, "Samuel thought exactly the same thing." That comment was enough to cause Eli to begin screaming all over again as the bartender had to push him back to the top of the staircase.

Finally after minutes of continual shouting, Eli began to calm down as the bartender asked, "Do you want to continue coming here or do you want me to bar you?"

Eli argued, "That fucker started it Randy, you fucking know that!"

"But it was you who launched the glass at him dude…"

"Did you hear what he fucking said?!"

Randy pinned him to the wall and screamed, "Look!" Eli was silent as Randy seethed, "You're treading a thin fucking line between coming and never coming back so don't fucking push me!!"

Eli then exhaled a few seconds later, "I'm sorry man have you seen him?"

Randy asked, "What?" It seemed to ease the tension between them and Randy sighed, "What's going on with Dutch Eli?"

Eli wriggled himself free and headed down the steps as Randy watched him head down the stairs. When Eli made it out to the sidewalk he donned his sunglasses while his stomach began to turn. Beads of sweat ran from his forehead as he quickly wiped them off with his sleeve, the sun bright in his eyes. To him the day felt like a typical summer day pulled out of any American film that used them as a precursor to complete disaster. It was that part of the feeling that Eli hoped to God he was wrong about.

After he's snorted a small bump of coke he walked down Jasper Avenue to Dutch's apartment complex. He turned into the building's lobby and buzzed his number. A female voice answered as Eli explained it was him. He then swung open the door and once inside the elevator he opened the small bag of cocaine, took the end of his key, and shoved another small pile into his nostril. When he arrived on the twelfth floor he went up to the door and knocked. "It's opened!" she called out as he turned the doorknob and pushed his way in.

Aimee looked at Eli and grimaced as she said, "You look like absolute garbage."

Eli sighed and said, "Tell me something I don't know."

Aimee bit her lip and asked, "Have you even seen Dutch over the past few days at all?"

Eli shook his head no as she asked, "Did he tell you anything was going on?"

He shook his head again and replied, "I think he was having troubles with the boyfriend."

She sighed and replied, "Fuck" as she began to pace back and forth.

She went to the living room and motioned him to follow. She sat on the couch, him on the love seat opposite her. She said, "It's the fucking most ridiculous thing. He never ever disappears without saying anything and he never told me him and Antoine…"

Eli then asked, "What do your parents think?"

She blankly said, "So far nothing. Well, dad doesn't. He's thinking that this is finally an excuse for him to stop funneling money to him." Aimee then said, "Mom…well mom looks like the worried one." Aimee sucked in her breath and added, "Mom has always been the rational one, but I think finally she's starting to truly come around."

Eli sighed, "Too little, too late…"

She threw her arms up in the air and groaned, "Fucking typical ignorant politician. Dad thinks the way to solve any problem is to avoid it." She continued, "Between you and me, we're the only ones who really knew him." Eli could trace the lines on her face. The same lines their mother had. It was beginning to appear that the family secret that their father had tried to keep all this time was beginning to crumble.

Eli explained, "I checked the lounge up above Pink Bar. I also checked both bathhouses and I didn't find him."
"And he hasn't been at work for the past few days…"
Eli offered, "I'm going out tonight so I could pop by the Cactus as well as Vivid."
"All right. Search what you can. Please keep an eye out for him and let me know." Eli stood up and hugged her as he could feel her begin to sniffle, a few of her tears escaping down and onto his shirt. He didn't even quite understand why he did it, but he knew that this particular moment empty gestures were not appropriate.
He whispered, "Stay strong"
She replied tearfully, "Thanks." She then pulled away. "Go shower. You stink."
Eli cracked a faint smile as she snickered, closing the door behind him.

Eli only began to get angrier as he punched the glass mirror in the elevator, creating a web that reached to the far corners of the wall. He sighed and began to walk out when it finally reached the main floor. When he left the lobby he paused for a moment and looked around. The world had not changed. Eli wasn't sure as to what he expected. Whether it was an ominous black cloud or suddenly for Dutch to reappear, neither had happened. Eli's mind wandered back to Keith's comment about crystal. He was beginning to piece together what had been said and what Dutch's behavior had been like over the past few weeks. He let out a sigh as he walked back to the car.

When he was ready to open the car door he felt his phone vibrate. When he looked it read the number was restricted. He picked up the line and said, "This is Eli."

The voice on the other end snapped, "Hey Eli, you never told me what you wanted with that medical file I had my girl procure from the clinic."

He recognized the voice immediately and said, "E I'm so glad to hear from you. Do you know where Dutch is?"

E was silent on the other end momentarily. He then replied, "I haven't seen him. But if you do see him tell him he owes me a lot of fuckin' money."

Eli asked, "How much?"

"Six hundred."

Eli then verbally launched into him. "Six hundred for what? That fucking poison you've been pushing down his throat for how long since we've been buying from you? How much have we purchased from you E? Considering we stayed loyal with you after your arrest, multiple busts at multiple clubs, and that you pissed away our money considering you fucking sold our supply to someone else multiple times E. You can't even show your face in fucking public because you're so dried out and you've made a reputation of fucking your customers over. E if I knew what kind of squalor Dutch was buying from I would have put an end to it a long time ago. If I ever catch you out on the fucking street not only will I kick your ass but I will fucking needle it to you to the point where whatever is left of your poor little heart explodes. Now if you'll excuse me I have someone to find. Fuck you very much." And with that he hung up the phone.

Later that night when arrived at the bottom of the steps at the Pink Bar, he asked the door person, "Have you seen someone come in, bleach blonde hair, about my height, a little meatier?" The door person shook his head no as Eli walked into the main area of the bar. A Whitney Houston remix jumped and leapt out of the speakers and around the club. Eli felt unwelcome as he noticed people taking awkward glances in his direction. He looked himself once over to ensure that nothing looked out of place. As he waked over to the back bar and ordered his first dink, he looked up and over to where he spotted Samuel conversing with Keith, Paul and the rest of the group. The sight of this only made Eli angry as he finished the remainder of his drink, quickly ordering another one.

Three drinks in and Eli began to walk towards the bathroom where he quickly pulled out a bag and his car key. After some more coke he sighed and decided to wander over to the bathhouse.

He headed up the stairs and out the door and as the bouncer let him out onto te sidewalk he heard in a threatening tone, "Restaurant full of cats, eh?"

He turned around and his face was met by a fist that embedded into him, causing him to stumble backwards. He could only make out a scream as he landed onto the concrete, the feeling of warm blood starting to rush to his head. He felt a couple of kicks to the stomach as he could only groan in pain. He spat out whatever blood started to surge into his mouth as he felt two or three more kicks, leaving him a crumpled mess on the concrete.

He closed his eyes as he heard, "Fucking faggot!"

Eli only watched his attackers walked away. After a few minutes the bouncer came out and asked, "Are you okay?"

He groaned, "Help me up..."

As the bouncer helped him to his feet, Samuel had seen what happened and quickly rushed over. "Are you okay? he asked.

Eli asked confusedly, "What the fuck just happened?"

Samuel replied, "Looks like you pissed off half of Chinatown." He then tried to joke, "Did you tell them the chicken balls were made of cats or something?"

Eli shot him a dirty glance as he took the cloth that the bouncer had neatly wrapped some ice inside. Eli sat down on the step beside the entrance as Samuel mentioned, "I assume he hasn't been found."

Eli nursed his face and said, "I didn't think anyone else was looking for him." He then finally turned to Samuel and said, "I thought you didn't want anything to do with me..."

Samuel said, "I feel sorry for you. Misery loves company." Samuel explained, "I ran into Aimee. She was starting to put up some missing persons posters."

"Oh fuck..." Eli groaned as the ice shifted, the water starting to trickle between his fingers.

"Where have you been looking?" Samuel asked while Eli remained silent.

Eli deflected Samuel's question and asked, "So when did you start full fledged sleeping with the enemy?"

Samuel looked at him and sighed, "So this is what it's all about eh? I am friends with the A-gays and all of a sudden you have hurt feelings."

Eli started to stand up and Samuel grabbed his arm. Eli looked down as Samuel asked, "Eli, do you know why you and I could never make it official?"

"Because you used to manage a fucking fast food joint?"

"Wrong Shithead. It was always about you Eli. I tolerated all of the bullshit, the excessive drug use, the way you tended to fuck over everyone else around you and still came out on top. No Eli, the reason why we could never be a couple is because you are so skin deep to everyone that everyone can see right through you. You're never fucking happy with what you've got, and in your quest to be happy, you've fucked a lot of people in the process. Personally I wouldn't be surprised if Dutch never came back. He never deserved the shit you put him through. You're a self-destructive waste Eli. I hope you realize that sooner rather than later."

Eli pulled Samuel up as he then tried to stretch out the pain from the attack. The water from the ice started to dribble down his arm as Eli said, "God fucking dammit, where the fuck is Dutch?!" Samuel was silent as Eli continued to nurse his eye. Finally after a few minutes he took the melting rag and threw it down on the sidewalk.

He began to walk away as Samuel shouted after him, "Where the fuck are you going?!"

Eli shouted, "To the fucking bathhouse!"

He walked down Jasper Avenue, despite the pain he was experiencing, past Earls and the synagogue, further west just before Jasper turned into 124th Street. As he found the bathhouse entrance, he quickly sped down the stairs, nearly slipped on the bottom steps, but managed to regain composure. When he arrived at the window, the attendant motioned to him. Eli sheepishly smiled as he handed him his credit card. After a few moments the attendant pressed the buzzer and Eli pulled the door open, grabbing his towel, condom, lube and key to his room.

Once he locked the door to his room he quickly undressed, neatly folding everything up. He checked his pockets to see what he had left. As he pulled the baggie out from his pocket he saw the minor amount left sighing, "It's going to be a long night." He then placed the baggie back into his pocket in his pants and wrapped the towel around his waist.

After quick tours down each of the bathhouse's main aisles, he walked into the shower area that was deserted with the exception of three people in the hot tub. He walked into the shower stalls and closed the frosted door behind him. He turned on the water and sat on the stall floor, knees to his chest, head down.

Eli was beginning to feel a layer of film cover his body. He continued to sit there as the flow from the shower matted his hair, trickled all over his body and down the drain. He then held his head up towards the shower head, letting the water peel away the anxiety and frustration that seemed to be visible on the surface. Eli didn't want to move from the shower stall, the warmth of the water that rushed down over his body keeping him convinced to stay. After ten minutes he the stood up and planted both hands apart on each side of the stall, the shower still spraying down his back. He watched the water drip down off him in strand-like fashion as he once more held his face up to the shower head, the pressure beating down on him more intensely. Minutes later he turned the shower off and stepped out of the stall, drying himself off as he began to notice more people filing in and out between the wet and dry saunas and the whirlpool.

He decided to venture into the hot tub first, the hot water swirling around him as he sat back and stretched out. When he exhaled he rubbed his nose briefly and watched as people passed by the entrance. The water and pressure felt good on all of Eli's muscles as he leaned back against the edge. He didn't want to move from where he was. As the knots began to loosen he blankly stared at the entrance and watched men of various shapes and sizes move back and forth. He let another twenty minutes pass as finally he stood up and began to move out of the hot tub. Just as he reached for his towel he spotted someone younger slowing down and peering in as he smiled at Eli and waited outside the doorway.

Eli walked out the entrance to the sauna area and looked at the stranger as he looked up and smiled at him. Eli moved closer as the stranger inched up a bit further and they locked in a deep, passionate kiss. He was just a little shorter than Eli, light brown hair, rail thin, and freckled on both cheeks.

When he pulled away he smiled and asked, "Have you got a room?" Eli nodded as he then reached under the stranger's towel and briefly moved it away to reveal an already hardening penis underneath. The stranger pulled away and readjusted his towel as he said, "After you?"

They walked out over to the main area where Eli immediately stopped as he watched the flat screen television. Four or five men were all clad in towels as Eli couldn't help but watch the screen. The news anchor announced Dutch's disappearance as the stranger beside him watched in astonishments the anchor detailed how Donald Bryant had been missing since Monday.

He only made out pieces of the monologue as the stranger said, "They still haven't found him yet eh?"
Eli only shook his head no as he then heard, "His parents must be really heartbroken that he's gone."
Eli then said, "They're not." As Dutch's parents had now graced the screen Eli explained, "His father is a dumbfuck redneck politician from Calgary. Didn't give a fuck about him whatsoever."

The stranger observed, "They look pretty authentically worried to me." Eli then argued, "It's because it's his political career on the line. He's been so busy keeping him a secret that they're like deer in headlights."
The stranger said, "I heard that kid was really fucked up. Huge crystal queen. His best friend treated him like shit. Apparently he drugged and raped some eighteen-year old and forced him to watch."
He then looked over as Eli began to walk towards his room. The stranger asked, "Where you going?"
Eli replied, "Home. Have a good night."

LOVE'S SWEET EXILE - DISC 25: fourteen minutes, twenty-nine seconds

"I always think it's going to happen like this."

"I'm at Factory on a Saturday night, only a little high. Just high enough that I'm aware of my surroundings. It's an amazing night and I'm feeling the MDMA dance and massage my body. Everything is in its right place. The music is peak-hour hands-in-the-air trance, dancefloor full and everyone around me is a mass of sound vibrations mixed with glow-sticks and old school candy bracelets. While I still carry an emptiness that has continuously haunted me all these years, something is definitely different this particular night. I try to ignore it but I can't help but feel that something is about to happen."

"It's that point I slow down and turn round to see Eli standing there, black t-shirt and pants. His eyes fixed on me as he comes up to me, not dancing. After a few minutes when the shock has worn off, I only ask, what the fuck is he doing out at Factory."

"And that's when it spills out…"

"He tells me that he's been in love with me. That he's been in love with me for the past two years. His story then changes to five, then six, then finally the expression on his face gives it away completely. He admits he's always felt this way, since we met. And that all of the empty sex over the years hasn't amounted to the feelings he's had for me. He tells me he's been stupid all of these years and he asks me if I can ever forgive him. He swears up and down he'll make it up to me, which is why he came and tracked me down at Factory. Because he knew how much I loved this club and music, and above all why he's willing to adapt and change."

"And when he leans in to kiss me, this is where it ends. I snap out of it because Eli doing any kind of 360 degree turn like that is near impossible. Everytime I rewrite the scene mentally the years start to add up. I guess I'm the creator of my own fiction…I just wish I didn't have to bear this cross anymore. I just wish he would finally come around…"

Chapter Thirty-seven

Eli knew there would be questions and lots of them as he stood on the escalator and gazed upwards, his sunglasses shielding part of the bruises on his face. It throbbed as he sighed after spotting the entrance.

When he made his way into the lobby Dawn's expression was smug as he asked, "What's the good word today?"

Her gaze shifted to the screen as she replied, "There's police officers in this morning. It looks like Dutch hasn't been found yet."

Eli sighed, "It's been this long I don't think they'll ever find him."

She then asked, "Do you not care that your supposed best friends is missing?"

He inched his sunglasses down a little and replied, "It's why after every shift I still go looking for him." Eli scanned his badge and walked in towards his desk as Daniel quickly glanced over and then turned away, shuffling up the steps and back up towards the collection area. As people noticed that he arrived the floor became really quiet. When he looked down at his keyboard there was a piece of paper under his keyboard. He pulled the half – folded sheet out and opened it. The paper was his employee badge profile, with four lines running vertically over his face. The words BREAK FREE FROM COCAINE under the picture. His anger began to well up as he then looked for any sign of Stewart in his row.

Just as his anger was about to boil over the surface, his concentration was broken by Natasha. "Eli, in the conference room please." Before he could reply she quickly walked back over to the conference room.

Eli folded the note and stuffed it into his pocket as he waked over to the conference room. He was greeted by Natasha, Lance, Marie as well as a younger looking police officer. Eli moved to the nearest chair across from the officer as he looked up and explained, "I'm Officer Boyd, Eli. I just need you to answer some questions in regards to the disappearance of Mr. Bryant."

Eli was silent for a few moments. "What do you need to know?"

Boyd began, "When did you last see Donald Eli?"

Eli thought for a moment then responded, "I last saw Dutch here in the office last Monday."

"Did he seem okay when you had seen him?"

Eli adjusted his sunglasses and continued, "He actually looked quite strung out. He…" Eli fell silent again and looked around. "He just had a falling out with his roommate and ongoing family troubles."

"What kind of family troubles did Mr. Bryant have at home?" Eli said nothing as he bit his lip.

He explained, "His parents disowned him for being gay when he was seventeen. His father is a high-profile conservative politician in Calgary."

Boyd asked, "Would they have any reason to hurt him that you're aware of?"

"All I know is his father bought him a condo here in Edmonton. It was a bribe to keep his mouth shut."

"What about Dutch's boyfriend? Did you know anything about that situation?"

Eli suddenly became uncomfortable as he slowly inhaled. He glanced around the room and then blurted out, "From what I understood there were some issues in regards to him. They'd gotten in a fight before I'd seen him." He stopped and then said, "He'd received some upsetting news."

Boyd stopped writing on his pad. "Do you know what the news was?"

"You'd have to ask him. He would know better than me."

"Eli, Mr. Bourassa boarded a plane back to Montreal the night Mr. Bryant disappeared."

"Shame."

Officer Boyd sighed in frustration as he explained, "We found a small bag of ketamine, two bags of crystal methamphetamine, and five tablets of ecstasy in his top drawer in his room." Eli at first was silent as he wasn't sure what to say. Once Boyd had mentioned crystal, Eli had no suitable reply.

He responded instead with, "Dutch had disposable income, therefore liked to recreationally consume illicit substances."

Lance grunted while Eli shot him a glare across the table.

Boyd asked, "Did you know Donald did drugs?" Eli only nodded.

"Did he do them around you?" Eli shrugged. Boyd then asked, "How did you get that bruise on your face?"

"Because I told some dirty Asian fuck he served cats in his restaurant."

The conference room fell silent as Boyd breathed, "Right…" He then closed his notepad as he looked at all of them. "There hasn't been a lot we've been able to go on. We're looking but right now but every indication has gone cold." He then stood up, pulled out a business card and laid it on the table, pushing it towards Eli. "If you have any questions or information, please get in touch. We're looking to locate him as soon as we can." Eli was silent as Officer Boyd left the room, closing the door behind him.

Eli went to stand up when Lance snapped, "Sit back down Eli we're not fucking done." Eli said nothing as he sat back down.

He calmly replied, "That's so HR of you."

Lance opened a file and asked, "Eli where did you get the STD results from?"

Eli replied, "I don't know what you're talking about."

Lance said, "Oh Eli, see I believe you do. Because when we contacted Capital Health, it seems that Antoine Bourassa's test results were very different from what you placed on Dutch's desk." Lance continued, "In addition they had investigated the clerk who had provided these false files on suspicion of fraud. Turns out your drug addicted clerk snitched." Eli cringed as Lance also pointed out, "Rumor has it you also drugged up a co-worker's younger brother and proceeded to rape him."

Eli argued, "Lance, if you're here to try and fire me on hearsay…"

Lance then added, "We also heard reports you also coerced Daniel into having sex in the men's washroom."

Eli scowled and replied, "That was consensual, and I'm not going to let you crucify me over gossip."

Lance grimaced, "Well I do have something here from the fact file." He looked at Eli and leaned forward. "A lawyer from Merchant, Williams, and

Noble was in the office today. Stewart has filed a harassment suit against yourself and Go Credit."

Eli suddenly asked, "What?"

Lance elaborated, "We pulled all of his e-mails in addition to a file that was sent to us from Dutch's computer. There's some pretty inappropriate stuff in those e-mails from you, quite malicious actually." Lance continued, "It also seems you made some degrading comments about his sexual orientation and teased him consistently. In addition to spreading gossip which has resulted in a poisonous work environment…"

While Eli looked attentive on the outside, internally he'd tuned out Lance's point by point execution. He sighed, remained silent and stone-faced as Natasha's comment brought him back to earth when she raised her voice. "You, out of all people, Eli should know better when it comes to respect in the workplace. I've seen you evolve from customer service representative to retention specialist and now you've gone and fucked this up by being careless." Every word, every inflection pierced him as she continued, "Now not only do I have one representative fallen apart on me on the floor Eli, I've got another one who mentally fucked off and may never come back."

By this point Eli's guard had been ripped down to shreds by Natasha. He in plain view had been broken. Eli yanked his sunglasses off from his face and they bounced off the table once and slid to the card left by Officer Boyd. Eli rubbed his forehead as all the words came back to him, and all at once. Eli envisioned Dutch, Natasha, and Samuel, all towering over him, chanting their condemnations while Eli cowered in fear and pain. It was enough of a mental picture to leave him at a loss for any response. Up to this point he had successfully ignored his past sins, but this meeting in the conference room had now uncovered all of it.

Nothing seemed to process as Eli finally looked up. He mumbled something about needing air to them, and slowly staggered out. As he left the conference room, everyone who wasn't on the phone, or in conversation, cautiously looked over as he inched back to his desk. Ariel looked over at him while Eli noticed that Stewart's desk was empty. He opened his desk drawers and slowly glanced around.

He then reached into his bag and pulled out a full bottle of water then asked Ariel, "Hey Ariel, have you ever heard of scorched earth policy?"

She was silent as he took a sip from the water bottle and then proceeded to pour the entire bottle into the opening of the computer tower. He explained as the computer hissed, snapped and sizzled, "It was a tactic used in World War II to prevent the enemy from using any of the country's natural supplies." Eli could hear a snap and crackle as smoke began to rise from his computer. He then dropped the bottle onto the floor where it made an empty thud and put his messenger bag strap over his shoulder. He then glanced up at Natasha, Lance, and Marie who by this point seemed to watch helplessly as Eli walked out of the office and back into the mall.

Chapter Thirty-Eight

Eli sat in his apartment and fidgeted with the small bag of cocaine between is fingers as he blankly watched the television and the images that danced around on the screen. It had been a week since Dutch's disappearance. The past few days had especially become a blur as he had missed work since the meeting between himself, Marie, Natasha, and Lance. He knew it was probably a mistake to not go. He reasoned that they would have sent him home anyways due to the pending lawsuit that now hung over his head. He spent the past few days searching and searching again all of the regular haunts that he and Dutch had ever been to in Edmonton. He would get home every night about midnight, lay out two lines of ketamine on his counter, and morning would find him curled up and in the fetal position on his bed, still in his clothes from the previous day. He would then wake up, shower and get dressed. But for whatever reason he felt as if the film on his skin was not washing off. He would scratch at his arms and his chest, leaving deep marks behind.

The television was an empty distraction. The last few days he had begun to feel restless. He walked out onto the balcony and looked around, watching people pass by his building. The air felt good as he deeply inhaled and leaned over the rails. Time passed and finally he made the decision to walk over to the Pink Bar. He changed out of his clothes and quickly showered as he unplugged his cell phone from the charger and carefully locked the door behind him.

As he walked out of the apartment building his cell began to vibrate as he looked at the call display. He answered it with, "Yeah?"

The voice on the other end said, "Eli, it's Aimee..."

Instead of snapping at her he asked "Is everything okay?"

She said, "No it's not fucking okay Eli."

He said, "On my way" and hung up the phone as he shifted direction towards Dutch's apartment building.

Eli began to feel uneasy as he walked up to the building's main entrance. He entered the lobby and towards the first available elevator and pressed Dutch's floor. It was a brief wait as he stepped into the hallway and towards the door. He knocked and called, "Aimee?" He waited as he then heard something inaudible, and decided to turn the doorknob and pushed in.

What only should have felt like seconds elapsed into what seemed like hours as Eli called out again, "Aimee are you there?"

She called out, "I'm in Dutch's room!" Eli walked over to the bedroom and looked in as she stood there tired, eyes fixed on him,

He asked, "What's going on Aimee?"

She was silent for a minute then explained, "I've been up for the past twenty four hours Eli, tearing apart his room, trying to figure out where my brother's gone." She pulled out a minidisc and said, "You know what I found? I found the minidisc recorder that was his gift for his sixteenth birthday. I also found about three boxes worth of minidiscs all titled Love's Sweet Exile in his desk drawer."

Eli scowled then said, "So fucking what Aimee? Look I don't have time for this shit if you wanna..."

He was stopped short when she clicked on Dutch's mouse on the desk, releasing a string of dialogue from the speakers. The more erratic the narrator sounded, Eli would become more visibly uncomfortable. It was as if Dutch had taken their friendship and deconstructed it piece by piece, frame by frame. The more Aimee pointed and clicked the mouse, Eli's breathing became heavier.

Aimee then said, "I'm sure you'll really like this part Eli." She clicked on another audio file which included Dutch's commentary to the backdrop of music.

Eli said, All right, all right…I've heard enough. Aimee, please stop the recording. Please turn it off…"

Instead she folded her arms and asked, "Where is Dutch Eli?"

Eli stammered, "I d-don't know Aimee I swear to God. I don't know where he's gone."

She wiped her eyes and said, "I listened to every one of these discs Eli. Every fucking single one. The way you treat people notwithstanding Eli, did you ever clue into the fact that he was in love with you?"

She then breathed, "After all of these years Eli, did you ever stop to wonder if he thinks the world of you?" She then clicked the mouse again as she played the last file on the computer that Dutch ever recorded. Eli shut his eyes as Dutch's screams shot out of the speakers, Aimee's hate filled expression still fixed on Eli.

She then said, "So this was going to be the greatest love story never told. And you just helped him write the very last chapter."

"I want the files Aimee."

"I ain't giving you shit Eli."

"Aimee, please give me the discs. I want the…"

"These discs don't belong to you Eli. They're my brothers and I'm keeping them."

"God dammit that's my fucking life on those discs!"

"YOU GET NOTHING ELI!"

She continued to scream at him, "This is my brothers life and I all have left of him and you want this too? You don't get the discs Eli. Understand you fucking get nothing! You. Get. Nothing!!" Eli did everything he could to hold it together while she began to fall apart. He would never let it show, especially to her. All Eli could think about was the string of narratives that Dutch had haphazardly created, stored, layered, and polished to become a mirror that at that point had reflected the things Eli had tried so hard to hide under his exterior.

Eli didn't wait to watch Aimee fall apart before his eyes. On any other day he would have stayed and watched as in slow motion she would unravel. But she had also touched a very deep nerve inside him that he was sure didn't exist. Eli knew that given the situation given he did not want to stick around. This time he ran for the elevator, slamming the apartment door behind him while he fished his pocked for the small bag of coke. In the elevator he grabbed his keys, scooped out a small pile, and promptly snorted it up his nostril.

When he left the building he decided to keep walking towards downtown. His bruise on his face began to throb in pain and he slowly followed the light grey clouds towards the office towers, his mind silencing all noise around him while he mentally pieced together Dutch's confessions from the audio journal he'd kept. As he looked up, it was as if the people who passed by him on the sidewalk were able to directly able to stare into his soul. Eli's face read that he was emotionally naked and no matter how hard he tried, he was unable to purge himself from the varying degrees of Dutch's voice, the screaming confessions of hurt and longing that up until this point, Eli had purposely avoided.

His walk ended at a lone bench facing north on the most southern point of Churchill Square. Under a glass canopy and nestled between Three Bananas Café and the LRT entrance, he leaned back for a few minutes, gazing blankly at the clock that stood on the tower of City Hall, then down to the wading pool and fountain where Eli vividly remembered dunking Dutch upon the first week that he had been exiled to Edmonton. His surroundings were still on mute as the pain still throbbed. When he finally leaned forward he rubbed his face with his hands and sighed, staring blankly out at the fountain and City Hall. He then sat back as people slowly crisscrossed the open concrete area. A homeless person then came up to Eli and began to slur out, "Excuse me sir…" while Eli looked over and barked, "Fuck right off." The man's face whitened underneath the dirt caked on him as he abruptly sauntered away. Eli sighed again as he faced forward, eyes fixed on the buildings ahead of him, trying to ignore the pain that pulsed in his face.

Minutes stretched into what seemed like forever as a familiar voice asked, "What are you doing out here on your own?" Eli looked up to see Peter's familiar face looking down at him as he sat on the bench next to Eli.

Eli then blurted, "Please promise me you won't ask for money."

Peter let out a small chuckle and replied, "I don't need any money. I have love, and a lot of it. I'm a good person." As Peter adjusted himself to a comfortable seating position on the bench he explained, "I've been nothing but good all of these years, and trust me the more good you do, the more it comes back to you."

Peter seemed to almost zone out for a few moments and when Eli glanced over he began, "You know those people over at The Pink Bar, they're not good people." He stomped down his cane and rambled, "They treat their paying customers like garbage and talk about you behind your back. I've been a good paying customer of theirs all of these years and all they do is talk shit about them." He then repeated, "But that's okay because I'm a good person. They damn well know karma gets everyone in the end."

Eli groaned then leaned forward. He asked, "Fucking Christ, where the fuck is he?"

Peter asked, "Who?"

Eli sniffled then explained, "I thought you would have heard by now. It's been two weeks." Eli swallowed then explained, "Dutch vanished. He disappeared two weeks ago." An uncomfortable silence then sat between them on the bench while Eli leaned forward and started to pick at his hand.

Eli pondered, "It's insane that it's been all over the newspapers and TV. Two weeks ago his parents didn't give a fuck about him because he was out of sight and definitely out of mind. Now the cats out of the bag that he's vanished…" When Eli stopped there was silence and he began to explain again "Funnily enough no one's mentioned how shitty the relationship with his family was because of the minor detail that he's gay."

Peter then mumbled, "It'll come out soon enough. Secrets like that don't stay in the political closet for long."

Eli said abstractly as if he hadn't really heard Peter, "His mother at least is being genuine about her grief. She at least gives a fuck about Dutchie. Aimee, there's no doubt in her mind she loves him." He then looked over at Peter and said, "It's his father that's putting on the act. When he won his seat in the last election, we watched the news feed online from work. You'd have thought the Flames won the fucking Stanley Cup judging by the insanity from that victory party. But amongst all that Conservative blue one person was missing on that podium. That person was Dutch."

He paused for a moment then said, "Dutchie was so gutted when his dad gave the victory speech. And in it he thanked his child. I mean, really? Who the fuck has the sack to refer to only one child when in all honesty it was supposed to be two? It was bad enough he told Dutch not to come within a fifty kilometer radius of Calgary during the entire campaign for fear of fucking the election for him. And then to just write him off on television like that, like he never existed, so fucking harsh to just break his heart like that." Eli said, "It was that point I realized how much he loved his family, especially his father. Despite everything that had happened he would still want to see his father succeed."

"The sad thing is this fucking disappearance will probably secure him another term in the legislature. And once again redneck Alberta will breathe a collective sigh of relief."

Peter pointed out, "That might not be the case. Karma will get him in the end. "

Eli stared back out into nothing and after a few minutes of silence Peter then breathed in near zen-like fashion, "He's in a better place."

Eli glanced over, "A better place?"

Peter then turned to him and said, "There's always a better place." The comment vaguely resonated with him as Peter began to slowly stand up and pushed his cane forward.

Peter then looked at Eli as Eli asked, "How do you do it?"

Peter replied, "Sometimes surviving is all you can do. I've survived a lot, and all I can tell you is that sometimes you just need to keep moving. The trick is to learn from your sins, and keep breathing."

Just before Peter walked away he said, "It's just the fact that you survived, is all that matters." Eli could only sigh as a couple of tears escaped onto his cheek while he watched Peter slowly shuffle away. As the clouds began to darken overhead and the sounds of distant thunder began to echo, it was at that point Eli realized one horrible lonely truth.

Dutch was never coming back.

Chapter Thirty-Nine

E stood at the kitchen counter as he shakily took a small bottle, almost resembling a medicine bottle and slowly poured a minute amount of clear fluid into its cap. His hands shook a little as he'd been up for hours, maybe days. He wasn't so sure anymore how long it had been. As he set the bottle down his heart raced as the sole diet of methamphetamine coursed through his veins. In his nervous seclusion he'd managed to clean through his apartment, neatly sorting everything while his mind raced with thoughts that Dutch's disappearance would mean that Edmonton's finest would be looking for him. He reasoned that Dutch would have carelessly stored the drugs and as the police scoured for clues they would find the chemicals and Eli would trace it back to him. He was almost certain of this.

He knew that Eli was right. They had been loyal customers through a lot of E's personal drama. He knew that money was money, but at the same time in a fickle industry where drug dealers can be switched like major coffee chains, Eli and Dutch's loyalty was essential. He had saved the newspapers with all of the headlines that had announced Dutch's disappearance. E hadn't thought too much of it except wanting to piss all over the newsprint that displayed Dutch's last color picture on the front page. He thought in the back of his mind that Dutch would say aloud through the picture, "If I'm gone, then you're fucked."

E stared at the cap for a few minutes, and then finally swallowed the cap full of fluid. The tinny taste nearly made him vomit as he grabbed the beer that sat on the counter and chugged half the bottle. It helped a little as he walked over to his couch and plopped down. He knew it wouldn't be long as he could feel the GHB start to pull him down to the floor, attempting to negate the effects of the crystal. E still seeing sudden blotches of black as in the background he saw a huge flash of light beam into the living room from outside, then the sound of thunder that shook his living room. He stood up, walked back into the kitchen, and shut off all of the lights. Just before he passed by the counter he saw the bottle of GHB. Reasoning that another swig wouldn't hurt he picked up the bottle and swallowed the equivalent of another three capfuls. His body by this point had started to wrestle with whether it wanted to be on accelerate from the crystal, or in park caused by the GHB.

He sat back down as the rain began to make tapping noises on his balcony and windows. He briefly glanced at the rain that had now begun to cover the balcony, then noticing the disfigured bars shuddered and tried not to remember that evening. He looked at the Edmonton Journal from this morning. It was a photo of Dutch's anguished parents looking on with determination while the above headline screamed PARENTS OF MISSING SON HOLD OUT HOPE. Etienne grunted and put the newspaper beside him as the chemicals finally slowed down his heart. His muscles unwound and he laid back as if he was a rag doll haphazardly propped up.

E was so enwrapped in his high, barely able to move and could only focus on the sounds of the thunderstorm from outside that he'd completely forgotten about the apartment door being unlocked and missed the sound of the doorknob quietly being turned open.

When he slowly looked up he saw a silhouette completely in black which blended into the darker corners of the room. E exhaled and silently cursed that he had smoked far too much, which resulted in the apparition that seemed to have stalked him. He rationalized that he could turn on the lights, which would result in him giving in to the paranoia that had manifested itself from years of meth use. Even if he wanted to, he could barely move, the GHB grounding him as he saw the silhouette move yet again. He sighed and watched as he tried to decipher anything that remotely looked like a physical being that crept out from the shadows.

That moment, he felt the first blow to his ribs. Something metal cracked against his chest as E twitched as it made contact. Seconds later another blow struck his chest again, this time E beginning to feel a warm rush of blood that first began to drip from the sides of his mouth, then fountained up with the third and fourth blow, covering his face, running down his chin and down onto the white t-shirt that had already been stained by four days worth of wear. E coughed up some more blood as he tried to formulate the word, "Sto…" As the metal object struck three more times, Etienne realized that he would be unable to fight back as the GHB coupled with the pain of his rib being broken.

His body made snapping noises with every subsequent blow as Etienne lost count. He could only mumble his pain as piecing together his words had become impossible. It took one more blow to the chest and a snap that couldn't be ignored as Etienne leaned his head over to the side, blood running from the corner of his mouth, dripping onto the newspaper photo that sat beside him. The last thing he remembered was the flash of lightning that illuminated the empty room, a cool breeze wrapping around him as he sputtered and stopped breathing.

Chapter Forty

Eli couldn't remember the last time it had been so bright outside.

Since as far back as Eli could remember, whenever he'd taken an excursion from Edmonton International Airport the skies were always ominous and grey. Grey when he departed on the plane, grey when he arrived. It had been three years since Eli had been on a plane. He wondered if he would ever come back to clear skies over Edmonton.

He glanced at his plane ticket, then over to the newspaper whose headline read BRUTALLY MURDERED DRUG DEALER FOUND IN APARTMENT. The photo showed an anguished police officer while police tape ran across the entrance of the building where couple of random neighbors look on. Eli scanned the article underneath, another headline that read CONSERVATIVE MP SON EXILED FROM FAMILY. The article was by large an interview with Dutch's sister Aimee, pulling the family closet door wide open and cleaning out every damaging skeleton that concerned Dutch's father and his non existent relationship with his son.

When he thought it was too painful to read, he then shifted his gaze to the blue skies. His eyes began to sting as he donned his sunglasses. His flight wouldn't leave for another two hours yet. Eli still felt very much at a loss. Three weeks had passed since Dutch's disappearance, and Eli still couldn't focus. He'd haphazardly texted Samuel in a blizzard of cocaine and ketamine days before. Eli's phone in return was deathly silent.

As he sipped his coffee he leaned back on his seat and fidgeted with the cup. He had never realized how busy the airport was for Edmonton. People continued to walk back and forth, and into the security area as he sighed and continued to blankly focus at the planes and runways. His scattered thoughts were interrupted when someone sat down beside him and said, "Your sister told me you'd still be here."

"I'm surprised you even came."

Samuel fidgeted with his sunglasses as he looked over at Eli. "I figured no one was seeing you off. So…" Samuel then picked up the newspaper and quickly glanced at the front page. "I can't believe how fucking nuts this is. They found this guy dead in his apartment four days after when the landlord came to pick up the rent. Guess someone offed him pretty good. The only thing they found was the newspaper articles about Dutch's disappearance." Eli was silent as Samuel asked, "What do you think?"

Eli sighed deeply and then replied while staring out the windows, "He might have pissed off a supplier, or a very powerful customer."

Samuel then asked, "Was Dutch one of his?" Eli nodded as Samuel then asked, "You don't think he…"

Eli only shook his head. "Wherever Dutch went, he definitely didn't disappear just to fuck up E."

"What do you make of the article about Aimee?" Eli looked at Samuel and said, "Apart from knowing who has the balls in the family…"

He then blurted out, "It was a long time coming. You can't exile a family member and just think nothing's gonna happen." Eli sipped his coffee. "I never understood how his family still held it together all of these years. Seems like he was the glue." Samuel rested a hand on his shoulder. "She's filing for divorce. All she wants is the apartment and spousal."

Samuel was quiet for a few moments, then murmured the words, "Love's Sweet Exile…"

Eli said, "It's a song from a Manic Street Preachers album." He then explained, "They were his favorite band."

When Eli looked back out he said, "I remember when he wanted to go to London to find Richey. Richey was the band's lyricist who just fucking vanished into thin air years ago. He wanted to see the exact location and trace his steps. I thought Dutch was crazy. Not so much anymore…"

Eli fidgeted with the now empty cup as Samuel asked, "Where do you think he's gone?"

Eli shrugged and said, "Could be anywhere."

"And where are you going?"

Eli was silent as he stared down at the floor. "I don't even know. I'm off to spend time with some family in Arizona. Maybe dry out for a bit. I don't even know anymore. I'm so fucking scared I'm going to kill myself before I get to where I need to be." He fell silent as he could feel Samuel's hand start to massage his shoulder. Eli then said as he looked back up at Samuel, "Everyday I wake up and all I can hear in my fucking head is Dutch's last words all neatly compiled from the audio journal he kept." His voice started to quiver as he continued, "The last thing I remember is him screaming at me. Him screaming out why I couldn't love him...it was that moment I realized I'd really fucked up. Everyday those fifty seconds play over and over like a loop in my head. It continuously reminds me of how much of a fucking failure at life I am."

Samuel cautiously asked, "Did you know?"

Eli stared down at the floor again. "I think in the back of my mind it was always there. But..." He stopped and after a few minutes said, "I was in such a chemical haze I don't think I would have been able to acknowledge it. Not until now..."

"Until it was too late."

Eli added, "The least I could have done is let him have happily ever after with Antoine. I at least owed him that much."

Samuel said, "I'm sure he'll forgive you Eli."

"I don't know about that Samuel. After seven years and a lot of the times he's forgiven me before." A couple of tears streamed down his face. "I'm a fucking horrible person Samuel. I guess I've always known it. Leave it to my best friend's disappearance to finally hit that point home."

Samuel mused, "Dutch's parents have set up a reward for finding him."

Eli flatly argued, "They'll never find him. If they think that some fucking reward is going to coax him out, they're sadly mistaken." Eli continued, "When I sold the majority of my shit from my apartment, I put that towards the reward. I gave it to my sister to give to the family cause there's no way they'd accept it if they knew where it was coming from."

Samuel then asked, "What about everything else?"

Eli replied, "Stored it at my parent's house."

They were quiet, Samuel finally asking the question he knew was on both of their minds. "Are you ever coming back?"

Eli grimaced and replied, "When I stop hating myself."

Samuel was silent for a few minutes. He then offered, "If you ever want to talk where you are…"

"I know where to find you."

The overhead announcer indicated the boarding of Eli's flight as Eli stood up. "I guess this is goodbye." Samuel nodded as Eli fished in his pocket and pulled out his employee badge from Go Credit. He held onto it and after a few moments said, "If you can, please tell Dawn to let Antoine know I am truly sorry."

He placed it into Samuel's hand as he put his sunglasses back on while Samuel hugged him tightly. For those few minutes, Eli felt like that weight had been lifted off him, if only for that moment. Samuel then pulled away as Eli slowly began the walk to the security terminal entrance. After a very brief search he slowly walked over to his gate and presented his ticket. When he finally stepped into the plane and sat down he opened his passport, where the badge of a familiar face was nestled.

It was the only thing he had left of him.

Acknowledgements

After eight years of a first draft write, another year of working through the second draft, and another four years of enforced patience, *Drowned World* finally became a published reality on July 2 2009. While I was in Montreal soaking up inspiration for my next book, the passing of one of the world's greatest pop icons shortly after my thirty – second birthday signaled the end of a chapter and the beginning of another. It goes without saying, the initial road hasn't been without its many twists and turns. In between green tea lemonades at my favorite Starbucks on St. Catherine's and Visitation, and sangria on the roof of the Sky Complex, I had the time to formulate a list of *un grand mercis* to those who have made me feel blessed to be sharing my stories with the world.

First and foremost to everyone who bought, read and supported *Drowned World*. Thank you for being the beginning of the journey and being the witness to the bigger picture, especially to those who have kept the faith all these years.

A very huge thank you to my family and friends who have generously given their love, feedback and encouragement. There are so many of you that I can't thank you enough…especially mom whose genuine enthusiasm and support for *Drowned World* helped me open the door.

Trafford Publishing, especially Josh Spears and Jenny Bacurnay who made it their sole purpose to see *The Heart's Filthy Lesson* through. Also to

Steve Furr who was there to smooth all of the bumps and ensure *Drowned World* finally saw the light of day.

To those who doubled as cheerleaders during the creative process: Stephanie Pryutliak, Joanne Paisley, Elaine Perri, Tara Catalano, Tara Carlson, Rheanne Bedard – Schilling, Vivianne Bridgeman, Karen Dyck, Jenna Kostiuk, Morgan Lindgren, Alex Pedden, Anne Evans, Cheillah Kranic, Nevena Plemic, Cam and April Rigsby, Christopher Lauzon, Cortney Dietze, Annette Lapointe, Staci Cadieux, Shannon White, Antoinette and Dale Gonzales, and Angela Sykes.

To Jamie Knox, whose friendship and support over the years has made me rethink Chinese food and provided me with a gift of proper sleep. From the bottom of my heart, thank you and all the best as you begin your next chapter this summer.

To those friends who the first test audience for *Drowned World*: Mitch and Jessica Bloos, Jason and Kara Garvey, Ross Corriea, Andreas Much, Daniel Kavanagh, Sandra Haroun, Tina Achorn, Sandra Haroun, Lindsey Heightington, Wendy Frietas, and Debi Mayes.

To my Flatland/Edmonton electronica family, there are too many of you to name. Thank you for being a different kind of audience since 99. Words cannot express how grateful I am to you for allowing me to express a different story through the music.

Especially big thanks to Michael Babb, Nicky Delgado, Garrett Friesen, Loreen Douglas Alison Braun, Jeff Galaxy, Jamie and Cheryl McCormick, Adam Bradley, Anthony Kwok, Kim Drake, Greg Hluska, Robbie Picard, Marshall Catterson.

To my Montreal family: Joshua Levin, Jimmy Rheaume, Nadia Mazza, Alexa-Love Tremblay, Mariette Bohemier, Patricia Bissonette, Ana Cuadra, Kim Vallee, Evelyne Mazza, Lisa Fiorilli, Gabriel Auger, Dawn Cathcart and Lisa Mayes.

To my amazing editor Sean Rasmussen, for seeing what I saw and helping me to correct the little bits that I didn't see. Your expertise has been greatly appreciated on The Heart's Filthy Lesson. Much love, Shelli-Anne.

To Alex Burdeniuk, who came in at the eleventh hour and was my extra set of eyes. Sorry, you don't get a copy with all the bad words blacked out

A very special thanks to David Fortier whose love and friendship saw me through a very difficult time.

A special tip of the hat to the genius of Matthew Good, whose album Hospital Music was one of the many pieces to the soundtrack while hammering out *The Heart's Filthy Lesson*.

To everyone I've forgotten or not thrown on this list. Thank you for everything and even though you're not on the list, you're most definitely in my heart.

Last but definitely not least to Him: who continues to bless me, who I sometimes take for granted, and should be more the steering wheel instead of the spare tire. Much everlasting love.

CPSIA information can be obtained at www.ICGtesting.com
Printed in the USA
LVOW081831301011

252738LV00002B/4/P